STEALING HIS MATE

ALIENS OF OLUURA

IVY KNOX

Cover art: Natasha Snow Designs

Edited by: Tina's Editing Services & Owl Eyes Proofs & Edits

❀ Created with Vellum

AUTHOR'S NOTE

Stealing His Mate is book 3 in the Aliens of Oluura series. Each book focuses on a new couple and their happily ever after but reading them in order is way more fun.

Here's book 1:
Saving His Mate: Aliens of Oluura

<u>Content Warning</u>

If you don't have any concerns regarding content and how it may affect you, **feel free to skip ahead to avoid spoilers**!

This book contains scenes that either reference or depict depression, abduction, graphic violence, as well as domestic abuse which may be triggering for some. If you or someone you know is in need of support, there are places you can go for help. I have listed some resources at the end of this book.

CHAPTER 1

KATE

I should get up. I should get out of bed and meet the day. But I can't. There's no part of this day I'd like to meet. Nothing I want outside of my bedroom. And yet, staying here and falling asleep isn't an option either, even though I'm more exhausted and sleep deprived than I've ever been. Napping was once a beloved pastime of mine, but not anymore.

Turning onto my side with a huff, I pull the fur blankets up to my nose and stretch my entire body, my fingers and toes spreading wide. I smack my pillow with my palm and push the sides up into a poof for my head to sink into. The rain pelts the window, and the sky is a dark grayish purple, creating the perfect atmosphere for a lazy afternoon.

It's nice having a big bed all to myself. I just wish I had my dreams to myself as well. But nope, they've been shared with an anonymous dude since the moment I was brought to this strange little planet. I didn't invite this guy into my head, but whenever I fall asleep, he's there. Whatever I dream about, he sees it. Memories, random thoughts, fantasies—he gets a front row seat. And I know he's real because I've witnessed his dreams too. Memories and fantasies that make no sense in the context of my life but seem to align with his.

Why can't I sleep and dream like a normal person? Ava and Chloe have no idea how lucky they are. Then again, I've never been lucky, so I shouldn't be surprised that this is my life now.

My stomach growls the moment I finally get into a comfortable position, and I groan in frustration. "Fine," I reply to my stomach. Swinging the furs off my body, I climb from bed. I rush down the steps, and reaching the front door, I shove my feet into my boots and tug my thick, black cloak over my shoulders.

Maybe Chloe will be up for lunch, I think to myself, trudging through the damp moss. I make it onto the main path of the village and knock three times on Varrek's front door.

Normally, I'd check with Ava first, since Chloe and Varrek are newly mated and constantly fucking like bunnies, but she's been holed up with Ahlvo at a house by the lake for the last week, making sure his leg is healing properly.

No one answers the door, so I knock again, this time louder. It's possible they're not ho—

"Oh god, Varrek! Right there," Chloe screams from upstairs.

Ah. They are home and very much occupied.

I roll my eyes and drag my feet toward the meal hall by myself. It's not that I'm not happy for her. She just learned she's pregnant with Varrek's baby, and I'm thrilled for them. She's going to be a wonderful mother.

I just miss my friends.

I get that Ava and Chloe are both happy with their alien boytoys and planning their futures, but I don't see them as much anymore and that bums me out. It's not like I have many people here I can talk to.

"Morivikka, Kay-teh," Bruvix calls as he drops his dishes into a bin and leaves the meal hall to greet me. "Where are you headed?"

"Hey, Bruv, just grabbing a bite," I tell him, forcing a smile.

His dark blue eyes narrow at me as rain falls on his already damp hair, causing it to curl slightly around his pointed ears. "You are morose this day. Why?"

"Oh, it's fine. I'm fine. Just tired."

He grunts quietly and walks at my side toward the meal hall.

"Didn't you already eat?" I ask.

"You think I cannot fit another meal into my belly?" he replies, patting his flat stomach. I'd call him a liar and point to his eight-pack abs as proof, but these Trovilian males are huge, and I've seen how much food they can put away.

So instead, I scoff and say, "I don't doubt it."

"Besides, I will enjoy eating with you," he says with his version of a smile. Bruvix is frequently in a bad mood, but I've spent enough time with him to learn what it looks like when he's not. One side of his mouth quirks up slightly—the side that doesn't have a long scar running through it—then a laugh line appears on that side, framing his soft mouth, and his eyes twinkle.

The rain picks up as we duck under the roof of the meal hall. Stray leaves blow in an erratic circle above our heads as the wind quickens, and the skies darken even more. Several members of the clan deposit their empty plates into the dish bin before hustling to their next destination. But like most days, I hear a few whispers behind my back as I get in line for food. "Kay-teh" and "draxilio" and "biyiio," which is Trovilian for "odd," are the words that stand out, and I do my best to ignore them as I focus on the smell of grilled meat covered in spices and sweet, freshly baked bread waiting to be dipped in a savory sauce.

"Ah, the little red one," Nalba says as her eyes land on me. "Morivikka, Kay-teh," she says before dropping her plate into the bin.

"Hey, Nalba," I reply. She cuts in front of us, which would normally piss me off, but watching Waldric nervously compliment her and offer her a pile of junasii bread to take with her is solid entertainment.

Once Nalba leaves, Waldric straightens his apron and finally notices Bruvix in line behind me. "Back already, Bruvix? I did not realize you held my cooking in such high esteem."

"O fah. Cease your preening, Waldric. I am here to eat with Kay-teh," he says, his tone cranky as he hovers over the fresh basket of junasii bread Waldric just pulled off the fire pit. Then he softly adds, "The bread *is* good this day, however."

Waldric smirks as he places three slices of bread on Bruvix's plate along with a cup of viiki spread. We grab seats in the center of the food hall where we're completely covered from the rain, and I start stuffing my face the moment my butt hits the bench.

I stop to take a breath, and I notice Bruvix nibbling slowly as he watches me. "What?" I ask with my mouth full.

He sighs. "While I find your voracious appetite impressive, Kay-teh, I would like to know what troubles you. Have I not yet earned your trust?"

He has. Since the day we landed on Oluura three months ago, Bruvix has been one of the only clan members to welcome me. To really make me feel at home here. The rest of them eye me warily, or think I'm crazy, and for a while, they thought my dragon sighting was total bullshit. That I was making it up for attention. Until the dragon left me a headless tr'gory corpse on the edge of the forest, that is.

But Bruvix always says hi to me, he believed my dragon sightings were real the entire time, and despite being a generally unpleasant guy, he makes me feel like a person, not a nuisance.

"It's not that I don't trust you," I tell him. "It's… it's a problem you can't solve. Something I need to work out on my own. And it'll all go away once I get a decent night's sleep."

He pauses, dropping his bread onto his plate. He clears his throat and lifts his chin, looking proud of himself. "I can assist you with this. We shall mate and it will relax your body. My cock is available to you."

Um.

"Mating relaxes the body. A relaxed body is able to sleep soundly," he explains, then tilts his head to the side. "Do you prefer to be fucked from behind?" he asks as he looks toward the sky. "I have some time now."

How romantic.

"Thanks for the offer, Bruv," I reply with a smile I can't hide. This must be his best attempt at flirting. "I'll keep that in mind."

Bruvix nods once, and his face settles back into his default scowl. We finish the meal in silence, but it's a comfortable silence, despite his supremely unsexy offer left on the table. He walks me back to the house, and I give his elbow a friendly pat before I head back inside.

It's not that I find Bruvix unattractive. He's covered in scars, but those don't bother me in the slightest. Honestly, if I hadn't spent the last two decades abused in every possible way by my almost-ex-husband, Dennis, I'd be very into the idea of casual sex with Bruvix. He's rugged and ripped and his eyes are this captivating shade of dark blue that reminds me of the ocean. The part of the sea with nothing in sight for miles, where only the toughest ships can cross. The part where deep below the surface, there's just as much mayhem as beauty.

However, the section of my brain that registers lust and romantic love is long dead. Or rather, a decomposing corpse beneath the dirt that's starting to flake apart. I haven't had stirrings of anything resembling lust or love in several years, and I have no interest in trying to resurrect them. I'm fine on my own.

Anything else would be too hard, too messy, and not worth the risk.

"Hiya, gorgeous," I greet my bed as I kick my leggings off and flop onto the furs, wearing only my long-sleeve beige tunic that falls halfway down my thighs. My belly is now full of carbs and meat and sleep feels impossible to resist. "Here we go," I mumble as exhaustion takes over and pulls me toward my mystery dream guy.

* * *

"Niro!" I gasp as I snap up in bed. Sweat coats my skin, yet my body shivers uncontrollably. My dream guy with the shimmering blue scales and horns and black hair…his name is Niro. Niro…something. I already forgot the rest of it, but I remember the first part.

The rest of the dream hits me in pieces, and I shudder as I put them together.

Flames. Naked aliens with orange skin and fins on their arms locked in a giant bird cage. Cries for help. More flames.

Then the dream plays out in order as I remember it fully: Niro as a boy. A male alien in a white, floor-length robe yelling at Niro for picking up a stuffed animal he found. Niro's small lip trembling. The male yanking the toy out of Niro's hands and shoving him to the ground. Niro being led into a room with a humongous cage hanging from the ceiling. The aliens in the cage screaming for help. Niro's first shift into his dragon form.

The male telling Niro to "fulfill his purpose." Niro opening his mouth and unleashing a stream of bright red flames onto the cage. The screams getting louder. The smell of burning hair filling my nose. The look of melting flesh. Dream Niro watching me with a tortured expression as I witness this gruesome memory unfold. The male in the white robe smiling once the room is silent, the flames die down, and there's nothing left in the cage but ash and bone.

The male approaching Niro as he shifts back into his humanoid form. The male calling Niro by name, patting him on the shoulder, and congratulating him for a job well done.

That's all my brain could handle, apparently, because then I woke up.

"Niro." I hiss the name this time, disgusted by what I've seen. Did he really do that? Did he murder those people by burning them alive?

A choked sob escapes my lips as I push the covers off my body. Pinching my eyes closed, I try to erase the images from my mind as I pace across the cold wooden floor of my room. I glance out my window, trying to figure out what time it is and how long I've been asleep. It's dark, but as I peer through the narrow crack between Varrek's house and the one directly in front of ours, I notice members of the clan still milling about on the main path, so I'm guessing it's around dinner time, possibly a little later. I've been asleep for a few hours, as best I can tell, yet that horrific dream felt like it lasted a lifetime.

Of all the people in the universe, my dreams have to be linked to a murderer. Fan-fucking-tastic.

Why. *Why* is this happening? And why me? All I want is to get some sleep. Is that really so much to ask? I feel like I'm losing my shit and the walls of my room are starting to close in on me.

I race down the stairs wearing just my tunic, and without putting on pants, I quickly toe on my boots, the backs crushed underneath my bare heels. I stumble outside and lean my back against the side of our house. Taking a few deep breaths, I let the smell of newly fallen rain fill my lungs. I fix my boots and then continue toward the main path.

Peeking around the side of Varrek's house, I make sure the coast is clear. I can't run into any clan members and be forced to make small talk. Seeing Chloe or Varrek or Bruvix would be worse, because they'd notice how freaked out I am and ask all kinds of questions I wouldn't know how to answer. I just need a few minutes alone.

A short trek inside the tree line, I find my favorite tree and lean against it, not caring that it's wet from the rain and soaking through the back of my tunic. This is where I come after every unsettling dream with Niro. It's my secret spot. The tree is one of the tallest in this cluster, its light gray trunk twice as wide as my body, with smooth bark that feels like suede.

I continue to pet my tree until the snap of a branch pulls my focus. I turn toward it, and spot one of the Hexrins peeking through the bushes at me. It's the tiny female with the spiky burgundy-red hair who looks like a teenager. I'm pretty sure her name is Jobaki. She seems nice enough, and since the Hexrins are viewed as outcasts among the clan, I can relate to them on that level, but I've noticed a few of them following me around the village lately, including her, and I don't love it.

All I want is a few minutes of peace and quiet outside the house so I can process the fact that my dreams are linked to a fire-breathing killer, and apparently, I can't even have that. The clan doesn't trust me —that much is clear.

My chin dips to my chest, and I sigh. These people don't like me, and yet, I'm stuck here. Though, despite seeing very little of outer space, Oluura seems like the safest place for a human woman. I'd rather be followed around and unable to sleep than end up as some freaky alien's sex slave on another planet. And I certainly don't want to return to Earth.

I should be grateful, I suppose.

That doesn't make me any less frustrated right now, though. I stomp through the brush and past the trees onto the main path, making sure Jobaki and anyone else within earshot knows I'm not causing any trouble and merely heading back home for the night.

My eyelids feel like they weigh fifty pounds each. I rub them as I pass Jobaki and shout, "I just want to sleep! Can you leave me alone! Please?"

She curls in on herself at the volume of my voice, and I feel like a jerk. That's the body language of a girl who knows pain too intimately. I'd recognize it anywhere. But the guilt evaporates when I remember she's the one who followed *me*, and I'm entitled to call out someone's creepy behavior.

Crossing my arms over my chest, I walk as quickly as I can to get back home. Once I'm inside, I fall to my knees.

Why is this happening?

The words play over and over in my mind as I press my tightened fists against the floor. I rock back and forth on them and watch my knuckles turn white under my weight. My bones feel brittle, like they could crumble as easily as crackers. Exhaustion is so deeply embedded in my body that I feel it even in my eyelashes.

The only thing I want is rest. To fall asleep and stay asleep. And to wake up not remembering my dreams like a normal person. I grab a nearby towel and shove it against my mouth as I scream into it. Pulling it away, I take a deep breath, and laughter bubbles out of my throat. *That feels good.* I cover my mouth with the towel again and scream over and over until my voice cracks and tears stream down my cheeks.

With my scream towel in hand, I climb the steps to my room on the second floor and take a seat on the edge of the bed. My gaze finds the stack of half-finished sewing projects I'm working on, and I grab the one on top. Zohma and the rest of the sewing circle don't seem to mind that I've brought my work home with me, which I'm grateful for since I haven't been able to get work done on a regular schedule.

My fingers fly as I add a stretchy cloth band to the waist of Chloe's leggings. The band is part of a tunic I cut into scraps, and it will accommodate Chloe's growing bump. I let my gaze go unfocused as I pull the needle out and weave it back in along the seam, the repetition comforting.

Sewing is a skill I learned as a kid. Growing up poor, you learn quickly how to fix things that are damaged; otherwise, you go without. I continued to hone this skill as I got older, adding monograms and symbols to my clothes at first, then creating entire outfits from fabric scraps. I had hoped I could turn it into a career as a costume designer, but that was back in college when my future looked bright. When I had hope.

Now, twenty years later, I'm just trying to make it through the day and contribute to the clan however I'm able.

When I reach the end of the seam, I knot the thread through the stitch and tie it off before moving to the other side and starting the process again.

Could this be considered a form of rest? Because I could sit like this for hours.

And I do.

The moment I realize I have to pee, the trance is broken. Dropping Chloe's leggings back onto the pile, I take care of business, pull on my pants, then head back outside. It's not like I have books or TV or a roommate to distract me from this nightmare I'm living. So, I might as well go for a stroll. It's around midnight, I would guess, and the village is silent. I find zero clan members on the main path, and relief washes over me.

The wind rips through the trees and lifts the bottom hem of my tunic, exposing my stomach to the cold air. I wrap my arms around my middle to keep warm.

As long as I stay within the tree line that borders the village on all sides, I'll be safe, and hopefully, left alone. I walk in the opposite direction of my favorite tree, toward the training grounds. Every few steps, I look around to see if anyone is trailing me. When I find no one, I let my shoulders relax and my teeth unclench.

I reach the center of the training grounds and spread the soft dirt around with my booted foot, creating random shapes. I start with a figure-eight, then move onto staples from my teen years, including the blocky Superman S and the transparent cube.

Letting my eyes close, I feel eternally grateful for a moment of peace. The cold air brushes against my cheeks as I lift my chin, and a shiver runs down my spine.

A heavy drop of rain splashes in the middle of my forehead, and soon, the rain peppers my face and hair, and I let it.

In the next breath, everything changes, my moment of peace stolen from me.

A massive hand closes over my mouth, the skin rough and calloused against my face. My nose fills with a crisp, earthy scent. Before I can react, the hand grows into an enormous claw, wrapping around my entire body, and I'm lifted from the ground.

CHAPTER 2

NIRO

The human female groans, her head lolling sideways as she remains hunched and unconscious in her chair. She shivers again for the tenth time since we first arrived in my caves earlier this night. While I am tempted to wrap a blanket around her small shoulders to comfort her, I will not show this witch kindness she does not deserve.

She is ours. Care for her, the draxilio within me commands. The side of me that can shift into a winged, fire-breathing beast has been drawn to this human since she first appeared in my dreams. It is the reason he continues taking me to the village filled with golden-skinned beings whenever I shift forms. But since I am in my flightless form now, I ignore his words and focus on my task: having her break this spell she has cast over me.

I do not know how she slips inside my mind when I am asleep, but she has, and now she has seen my past. She has invaded my privacy. I will not allow this deception to continue.

She must be a witch sent by my handlers to observe me and ensure I have followed the rules of my banishment. That is the only explanation.

How else could this strange-looking creature successfully access the darkest parts of my mind? Through a great deal of research on humans, I know their bodies are weak and their lifespans are short. I do not recall anything in their history about magical abilities, but perhaps this unique talent she wields is little known.

She groans again, as if in pain, and I decide I have had enough of her attempts to make me feel remorse. I wave a vial of tyrapkoi oil under her nose, and her head jerks up instantly after breathing in the bitter, strong scent, her spine straightening.

"The fuc—" she murmurs, her voice hoarse and throaty. I ignore its effect on my body and watch as she whips her head side to side. The eye coverings I applied the moment we arrived and the bindings of her hands and feet to the chair beneath her are to ensure my safety. The extent of this witch's power is unknown to me, and I refuse to let her have her way inside my dwelling.

"Where the fuck am I? What are you going to do to me?" she screams as she pulls against her binds.

I cross my arms over my chest and sit back on the edge of my worktable, wondering when I should remove her eye covering. Perhaps I may leave it on. My research has shown humans are troubled with extended periods of silence. If I keep her vulnerable like this and do not speak, maybe she will be compelled to confess all her secrets.

The table creaks under my weight, and her chin juts out in my direction. "What do you want from me?"

I give her nothing.

Her lip trembles slightly, and she continues. "Are you going to kill me?" Her nostrils flare and a tear rolls down the side of her small nose. "Look, I don't have any money, okay?"

Money is not what I desire.

"And I'm not talented or smart."

She has proven she is both.

"And… I'm dying."

My muscles tense. The draxilio grows restless within me.

I remind him she is not ours. We feel nothing for this human.

He growls, fervently disagreeing.

"It's a horrible disease. I know I don't look sick but...it's a sexually transmitted disease. Very contagious. So if you were thinking of raping me, well, that would be a bad idea," she continues to speak in nonsensical context. "One day, I looked in the mirror and boom, there were hundreds of tiny spiders crawling out of my butt. Crazy, right?" She gulps, trying to come up with more foolishness to add to this obvious lie.

"You do not want butt spiders, trust me. Very itchy. And...and it's spread to my vagina too. That's where they spin their webs. So not only will my pussy-web trap your pecker, or whatever you're packing, the spiders will also destroy your ass. Complete annihilation of your asshole. Yeah. It's a rare disease, I'm told. They're still learning about it. It's called..." she swallows a lump in her throat, "rectal arachnidosis."

I nod, trying to hide my smile, though she cannot see it. What other fabrication will she share next?

But instead of continuing with her tale, she yells, "Bologna foot! Bologna foot! Ava! Chloe! Help me! Bologna foot!"

Her shouts pierce and hurt my ears. This I cannot take. I rip the covering from her eyes and lower my face directly in front of hers. "Enough, human."

Her chest heaves as she stares at me, confusion and rage swirling in her light green eyes. "You," she snarls. "Should've guessed."

"You act as if you know me, tiny one."

"My name is Kate. And I know enough."

Kate. My draxilio hums in appreciation as I let the name settle in my mind.

"You certainly do...Kate."

Our eyes behold each other's, defiant in our refusal to be the first to look away. As odd as this creature appears, I find her fascinating. Her flesh is pale, covered in small brown spots that cluster on her nose, her chest, and arms. If her clothing were removed, where else would I find those brown spots? Are they all over her light, delicate skin?

I shake my head, cleansing those thoughts. Her lip curls up on one side, pleased she has won the stare-off.

"So why did you kidnap me? Am I about to be burned alive in a cage?" she asks, her tone biting.

"Kidnap? Is that what I did?" I reply, raking my fingers through my hair.

"Uh, yeah. You took me against my will. And you fucking drugged me. Which is messed up on so many lev—"

"I did no such thing," I interrupt, disgusted by the accusation. "There was no need. Your flat teeth bit the flesh between my claws when I covered your mouth, you saw my blood, and then you fell unconscious."

She does not seem surprised that the sight of blood caused her to faint, and her anger is slightly deflated at this information, but she tries to mask it with pursed lips. "You're still a kidnapper," she says.

I return to my chair at the worktable. I sink into the worn brown material and lean toward her, placing my elbows on the smooth top. "Aren't you too old to be 'kid-napped'?"

Kate's jaw ticks, and I hear the grinding of her blunt teeth. "Wow."

"The average human woman lives approximately eighty Earth years," I continue. "I would estimate you are halfway through your life. Forty? Fifty, perhaps?"

Her silence stretches on.

"So wouldn't the proper term be 'abduction'? I abducted you, yes?" I ask.

"Okay, that's enough," she says, her mouth dropping open. "I'm pretty sure the term has nothing to do with the age of the victim."

I shrug. "Your language is arcane and contradicting, much like your society."

"I'm thirty-nine, dick," she says.

"Close enough," I reply, walking back around to stand in front of her.

She pinches her eyes closed. "Whatever. What do you want from me?"

"Answers, Kate," I reply, slamming my palms on the arms of her chair, caging her in. "I want answers."

Kate throws her head back and sighs. The dim light from the candles in this room cast a glow around her, and I notice she has the same brown spots along the elegant curve of her throat, just fewer of them here. Seven. I count seven.

"Fine," she grumbles. "What's in it for me?"

For *her*? Is she deranged? "Perhaps I will not kill you. Is that a satisfactory trade?"

"I don't think you want to kill me."

Perhaps I am wrong to assume she is smart. Or maybe this human is dangerously arrogant. "You have seen what I am capable of. I have killed countless others since that first group of laxakauvus in the cage. So many, I do not know the number. So many, their faces are a blur. What makes you think I would spare you?"

Kate smirks and shakes her head slowly, her shoulders slumping in defeat. "I don't know. Maybe I'm just too tired to care about anything anymore."

I understand this feeling. This bone-deep exhaustion I notice in the dark marks beneath her eyes and the sagging curve of her spine. I have felt it as well. It tears away any semblance of sanity and self-preservation that remain.

I let out a sigh. "Tell me with whom you work and how to sever the spell, and I will allow you to return to your little village," I say with a dismissive wave of my hand. I have no interest in hurting her or the golden ones she lives among. I wish to be left alone to serve my penance.

"What?" she asks, her thick brows, the same striking red as her hair, raise and curve. "I have no idea what you're talking about."

I place my face in my hands. Must we continue this? "The dreams."

"What about them?" she asks.

"Ours are linked. You see mine and I see yours," I clarify for this unintelligent being. "This is bewitchment you created, yes? Tell me who hired you to enchant and observe me."

Kate laughs, the tone high and the sound unhinged. "You think *I* did this? And I'm some kind of witch? Why in the ever-loving fuck would I want access to your homicidal memories? To watch you hurt innocent people? You think it's fun for me to fall asleep and be trapped inside your mind? Or to have you loitering inside mine?" Her eyes narrow, a line appearing between her brows. "Do you think I enjoyed you being there when I dreamed about getting my first period at Tommy Benson's pool party?"

I still do not understand why Kate's cheeks turned that deep shade of crimson when I watched her recall the afternoon her blood cycle emerged. Or why the young males in the dream were so repulsed by it. It is a natural biological function for females of many species. Why should she be ashamed? "Possibly not, but there are many on my home planet who desire confirmation I am living a miserable existence on this prison planet," I tell her. "My handlers, specifically. They hired you. Admit it."

"If I'm being honest, I didn't understand most of that," she says, her nose scrunched. "But I can tell you that nobody hired me. I'm not a witch. And I have no idea why our dreams are linked. Since it started, my existence has been pretty miserable too. If I could put a stop to it, I would. Right fucking now."

I study her closely, searching for any manifestation of dishonesty. She is not sweating, not fidgeting (not that she can with her hands bound), not avoiding eye contact. As I focus on the sound of her heartbeat, it does not appear to increase its speed. She speaks truth.

"Very well, Kate. Then it appears someone else has placed this curse upon us. We must find them and hold them accountable."

"Oh yeah? *We?*"

I grunt in concordance.

"Well, who's your top suspect, Niro?" she asks as I slowly approach.

"That is not my name," I tell her. "My name is Nirossanai Dexii iy Prava."

"Yeah, I'm still gonna call you Niro."

"Why?" I ask.

"Because it seems you don't like it."

If I continue to argue with her, she will assume she is right. I suppose it matters not. Hopefully, we shall part company soon. Once we find the caster of this spell and have them break it, we can return to our lives. "Very well," I tell her.

I crouch behind her chair and unlock the chains around her booted feet. "I believe my sister may have information on this. She might even be the culprit we seek. Magic has always interested her. We will go to her home tomorrow. We leave when the sun rises."

She kicks her freed leg up and rotates her ankle in small circles. "Think it's smart to free me? What if I try to escape?" she asks over her shoulder.

"You are welcome to try. If you find your way out of this cave system and locate the entrance, you are free to leave." I unchain her other foot. "But you will find only the heat scan of my body opens the passageways." I swiftly unlock the bindings that hold her wrists, and they fall at her sides. "The exterior pathways at this altitude are narrow. One wrong step will send you down the side of the mountain. Your frail human body would not survive the fall."

She rubs the delicate skin on her wrists, shooting me a look of pure fury.

"Besides, you want this to end just as I do. You wish to sleep well once again?"

She nods, and then as if for the first time since she awoke, she starts to take in her surroundings. I follow her eyes as they roam my workroom, taking in the ewers, textured tapestries, sacred stones, and other items that remind me of home. Then her eyes stray to the corner where several screens monitor the surface of the mountain from peak to valley, scanning for heat signatures, limb prints, and anything that would indicate an intruder's presence.

"Nice place you got here," she says, her gaze still drifting along the walls and to the thick coverings on the cave floors.

"It is," I reply, trying to anticipate her next move. Part of me wishes to stay inside her mind while she is awake too. It would certainly be convenient in this moment.

She points to one of the lanterns. "You have electricity? Inside of a mountain? How?"

"I do," I reply. "Sufoian technology is complicated. I doubt your brain can comprehend such intricacies."

Kate scowls and rises. "So… looks like we're going to be roomies for a bit. Is there a bed I can use?"

"Yes, you may stay in my sister's old room. I will take you to it."

Before we reach the open entryway of my workroom, Kate spins on her heel, grabbing the light blue sgiliatoorye ewer from its podium and lifts it above her head. I suck in a breath.

"I will smash this ugly-ass vase," she threatens. Her eyes hold nothing but vengeance, and I am powerless in this moment to stop her.

Though she is a fraction of my size and easy to overpower, I am not close enough to grab the ewer from her hands. I would have to take a step toward her, and that single movement might cause her to react in a way I do not want. That vessel holds many memories; the only ones from home that are not filled with sadness and fear, and it will crush me to see it destroyed.

"Kate," I say, my tone pleading, my hands raised in surrender. "Give that to me."

"No! You don't get to talk right now. Got it?" she shouts, lifting the ewer as high as her short arms can reach.

I bow my head so she knows I am listening.

"I'll go with you to your sister's or whoever we need to see to break this link between us. But we will not sleep at the same time on this trip. I don't want any more dreams with you in them. And if this spell isn't broken in three days, you're taking me home. Back to the village. Deal?"

"I cannot promise it will be rectified at that time." I tell her only true words. I swallow. I never should have untied her. This female is clearly suffering from a state of rapid psychological deterioration.

"I don't care. There are people I care about in the village, and they'll start to worry if I'm gone too long. You need to take me back so they know I'm not dead in a ditch somewhere. Understood?"

"Yes."

"Give me your word! Or I'll smash this thing into a million fucking pieces."

I place my hand over my heart and look deeply into her eyes. "I give you my word. I will return you to your home in three days."

She breathes heavily as she stares at me for a long moment, and then lowers the vessel to her chest. She hugs it tightly against the pointed tips of her breasts, and briefly, I find myself envious of the object.

I extend my hands and she reluctantly places the ewer into them. Returning it to its podium, I let out a sigh of relief before turning to her. "You have now lost your leverage," I say. "What happens if I revoke my vow?"

"You might. But unless you plan on keeping me bound and blind-folded throughout this little adventure, you understand now that I can figure out what matters to you, and I can destroy it. Whether it's that extremely fragile and hideous vase," she says, looking around me at the ewer, "or something else."

"I am perfectly capable of manipulating you for my own gain," I tell her. She has no idea who she is dealing with. "You think this is a skill only you possess?"

Her eyes dart away briefly before returning to mine. "No, but I'm very good at it. I learned from the best."

"Another lesson from your coven?"

She flashes her blunt teeth at me like a wild animal issuing a threat. "Not a witch. And no, I learned it from my ex-husband. Well, almost-ex-husband. I was nearly rid of him before I was taken from Earth. I hired a lawyer, moved into a place with roommates in case he tracked me down... I even filed the divorce papers."

I have learned that this term *husband* is used synonymously with *mate* among humans. "Your former mate taught you the art of cruelty?"

"He did indeed." Her green eyes turn cold. Hard. "I might not be able to breathe fire or crush you inside my palm, but I can find other ways to blow up your life. Try me."

I eye her warily. "You are much kinder in your dreams."

"And you're much prettier," she says, looking me up and down.

I chuckle under my breath.

"I might be an old woman from Earth, Niro, but I've also been without sleep for far too long. The last fuck I gave, I can't even recall."

We reach the hall outside my workroom, and she turns to face me.

"So which bedroom is mine again?"

"This way," I say. This may have been a colossal mistake.

CHAPTER 3

KATE

In all the times Dream Niro tried to convince me to leave the village, he never once mentioned that he lives inside a cave that looks more like a castle. What a terrible salesman.

As I follow him along the hallway, I notice what looks like gold pipes running along the tunnel ceiling, disappearing into the rock walls. Are they for water? Running water in a cave castle? Hell, there is enough rain on this planet to fill every cavern in this mountain, no doubt. The pipe traveling with us sinks into the wall several feet before the wood door that my host opens.

"Here is your room for the night," he says as I scoot inside the entrance. "You may lock the door like this," he adds as he points to the chain dangling on the inside of the door. Then he nods and mutters, "You will not see me until daylight." He closes the door quickly, leaving me to myself.

My bedroom in the village is nice, sure, but it's not like the room I'm in now. This room drips with opulence. The walls are a smooth cream-colored stone and between the gold lanterns giving off a dim, flickering light are velvet tapestries in rich shades of teal, maroon, and pale pink. There aren't any windows, which makes sense since we're inside a mountain. Plush carpets cover the dusty floors and are at least three inches thick; my feet sink into the softness. There's an empty wardrobe, a small square nightstand, and a chest, all with the same intricate black and white bone inlay design.

There's a faint scent that lingers, and it reminds me of eucalyptus—fresh and earthy and calming. I have no idea where it's coming from, but I love it.

But the best thing about this room is the bed. The canopy bed frame is made of a black wood with hand-carved leaves around the base and small birds perched atop each bedpost. The mattress isn't a mile wide, but it's close. I didn't realize there was a bed size beyond king, and yet, here one sits. I take three long strides before leaping onto the bed like a child.

The mattress bounces once, twice, and then settles with me in the center of it. Chills race up my legs as I feel my soaked, muddy clothes cling to me. My inner thighs are starting to chafe and itch and I'm in no mood for that level of discomfort.

I pull myself off the bed reluctantly, kick off my boots, and strip off my leggings and tunic. I don't typically sleep naked, but I *won't* sleep at all if I'm wearing wet clothes, which will ultimately make the mattress wet too. Plus, it's about ten degrees warmer in the cave than in the village, so birthday suit it is. Since Niro showed me how to lock the bedroom door, I won't have to worry about him creeping in on me during the night.

If he really wanted to break in here, I suppose he could rip the door off its hinges with his bare hands, but I'm choosing to trust him. If only because he wants me here about as much as I want to be here, which is not at all. He also promised that he wouldn't sleep tonight, so I can have my dreams to myself, and I'm very much looking forward to that. We'll have to take turns sleeping until we get this problem solved.

Nerves tighten my stomach as I think about meeting Niro's sister and the possibility of her being responsible for our dream link. I'm no stranger to sibling pranks, but I'm not a member of this dragon family, so it seems cruel to put this curse on me when she's trying to mess with Niro.

I hope she's nice.

Though if she's anything like Niro, I'll hate her the moment she opens her arrogant, pretentious mouth. Why did I expect Awake Niro to be as gentle and kind as Dream Niro? Maybe because Dream Niro doesn't talk very much. He usually just takes my hand when I dream about something sad, or holds me in his arms when I'm scared, whether we're in my dream or his.

Awake Niro, on the other hand, is about as warm and inviting as a frozen bag of shrimp. He's cocky and rude and ageist, and it doesn't matter how veiny his forearms are, or how silky his hair looks, or how his chest is so sculpted that he could probably stop a train with one flex of his pecs. He may not have drugged me, but he did kidnap…er, abduct me. He put his hands on me without my consent and that's not something I take lightly. Why not just swing by the village, introduce yourself, and ask, "Excuse me, ma'am, are you a witch? And did you happen to cast a spell that links your dreams with mine?"

Ugh, men.

I push most of the smaller throw pillows off the edge of the bed and place one between my knees as I turn on my side. Pulling the thick, downy comforter around my shoulders and under my chin, I moan at how good the crisp sheets feel against my skin. Maybe I'll sleep naked more often.

Then I close my eyes, take a deep breath, and begin my bedtime ritual.

Some people count sheep as they try to fall asleep. I prefer zombies. And I don't really count them; it's more about building them. Designing them. I picture them staggering toward me from whatever nearby graveyard they crawled out of, and I start adding details. The milky glaze over their eyes, their clothing filthy and torn, patches of skin on their faces flapping in the wind—revealing bone and tissue in various stages of rot beneath. Eventually, the details tire me out and I fall asleep. I've done this since I was a kid, and it works every time.

Perhaps my mind has always been a little bit twisted and dark.

Tonight's zombies are my favorite pro baseball team from 1995. Although, growing up in Boston, there's only one team you're allowed to root for, so it's not like I had a choice. But it wasn't a hardship because I loved every single player—from the sluggers to the relief pitchers. I watched every game with my dad and brothers that summer.

I still remember which players used chewing tobacco versus gum, who was the most superstitious, and who wore the tight knee-length pants, versus the full-length ones.

I add all these details to the zombie ball players that limp toward me from center field of the historic ballpark. They move as one, huddled together as they groan ominously and their limbs jerk. Their jaws snap at me, and I notice a tooth go flying onto the dirt as they cross the infield. My favorite pitcher drops the ball in his hand, and a gray, decaying finger falls with it.

As the best batter on the team vomits black bile onto his chest, the zombies start to fade, and I drift into a deep, restful sleep for the first time in months.

* * *

A loud and incessant knock jolts me awake, and I have no idea where I am or what's going on, all I know is that I'm pissed. My body tingles with desperation for more sleep, because even though I slept well, I'm so far in sleep-debt that I could pass out for at least a week.

I stumble over to the door, rubbing my eyes as I go. "What do you want?" I shout.

"It is time to wake, Kate," Niro says from the other side of the door.

Oh, right. I'm in the dragon's house.

"It's too fucking early," I grumble as I unlock the chain and pull the door open.

Niro says nothing. He remains perfectly still, apart from the slight heave of his chest beneath his dark charcoal T-shirt that fits him like a second skin. As his gray eyes travel down my body, it feels like a caress, and I briefly forget why I'm mad. I just let him devour me with his hooded eyes, waiting to see what he does next.

But *why* is he looking at me like that?

I look down and immediately understand. I'm completely bare-ass naked.

CHAPTER 4

NIRO

*D*id I exist before this moment? I cannot recall. I recall nothing, not even my own name, as I take in the sight of Kate's bared skin.

Beneath my gaze, her cheeks and chest flush, causing me to swallow the lump in my throat. I follow the trail of brown spots as they cluster just above her heavy breasts and then scatter farther down her body. Her nipples are a dusty, light pink, matching her small, thick lips. Her stomach is enticingly round, just like her hips—curves everywhere.

Eyes moving down, my mouth waters upon seeing her cunt, though it is hidden from my eyes by a triangular tuft of hair in a slightly darker shade of red than the hair on her head. Just as I begin fantasizing about exploring this sacred part of her, she releases a panicked squeal and pulls the door in front of her, blocking my view, and peeking her head around it so that is the only part of her I see.

As quickly as desire heats my blood, self-loathing floods my mind. I cannot have these thoughts for Kate. I am still convinced she is a witch. And even if she is not, she is not mine to long for.

Take her. Pleasure her. Make our mate feel good. The draxilio purrs at me from within.

I shake my head, coming back to myself, and clear my throat. "Um, we must leave soon in order to reach my sister's dwelling. It is not close."

Kate nods as her small fingers wrap around the edge of the door. "Okay, yeah. I'll, um, get changed and we can go."

I am still picturing the hair covering her cunt when she snaps her fingers, trying to regain my attention. "Yes, in the hall," I reply quickly. "In the hall, I shall be out here."

My feet take the rest of me down the hall and I pace outside my workroom, clenching and unclenching my jaw as my mind reels. Kate has never been naked in her dreams. Having seen her luscious body, I can affirm it is better than I ever could have imagined.

The patch of red hair between her thighs is an image I never want to forget. I am eager to study Kate's cunt, closely, and become an expert on how it looks, feels, and tastes.

Get ahold of yourself, you fool, I chide myself.

Right. This is not a time for scandalous thoughts. Kate is not my mate. She is merely a human I am inexplicably linked to for a short period of time. Once we break the spell, we will resume our separate lives. There is no reason for thoughts about her body.

Kate's door creaks as she closes it, and I stride down the hall to meet her.

Her eyes are bright, and her hair is pulled into two neat braids that hang down past her shoulders. Two strands hang loose down the sides of her face, and my hand flexes with the need to push one behind her small ear. She has on her same unkempt tunic, leggings, and boots from the night before, and I make a note to show her how to use my digital stitcher so she can have decent clothing options upon our return.

"Ready!" she says in a bright tone that seems forced.

"Good. Follow me," I say.

"Um, how are we getting there?" she asks as she trails behind me.

I turn slightly and flash her a grin. "We fly, of course."

"Riiiiight," Kate says. "And how am I supposed to—"

I don't let her finish her sentence as we step into the launch cavern at the far end of the caves.

"What in the..." Kate gasps as she enters behind me, looking around the spacious room. "How did you create this in the middle of a mountain?"

"It was open and exposed to the elements when my siblings and I first settled here," I tell her, "but over time, we removed the scattered boulders and added a mechanical glass ceiling with solar light panels that open when we shift to draxilio form and launch into the sky."

She nods with wide eyes and pursed lips. It looks as if she is trying to hide her astonishment.

"The ceiling is also programmed to close the moment we clear the top of the mountain," I add.

Kate scrunches her nose as she takes me in. "I mean, with the right tools, anyone can do anything, when you think about it."

I ignore her obvious barb. "I will carry you in my claws," I tell Kate as I walk into the center of the room and shake out my limbs, preparing to shift.

"Yeah...no offense, but that sounds terrible," she mutters, her eyes darting around the room nervously. "How am I supposed to hold on? What if you drop me?"

"I will not drop you."

She chews on the inside of her cheek as she crosses her arms over her chest.

I make my way to her and open my arms. When she is scared like this in our dreams, I hold her close. But as I get within reach of her, she takes a step back and the tension in her body is visible.

My arms drop to my sides, and I keep my voice soft. "This is the only way we can get to my sister. I know you are frightened, but I will keep you safe."

"Can't we just call her? You must have a phone or computer or something. Maybe we can interrogate her over video chat?"

I tsk under my breath. If that were possible, I would certainly prefer it. "Her electronic communication is unreliable, and we need answers now. I cannot wait a full moon cycle for her to return my message."

Kate takes a few breaths and rolls her eyes. "Fine. Let's get this over with."

I nod, relieved, and hold up a hand. "Stay where you are. I need space to shift."

She takes another couple steps back and leans against the wall. I return to the center of the room and wave my hand in front of the automatic sensor. The ceiling opens in the center, and the glass panels slide wide to expose the gloomy sky above.

I close my eyes and picture my draxilio form, the strength in my limbs and the deadliness of my claws. I picture my wings, wide and thick, as I glide through the clouds. Within a heartbeat, my body transforms. The moment the shift is complete, my nose is assaulted by Kate's scent. It is sweet and rich—reminding me of a pastry I used to eat on my home planet of Sufoi. In my other form, my senses are not as strong, and I did not know she smelled this good. But in this body, and being this close to her, I want nothing more than to press my large muzzle into her neck and breathe her in.

I must ignore the desire in my chest though, because this human is not mine, and we have a long journey ahead of us to my sister's dwelling. I must focus. I take two lumbering steps toward her and uncurl my front claws.

Kate stares at me wide-eyed and slack-jawed as she slowly approaches. I thought for certain she would be even more terrified than she was before, but her expression as she steps in the middle of my open palm is one of awe. I close my claws around her and bring her close to my chest. I hear her mumble something in alarm as I launch us into the sky.

I cannot speak to Kate in this form, so I will address whatever concerns she has once we land.

When we arrive, the midday sun hangs low in the sky. It peeks through the puffy purple clouds and shines down on the cliffside clearing above my sister's dwelling. My back claws dig into the soft soil, and I feel Kate smacking against my claws, trying to free herself. I release her, and she stumbles before falling to her knees and screaming something with her fist raised in my direction.

I shift into my flightless form, and race toward her, worried she has been injured on our journey. "What is wrong?" I ask, crouching beside her.

"Could you not hear me?" she huffs between panting breaths. "I've been yelling that I have to pee for the last hour! And I've been stuck in the same position the whole trip, so my legs are full-on pins and needles right now."

Kate rolls onto her back and kicks her feet up. Her kicks are awkward and her feet flop around as if no longer connected to her legs.

"We cannot communicate when I am in my draxilio form. I can understand what you say but I cannot respond in a way you will comprehend. And when I am in flight, the wind is too loud to hear anything at all."

"Ahh," she groans and hisses as she massages her ankles. "Okay, I suppose that's good information for the trip back." She rolls onto her belly and looks around. "So where's your sister's place? My bladder's about to explode."

I grit my teeth. She will not be content with my reply. "We are required to go on foot from here, down the cliff trail."

"Cliff trail?" she says, her voice rising to a nervous pitch. "Is it steep?"

"Yes. And uneven. And long."

She nods, her lips forming a grim line. "Of course, it is. Icing on this whole fucking turd cake."

If Kate is complaining now, I cannot imagine how she will react to the rickety foot bridge we have to cross. I offer her my hand, bracing for another biting remark.

Instead, she takes it and hops up and down once she is on her feet. "Okay, my feet are awake now. Turn around."

"What?"

"We're about to hike into the jungle, and if I don't pee right now, I'm jumping off this cliff. So. Turn. Around," she demands, drawing a circle in the air with her finger. She lifts the hem of her tunic and starts tugging at the waist of her pants as she steps behind a stout bush covered in purple flowers.

I do as she asks and walk a short distance away to give her more privacy. "I did not realize humans were so free with nudity."

"We're not. The peep show from this morning was unintentional."

"Yet you were mere seconds from pulling your pants down in front of me."

I hear her scoff, and I imagine the expression she is giving me is scathing. "I wasn't trying to show off my cooch. That's just how badly I had to pee."

Kate continues to mumble something in a searing tone under her breath. I shake my head as I walk a few more paces from her. I have a feeling our inability to communicate while flying in my draxilio form was a blessing.

She hollers that she is finished, and I return to her side. "May we continue?" I ask.

"Lead the way, blue man."

I bristle at the nickname, not because of what it is, but this is an intimate, familiar practice between beings who are close, and she already calls me "Niro," which no one else ever has. More than one casual name makes us seem like friends, or perhaps something more. I do not want her to be anything other than a temporary partner in this mission.

"Wait," she says, her heavy steps ceasing behind me. "Why aren't you naked?"

I turn toward her, my eyebrows rising in interest. "Do you wish for me to undress?"

"No," she replies in a loud, embarrassed tone. "That's not what I meant. How did you shift back while keeping your clothes?"

I look down at the garments I was wearing before I took flight in my draxilio form. It is a reasonable question. "Not long before our first shift, draxilios undergo a procedure to get a clothing block inserted here," I say as I point to the metallic insert on the inside of my left bicep. "It is activated when our bodies begin the transformation, and removes our clothing so it does not get destroyed each time."

She jerks her head back, surprised by my answer. "And it just puts your clothes back on when you're shifting back?"

"Yes," I answer. "As I said, Sufoian technology is complex. You would not understand."

"What if someone were to rip your clothes off before you fully shift?" she asks, a slight grin tugging at her lips.

Her expression is one I have not seen on her. It worries me. "Are you scheming to steal my clothes?"

Her eyelashes flutter in an innocent, yet wicked, gesture that tightens my stomach. "Maybe," she says. "Tit for tat."

There must be a language barrier here. I know the definition of the slang term *tit*, but not the last word. I do not understand the phrase in this context.

I surmise there will be many human words and phrases I will not comprehend from her as I continue down the trail, a careful hand resting on the hem of my shirt and the waist of my pants.

Not far onto the trail, I find that Kate's short legs slow our pace significantly. I fall back and wait for her to reach me.

"So how are you able to speak English?" she asks.

"As part of my research on your kind," I reply. "I learned many of your planet's languages."

"Right, and why were you so obsessed with my kind?"

I rub the back of my neck, trying to ease the tension that builds at this topic. "That is not information you need."

She laughs, the sound bitter. "So what? It's information I want."

"The human race is a subject I was required to study for a mission on Sufoi."

"What kind of mission?" Kate asks quickly, her tone stiffening. "Were you planning on invading our planet *Independence Day* style?"

"What is Independence Day?" I scan my memories at the familiar name. "Is that not a holiday celebrated in the United States?"

"Yeah, it's a holiday but it's also the best alien movie ever," she declares. "How did you study humans and not watch that movie?"

"You sound as if you are judging me," I tell her.

"Oh, I am. Big time. It was a staple of the 1990s."

I use my shirt to wipe the sweat dotted along my brow. "I watched no videos as part of my research. I only read texts."

"Well, you really fucked up there," she mumbles quietly. "What books did you read?"

"History texts, of course," I reply. What better way to gain an understanding of human behavior and how it has changed over time? "Some biology, as well." I turn back to face Kate, and find her nose scrunched, disapproval clear on her face. "What disturbs you?" I ask.

"Look, I don't know which history books *you* read, but if they're anything like the ones I was forced to read in school, they were all written by white men who painted their fellow white men throughout history as morally impeccable heroes," she says, frustration punctuating every word. "And that is…not the case."

She means the humans with light skin like hers. I did read about such things. Not extensively, but I am familiar with the different races on Earth and how the paler ones rose to power in certain areas of the planet.

"At any given time, pop culture is where you'll find our interests and behaviors more accurately reflected," she adds. "But even then, trends can quickly get appropriated and whitewashed unless you're paying attention."

I consider this. If Kate speaks truth, my basic understanding of the human race could be incorrect. In particular, most of what I have learned about human females. Is that why her mannerisms and phrasing seem so crass?

"Why have so few rulers on your planet been female?" I ask. I had noticed this in the historical writings, and I found it quite odd.

She laughs, the sound dry and mocking. "Because most societies hate women and treat them accordingly."

Yes, this is what I gathered. But it does not answer my question, exactly. "I shall rephrase: why have your females not found other means of rising to power?"

"Such as?" she asks.

"The first female queen of Sufoi assassinated the king and took the throne," I tell her. "She grew tired of the inequity among the people of Sufoi and refused to wait any longer for change to be made."

"Is that so?" Kate asks.

"Yes," I reply. "Queen Savanavi a di Buonoza is known as the most successful and beloved draxilio queen to date. When she died, her daughter took her place. Their rule ended when her daughter died without an heir of her own."

Kate stops behind me, and I turn to find her smiling widely. "Are you suggesting that women on Earth should just kill the men in power to get them out of our way?"

I suppose I am. "It would be effective, would it not? And have the males in power truly earned their place?"

She chuckles, shaking her head. "Damn, dragon. You keep talking like that and I'm gonna fall in love with you."

I am…perplexed by this response. She must be trying to be humorous. Because surely talk of murder would not fill her with such joy.

"Okay, enough politics," she says. "How long have you lived on Oluura?"

I grunt as I turn sideways to fit through dense brush on the trail. "My siblings and I have been here thirteen soliqs."

"Soliq? Is that like a year?"

I think back to how her people calculate time based on their planet's movement around their sun. Such a self-centered, small-minded construct. "Do you realize the way you keep track of the passage of time correlates with no other civilization? What you refer to as a year does not match any other known time keeping processes?"

"Well, excuse us for not knowing about 'other time keeping processes' when we hadn't figured out our planet was round yet." Her use of satire is peculiar. I did not understand that human concept until now. It seems her vernacular is mostly of this style.

"God, is it always this humid here?" she asks, groaning.

I do not reply, focusing instead on my footing.

Kate mutters, "If you've been here thirteen years, how old does that make you?"

"I am two hundred ninety-four Earth years," I reply after a quick calculation so she will understand.

She gasps, and I turn to find her bent over and leaning against the cliff wall as laughter shakes her shoulders. "Two hundred and ninety-four? You made me seem like a wrinkly old hag and your ass is almost three hundred?"

I approach her slowly, remaining silent until her laughter fades. "The average draxilio lives seven hundred years. And I am not an average draxilio. I am different. I will live longer than that."

Kate rolls her eyes dramatically, a smile still spreading her lips and says, "Of course, you will. It's always the insufferable ones that live the longest."

"So you will outlive most of your fellow humans then, yes?"

She folds her fingers down on one hand, then raises the one in the middle. It is clearly a gesture of some kind, and the look she gives me indicates that it should offend me, but it does not.

After a peaceful moment of quiet, she asks, "What's your sister like?"

"Must you continue with these questions?" I ask, rubbing a hand through my hair.

"Forgive me for wanting to get to know my kidnapper a little better," Kate replies. "We're in each other's heads every night yet we know very little about one another."

She is right, but what can be gained by the two of us creating a more intimate bond? I do not want that with anyone. I remain quiet as I continue walking down the steep path, bracing my hand on the cliff wall as I go.

"Fine. We just won't talk then," she snaps.

My steps remain careful and my tread light as I step over fallen branches and thick vines that cover the path. The moment I think Kate has grown accustomed to silence, she begins to whistle.

She is terrible at it. But that does not stop her.

My shoulders scrunch up toward my ears with each sharp, high-pitched *thoooooowwwwip*. The birds perched in the surrounding trees respond to her unsteady tune with their own piercing chirps. I am tempted to burn this entire jungle to the ground to cease this noise.

I stop in the middle of the path, my chin dropping to my chest. "Ask your questions. Your chatter is far less irritating than *this*."

"Easy now, you'll make me blush," Kate sneers.

I remain quiet.

"Okay, um, why is that vase so important to you? The one I grabbed."

"It was given to me by one of my handlers," I tell her. "A gift. This handler, she was…kind to me."

She says, "Hmm," and then adds, "you seem to have a lot of fancy gifts."

I chuckle at the spiteful way she says "fancy." It is clear she is resentful of wealth, but maybe she has never experienced it. The village she lives in with the gold ones certainly indicates as much.

"Any other questions for me?" I ask as we reach the entrance to the foot bridge.

She starts to speak but stops once she sees what lies ahead. "You expect me to walk across that thing?"

"It is stronger than it looks," I say, trying to sound reassuring. "I would fly us over, but the gorge is too narrow for my wings to extend."

Kate leans forward on her toes to look over the side of the cliff. I grab her by the shoulders and pull her back. "Refrain yourself. Looking down will not help your confidence or bravado," I tell her. The gorge we are about to traverse is deep, and what lies beneath is jagged rock. There is no comfort gained from looking at it.

I step onto the bridge, gripping the ropes on both sides. "Follow me. One foot after the other."

To my surprise, Kate follows closely, placing each foot behind mine the moment I move. "Good, good. Go slow," I tell her.

"Sure," she says between panting breaths. "But if this thing falls apart on us, I'm taking you down with me."

We have about forty wooden steps between us and the other side of the bridge. The slats are worn and connected by fraying ropes, just like the handles Kate and I are gripping tightly. I have repeatedly told my sister that repairs are necessary on this wretched bridge, but she insists that she doesn't use it often enough to put the work in. This may be the case, but it makes for a treacherous journey for visitors.

"Neither of us will die this cycle."

"Yeah, we'll see," I hear her mumble.

Then I feel Kate's small hand ball into a fist against my back, clutching my shirt. It is contact I was not expecting, contact I do not want, but it also sets my skin ablaze with need. No matter how my mind screams for me to have her remove that hand, I know the words will not leave my mouth.

My draxilio is extremely pleased.

She leans in with her next step, and I feel the hardened tips of her breasts brush against my back. My heartbeat quickens, and every thought is gone from my head.

My foot lands a bit too hard on the next wooden slat, and it snaps under my weight. Kate, still clinging to my shirt, falls forward as I drop through the new hole in the bridge, and she lands on my back.

She screams and wraps her arms around my neck as the step she was on breaks under her. The bridge jostles and swings, causing me to lose my grip on the rope handles, sending us down toward the rocky gorge below.

I wonder if Kate's bone-chilling scream is the last thing I will ever hear.

CHAPTER 5

KATE

I continue to scream at the top of my lungs with my eyes closed, bracing for impact. Just waiting for death to claim me. When it doesn't, my eyes slowly open, and I see Niro holding both of us up by the frayed end of a rope that dangles between the steps we broke and the ones that remain intact ahead of us. He grunts softly as his muscles strain, and I'm torn between kissing him all over for keeping us alive and holding my breath until we make it back to solid ground. I settle on something in the middle.

"We're not dead. Oh my god, we're not dead," I say into his ear, my voice shaky. "You saved us."

"I have done nothing yet," he replies through gritted teeth. "Just… do not let go of me."

I do as he says, being careful not to strangle him. The rope gives a little more, and a loud squawk escapes my lips as we drop a foot. Not a good sign for what's to come. We need an exit plan. "I don't think the rope can hold both of us," I say, studying the bridge ahead of us.

"Yes. It can," Niro replies.

Is he out of his mind? Is he trying to be encouraging or polite? This is not the time for either.

"Between my chubby, dimpled ass and your ridiculous bulk, we've got too much weight on this rope. We need to spread it out."

"No," he replies quickly. "I am able to climb."

"Mmm, I'm pretty sure you can't."

His grunt echoes throughout the gorge as he pulls us up another few inches. "Must you fight me on this *now*? I will get us across."

"Can you not let your stupid male pride get in the way?"

I spot an unbroken step that's not too far from reach and a plan starts to form in my head. "Can you swing us closer to that step?" I ask, pointing at my target.

"Yes, why?" Niro groans as he struggles to pull us up higher on the rope.

My legs still wrapped around his middle, I start to shimmy down a bit farther, coming around to the side of his body. "Kate, what are you doing?" he yells in more of an admonishment than a question.

"I have an idea," I start, panting and sweaty already. I duck my head around his massive bicep, and carefully place one arm firmly around his neck while leaving my other arm hanging free. "Swing us closer to that step, and I can grab onto it and pull myself across. We make our way to the end of the bridge, separately, and we won't die. Sound good?"

"You are sure you can do this?" he asks, his tone thick with skepticism. I know what he's thinking. Little old human me couldn't possibly have the arm strength to accomplish this. And that's fine, let him think that. I don't mind being underestimated.

"You have a better idea?" I ask.

A low growl rumbles in his chest. He adjusts his grip on the rope and pulls his legs together before swinging them in front of us, and then behind. He repeats this until we start moving, and I lift my hand out toward the step, readying to leap.

Once we have some momentum, I stretch my fingers as long as they'll extend and hold my breath. I reach for the step once we swing forward, but miss, my fingertips brushing the edge of the wood. "Next time. Be ready," I yell.

Niro grunts as his legs cut backward through the heavy misty air of the jungle. I can tell the moment we rush forward that it's enough to get me there. I clench every muscle in my body as I reach for the step, desperation and adrenaline pumping through my blood.

My fingers wrap around the outer edge of the wood, and my grip is like a vise as I release my hold on Niro's body, letting my weight swing forward as my free hand reaches for the next step. Once I grab hold of it, I stop, turning back to Niro with a smug grin on my face.

"Well, come on. We've got people to see and spells to break. Shake a leg."

His lips flatten into a hard line. "Why would I need to shake my leg?"

The moment I notice his muscles flex is the moment I realize I need to focus. I can't exactly be smug about this tiny victory if I end up falling to my death. I face forward and continue to awaken those old monkey-bar muscles I used as a kid to dominate on the playground.

Beads of sweat glide down my back and between my boobs as I make it about halfway, and I know I need to move faster before my hands get too sweaty to continue. I hear Niro close behind me, and it pushes me to keep moving.

I reach the second-to-last step, and my palms are slippery against the wood. I scramble to pull myself up, but every time I adjust my grip, my hands immediately start to slide. Tears fill my eyes as I struggle— I'm not sure I can climb out, and worse, I'm afraid that after all that showboating, I'm going to fall. Taking a breath, I focus all my energy on my grip, praying this is simply a mental hurtle I need to overcome.

I can almost touch the side of the cliff with my feet, and if I can just make contact with the soles of my boots, I'll be able to use that leverage to push up and reach the last step. Stretching my toes, I find a protrusion of rock that feels solid enough to stand on. The moment I lean my full weight on it, my boot slips and I let out a screech as my leg scrapes against the rock. I feel my leggings rip all the way up to my thigh, and I'm certain several layers of skin have been torn away, but that's the least of my problems right now.

I let out a strangled cry the moment my fingers slide off the edge of the step.

This is it. This is how I die.

But before I land face first on the sharp boulders below, I'm caught. I look up to find Niro's large hand wrapped tightly around my forearm, his gray eyes blazing with determination. He pulls me up as far as he can, then snakes his arm around my waist as he reaches for the final step. Once he has it in his grasp, he finds secure footholds along the cliffside to climb up.

"I have you," he rumbles into my ear as he presses my back against his chest. Goose bumps explode across my skin at the words, but I try to push the sensation away, rejecting the mere possibility that the sound of his voice could elicit such a reaction from my body.

It's the adrenaline. That's all.

He wiggles us through the opening of the slats at the end of the bridge, and slowly, he pulls us over the lip of the ledge. We collapse and roll onto our sides, finally able to breathe.

We separate, only slightly, and our chests heave as we take each other in. The light dances along his cheek and neck, causing his scales to shimmer. It finally starts to hit me that I was dangerously close to falling to my death, and if Niro hadn't caught me, I'd be a crumpled pile of bones. He saved me. I kind of hate that I needed him to save me, but I'm grateful he did.

"Thanks," I say through short, quick breaths.

His eyes travel down my body, and widen when they reach my leg. "You are bleeding," he rasps, his tone filled with worry.

I don't look down. I can't if I want to remain conscious. "How bad is it? Am I going to lose a leg?" I ask with my eyes pinched shut.

I hear him chuckle softly, and relief washes over me. Surely he wouldn't find anything funny if amputation was in my near future. "No, Kate. You will be fine." I peek one eye open as he pulls his shirt over his head and rips it into several strips. Then he starts tying the dark gray fabric around my shin.

"How did you think to do that?" he asks, undoubtedly in an attempt to distract me from the sight of my leg. "The swinging."

"There's a thing called *monkey bars* where I'm from, where you swing your body from one bar to the next," I tell him, keeping my eyes trained on his face. "I learned as a kid."

"Ah," Niro says with a smile, his eyes holding a warmth that looks almost like admiration. But that can't be right.

"Then a few years ago, I found myself married to a man who didn't want me to work. He even installed security cameras at our front door to monitor my daily activities, so I got really good at climbing the tree outside our bedroom window on the second floor so I could do odd jobs for my neighbors."

I'm not sure why I'm sharing this with him. Perhaps I'm drunk on extreme terror.

I've had one dream of Dennis that Niro has seen, but it was fairly tame. Just a flashback of a party we threw a few summers ago. He belittled me when I filled my plate with food, but that was it. I'm not sure Niro pieced together that Dennis was my husband.

"He did not allow you to work? Why?" he asks as he finishes wrapping the final strip around my thigh. "I thought human females had joined the workforce not long ago."

"Because he didn't like the idea of me meeting people? Or having my own source of income? Or saving enough money to one day leave his ass? I don't know, but it was probably a combination of all three."

"And his heart still beats?" Niro asks with a dry laugh.

I return his grin, but I feel it fade almost immediately. "Unfortunately."

The muscle in Niro's jaw ticks, and he looks down at the ground between us. I see his fist clench at his side, and I wonder if he's angry on my behalf, or just angry in general. Or perhaps our near death is affecting him as well. I want to ask him, but before I can, a rustling sound comes from the bushes a few feet away, and Niro lifts into a crouched position, ready to shift and attack.

A moment later, a tall, blue-skinned female emerges. "Nirossanai!" she greets him, excitedly. Then she says something I can't understand, in what I assume is their native language.

This must be his sister.

She looks to be around the same height as Niro with the same thick black horns poking out from her hairline. The round shape of her face and her wide-set gray eyes are just like his. Her silky black hair hangs like a curtain just past her shoulders but is completely shaved on one side of her head, with an intricate design etched into her scalp. She also has piercings on either side of her nose and through her brow, and a slim black tattoo that snakes around her right arm from shoulder to wrist.

Niro's shoulders drop and a relieved sigh whooshes out of him. "Yes. And barely survived the journey." He says in English as he stands, shaking the grass and dirt from his pants.

Her body is lean, but she still has curves that are proportionate to her frame. She wears very little clothing, which makes sense in this stifling humidity. An olive-green tube top covers her chest and the upper half of her stomach, and loose shorts of the same color hang low on her hips. Her skin has the same smooth but tough-looking scales as Niro's, in a rich blue that almost sparkles. She also wears ankle-high silver boots with buckles on either side. As she steps out of the bushes, her spine straightens and her chin lifts.

"Why did you not enter through the tunnel on the other side?" she asks, now speaking in English also.

"There's a tunnel on the other side?" Niro asks the question calmly as I scream it.

He offers me a hand and I take it as he carefully helps me stand. When I put weight on my leg, I'm relieved to find no deep aches or pains, just a persistent sting where my skin is scraped.

"Yes, our brothers helped me construct it. This bridge is far too old and fragile to use," she says.

My eyes roll so far back in my head I worry they'll get stuck. "Uh, yeah, it is," I reply. So fragile, we almost died.

His sister's eyes find mine as if just noticing my presence. She tilts her head at me, and then shoots Niro a strange glance. "What is this you have brought? A human? Is she a gift for me?"

"Kate, this is my sister, Alussanai Dexii iy Gwix. Alussanai, this is Kate. And no, she is not a gift for you," he says, his tone stiffening. "She is a problem of mine. A problem we have come here to fix."

"Oh, *I'm* the problem here? Please," I say to Niro. His default dick-mode has been reactivated, I see.

I turn to Niro's sister. "I…" I start. "May I call you Alu?"

"What a fun little version of my name!" Alu squeals, and I take that as a yes.

"He's a problem for me too," I add. Niro and Alu stare at me, then look at each other with raised eyebrows. "I just want that…noted."

"Very well. It is noted," she says. "And why do you assume I am capable of fixing this problem you share?"

Niro takes a step toward her. "Because I am quite certain you caused it."

Alu starts giggling, then eventually her giggle grows into a full howl of laughter.

Niro crosses his arms over his chest and his mouth forms a grim line. "Can you continue this," he says as he gestures at her leaning back with her hands clutching her chest, "inside? I have grown quite tired of this stickiness out here, and Kate is injured."

She nods, still laughing too hard to speak, and waves a hand at us to follow her.

Behind the bushes Alu emerged from is a narrow walkway that forms an S shape to Alu's small cottage. The pebbles that fill the path are lime green and match the exterior color of Alu's home. It's a one-story building with a layer of slender, dark-green leaves covering what looks like a bamboo roof. Alu pushes aside a large dark brown panel with hinges across the top, and I realize it's a sliding door.

The moment we enter, I notice just how not small this home is. From the front, it looks like an unassuming shack. But on this side of the door, it looks like a five-star villa in the middle of a jungle paradise. The opposite wall is a floor-to-ceiling window with a breath-taking view of a waterfall on the other side of the cliff. The living room has a sunken seating area in the center with a burnt orange couch that fills the circle, apart from a wooden table in the middle and a set of two white steps leading to the main floor. The couch is covered in plush velvet pillows and blankets in various shades of gray.

I also notice that whatever form of air-conditioning she has is on high, and the sweat dripping down my back instantly dries. More alien technology, no doubt.

It's also pretty messy. There are clothes and shoes and blankets tossed every which way on the furniture and all over the floor, and I hear Niro grunt under his breath at the sight. I get the sense that Alu is a carefree gal and clutter doesn't bother her. It certainly seems to bother her brother, though.

Alu tells us to remove our boots and take a seat as she slips through a heavy burlap curtain. She comes back a moment later with a chrome-rod bottle carrier hooked over her forearm. It looks like an old-fashioned milk carrier, but this one has a large glass bottle and three short, frosted tumblers, as well as a tall glass filled with a snack of some kind.

Alu places the carrier on the table in front of us. Niro helps take out the tumblers and pours a white creamy liquid from the bottle into each glass. Once the glasses are full, Alu places the snack glass in the center. It looks like popcorn or a nut of some kind, all puffy rounded edges in strange shapes, the color of caramel. Niro and Alu both drop two of the snack things into their drinks and lift their glasses, then look at me expectantly when I don't follow suit. I reach for my drink and sniff it, nervous as to what I'm about to put in my body. It smells citrusy, but still unfamiliar.

I toss in two snack things, lift my glass to theirs, and then pause. "Are you sure this is safe for humans?" I ask.

"I suppose we shall soon see," Alu replies with a wicked grin.

Niro, sitting to my right, turns toward me while shooting Alu a deadly glare. "It is safe, Kate."

This could easily be poison. And a perfect scenario for Niro to kill me, thus breaking our dream link, and then he could dump my body off the cliff in the middle of the fucking jungle. "Okay then," I mutter with a sigh. Alu and Niro take large gulps while I take a teeny, terrified sip.

The instant the creamy liquid touches my tongue, my taste buds become desperate for more. This drink tastes like a creamsicle with a hint of coffee, and I throw back the rest of it within three big sips, leaving the now-deflated and smaller snack things at the bottom of the glass.

Alu refills my cup and smiles wide. "You like?"

"I do. What is it?" I ask.

"It is called tibbi. It is the nectar of bokna fruit with some xid candies to balance the sweetness," Niro replies.

The only time I've put candy in a drink was back in college when my roommates and I added sour gummies to a bottle of vodka. That was a dreadful beverage.

"There's no alcohol in it?" I ask Alu. She looks at Niro who says something in their language, then she turns back to me.

"It is just juice," she says, then shifts her gaze to Niro. "So, what is this quandary you blame me for, brother?"

Niro leans forward and places his drink on the table. He rests his forearms on his knees and scrubs a hand down his face. "I remember your interest in magic, Alussanai. The way you studied it so intensely when we were younger. It would not surprise me to learn that you had joined a coven or learned to practice the dark arts on your own.

"If you have unleashed a magical spell on me," he continues, his gaze turning hard, "whether intentional or accidental, you must tell me."

A loud, screeching caw meets my ears and Niro and I duck as a red bird the size of my head dive-bombs the table in front of us. "The hell?" I call out as it steals a candy from the glass and flies in a circle above us.

Alu chuckles as she sticks an arm out. The bird lands on her forearm and its long claws curl around her blue skin. It sits there with its head tilting back and forth, blinking its cartoonish, three white eyes. "This is Mek," she says, introducing the bird. It pecks at her empty hand, and she winces in pain.

"This is a companion to you?" Niro asks incredulously as he takes a closer look at the welt forming on her skin. "It is a wild creature, Alussanai."

Mek caws at us once more before launching off Alu's arm and flying down the hall.

She shakes her head as a charmed smile forms on her face. "He arrived the same time as I. This is his home too. I cannot force him to leave."

"You can," Niro says, his tone hard. "You choose not to."

"Perhaps," she replies with a scoff, her brow furrowing. "So, you think I have hexed you?"

"I will not be angry," Niro vows, raising his hands in surrender. "But you must be honest with me."

Her eyes dart from mine to Niro's, not in a guilty way, but more like she's shocked he would accuse her of such a thing. "I am sorry, but I have no involvement with this hex you claim to be stuck in. And an interest in magic does not mean I have practiced it myself."

"You're into witchcraft?" I ask. It seems like sorcery is all around me lately. My Aunt Milly, who used to appear in my dreams before I was taken from Earth, the Hexrins, Niro's accusation that I'm a witch, and now Alu.

Alu tilts her head back, looking at the ceiling. "I just find it fascinating. The ability to influence another living creature without them knowing? That is incredible."

"You're a dragon shifter." I point out in a flat tone. "Who can fly." What could possibly be more incredible than that?

"It does not mean I am immune to the lure of enchantment," Alu replies. "And there are draxilio witches, you know…who can fly *and* cast spells."

Her gaze lands on Niro then. She cocks her head, pity tightening her features. "You suffer."

Niro chuckles, the sound raspy and defeated. "Yes. We both suffer," he says, pointing at me with his glass.

"What are you experiencing?" Alu asks, placing a hand under her chin. "I wish to know every detail."

I let Niro take the lead on describing our dream link. How it happens without fail when we're both asleep at the same time. How the person who falls asleep first makes the dream we witness together.

"What do the dreams feel like? Look like?" Alu asks intently.

"Well," I begin, "the setting is always the same. Niro and I are in this black void as we watch the dream happen in front of us, like on a movie theater screen, but there are no defined edges of the screen itself. I just know we can't cross into the dream because I've tried. There's a barrier between us and the dream. So we're powerless to do anything but watch the dream unfold."

"Do you dream the same thing each time?" she asks us.

"No," Niro answers. "They are never the same. Sometimes they are a compilation of images, sometimes they are fantasies, but most commonly, they are memories."

"This human has access to your memories?" Alu asks, her voice taking on a wary edge.

"Yep," I reply quickly. "And he has access to mine. And it sucks a bag of dicks."

Alu is about to finish her drink when she starts laughing. The sound of her giggle is muffled by the glass against her lips.

"You know, this wouldn't be an issue if you just slept during the day," I suggest to Niro.

"I am not a nocturnal creature. Why should I alter my resting time? You sleep during the day."

"No," I reply. I don't have a convincing reason to give him other than *I don't want to*, so I say nothing more.

"Precisely," Niro says with a huff.

Alu continues to smirk at our back-and-forth, and then her eyes brighten with excitement. "You should visit Bexossanai at his dwelling on the plains!"

"I see no logic in that," Niro says as if he'd only visit this person with a gun to his head.

"He has the draxilio archives," Alu says. "He takes good care of them. There might be information to explain this."

"I considered this, but no," Niro says, shaking his head vehemently. "I do not wish to see him."

Alu rolls her eyes as if this beef between Niro and this other guy is nothing new. "What other choice have you? Where else could this hex originate?"

Niro looks at me, and I shrug. Fuck if I know how this dream link was created. "If I had any leads, I would share them," I tell him.

"You go to Bexossanai and get the archives for us," Niro suggests to Alu.

She just laughs. "You think I am eager to fill my cycles with errands for my siblings? Just so they will not have to face one another?"

Ah, it's his brother. Interesting. I nudge him in the side. "Come on, Niro. You're almost three hundred. Time to start acting like an adult, don't you think?"

He sneers at me, revealing his gleaming white teeth. They aren't exactly fangs, but they aren't the blunt square shape of human teeth, either. They're somewhere in the middle, and only mildly terrifying.

"Kate needs to borrow your clothing," he says as he turns to Alu and points at my tunic and torn leggings with a grimace. "These rags are about to fall away, as you can see."

Rags? Asshole.

I try to brush it off, but my head dips slightly as the blood rushes to my cheeks in shame. It's not like I had time to pack before I was kidnapped, or planned to have my leg shredded by the side of a cliff.

But if Alu is judging the state of my clothes, she doesn't show it. She just beams at me and says, "Certainly! I have a piece you may acquire."

Then her gaze slides back to Niro. "You will go see him then? And check the archives?"

Niro's forehead wrinkles as he looks around Alu's living room. It's like he's searching for a way out of it but finds nothing. "You think this occurrence has happened before among our species?"

"It is possible," Alu replies as she climbs the steps next to the couch and heads to the kitchen. She bounds back into the room moments later and places a tray of bread and fruit and something stringy and black on the table and puts another bottle of tibbi next to the tray.

Niro sighs as he takes in the small feast in front of him and rises to stand. "I must sleep now. I do not know when I will get another chance if we go to Bexossanai's dwelling from here."

"Have a restful slumber, Nirossanai!" Alu calls as she pops chunks of the black stuff into her mouth.

"You will be safe here," he says to me quietly.

I'm not sure what to make of Alu yet, but she seems nice enough. Besides, maybe I can score some leverage by getting Alu to reveal some of Niro's secrets.

"Yeah, I'm good," I tell him. "Sleep well."

He dips his chin and retreats down the hall.

Alu refills her glass and slams the bottle back down on the table a little too hard. She lifts the bottom of it and there's a crack on one side, the liquid slowly starting to seep through. She gives me a sheepish look, and then starts chugging right from the bottle. She pauses to take a breath and says, "We must finish this one quickly, Kate."

I laugh, surprisingly eager to bond with her. I throw back the rest of my tibbi, and once my glass is empty, I lift it toward her. "Fill me up, bartender."

CHAPTER 6

NIRO

"Approaching from the back. You need to circle around the compound again, Alussanai, and keep yourself unseen," I tell her through our mental link. The moment we shift into our draxilio forms, my podlings and I communicate through thought, but only if we are all in our larger forms at the same time. It is why I cannot currently reach Kulissanai, my youngest brother, and it is creating a growing ball of nerves in my center.

"We cannot rely on him. How many times must I repeat it?" Bexossanai grumbles, echoing my concerns of late.

"He will deliver," I reply, trying to sound confident. "He does not engage during battle the way you do, but you have seen with your own eyes how his unique skills benefit us."

"Brothers, there are lights scattered through the treetops! We must investigate!" Alussanai squeals with excitement in our heads.

Bexossanai sends her a growl. "Those are leafcrills, Alussanai. Pests. Their noses light up at night." Then he sighs, loudly. "Can you remain focused? Our target is in the structure below and he must be taken care of. Do not ruin this like you always do."

I am about to chide him for being too tough on her when I notice from my position on the ground that Alussanai's command over her light-bending capabilities are waning, making her draxilio form visible to anyone who looks up. It is because she is distracted. Besides, Bexossanai works best when there is someone to complain about, so I refrain from correcting his rudeness.

I huff a breath from my enlarged nostrils and launch myself onto the second-floor balcony. We are running out of time to get this done. I shall do it myself if I must.

"What room did we determine he was in?" I ask Bexossanai.

He hovers just above the ground behind me, maintaining a safe distance from the structure to watch for approaching threats. "According to the king's report, the leader of this group of radicals hides in the section on the second floor, on the far side."

I glide past the nearest window and catch a glimpse of an empty bedroom with a large bed covered in pillows of various sizes and colors. "You would think a male who denies science so vehemently would not require this many comforts," I send to my siblings. "It is not as if there is anything of value tucked inside that skull of his."

Bexossanai chuckles darkly. "I see Kulissanai in the main room on the first floor, mingling amongst the others. There are hundreds of them. They must be readying to discuss the assassination plot of the king. He appears ready to release the gas."

I maneuver my draxilio to the darkened window. I am lucky this balcony is so vast, otherwise, I would not be able to remain in this form. Sucking in a breath, I release a small, steady flame onto the exterior beams of the structure. When I inhale once again, I notice the beams appear untouched.

Either these beams are covered in a fire-resistant substance, or this structure is protected by magic.

That is fine. A structure can be protected from flames, but it cannot be protected from a draxilio's massive weight barreling into it. Just as I rear back to the edge of the balcony, I hear gasps throughout the house.

"Kulissanai has released the gas," I tell Bexossanai and Alussanai. Every occupant in the compound will be unable to shift into their draxilio forms. We must act quickly before the gas wears off. "Take action,"

I say to them, then hurl myself, horns first, into the side of the structure, crushing wood and stone under my body.

I roll onto my clawed feet, landing upright as I search the wreckage for our target. I hear coughs and cries and pleas to be spared coming from downstairs. I ignore them all without thinking. It is what I was trained to do. When a scraping sound emerges from the room next door, I smile.

There he is.

I bust through the doorframe, making a hole twice as high and wide as the door, and find our target crawling across the tiles of the washroom, blood trailing from his hip. For a moment, I wonder how I should continue.

Shall I burn him alive like I usually do?

Or shall I shift into my flightless form and cut off his fingers and toes with my dagger, one by one?

Perhaps if we had more time, I would choose the latter, but once the gas wears off, every draxilio, including the shivering male before me, will shift and pose a potential threat.

As he bellows, "Please! What you have heard is a lie! I am innocent!" I unleash a ball of fire onto his face, and he is silenced instantly as the flames ravage his body. Seeing him suffer fills me with satisfaction, even glee.

I push my way through each door and wall that meets me as I find my way down to the first floor. The main room is the size of an arena with hundreds of flightless bodies on the floor, whimpering as they clutch each other. Kulissanai sees me and gives me a bored nod from behind his mask. He points his weapon toward the five males lined up next to him along the wall.

These must be the leader's underlings.

Then Kulissanai strolls casually out the front entrance and into the night.

The males look at me and I nod in the direction from which Kulissanai just left. They follow, nervously, timidly, knowing their lives are about to end.

"Alussanai, come watch the front," I tell her.

She lands with a thud beside me and pushes her short draxilio nose into the house, watching the rest of the group.

Kulissanai barks an order at the males to form a line. Once they do, my youngest brother shifts and settles at my side. We open our mouths in tandem and let the flames race out, melting the males from horns to toes until there is nothing but small piles of ash.

It is only when we cease our fires that we notice Alussanai yelling at the group inside. She is asking for their names, and what foods they like, and it is a signal that something has gone very, very wrong. Though she is not afraid of what she sees, she is curious, and it drives her to ask inane questions. It is a woefully inconvenient habit of hers.

I shove her out of the way to look inside, and I see beings in their flightless forms, but parts of them shifting in and out in strange ways. One moment, a large draxilio head atop a much smaller, flightless body. Or a being in flightless form crying as she looks down at her enlarged draxilio feet.

This should not be happening. "Kulissanai! Where did you get this gas? Come look," I demand.

He peers around me at the madness inside with nothingness in his eyes. Then he shrugs.

"Is this a side effect?" I ask impatiently. "I thought it was merely supposed to prevent them from a full shift."

"That is what I was told," he replies in a flat tone. "But we have clearance to kill them, so let us do that."

I sigh as I nudge him aside to take another look. I do not know how long this strange partial shift will last before they return to their full capabilities, if it has not permanently altered their bodies, that is. Regardless, we must end this now.

"Very well," I say. "At your stations," I tell my siblings, "and be aware that the exterior is flame-resistant. Find an opening. Focus on the main room of the first floor."

Alussanai moves into position above the structure, peering into the hole I left from the second floor. Bexossanai follows suit, but first busting through the wall on the far side of the compound, from the third floor down to the first. Kulissanai throws his clawed hand through the windows along the side of the compound, dragging it through the glass until there are no more windows to break.

"Ready," I say through our mental bond. The screams of those inside fill my ears, causing an uncomfortable itching sensation inside my chest. My training pulls at my mind, hardening my resolve.

"Ready," Alussanai says.

"Ready," Bexossanai replies.

Kulissanai is last, and in his typical dull tone, says, "Ready," just before we discharge our fire onto the compound. From all directions, bright oranges and reds light up the sky as we burn down the structure and the draxilios inside.

We make quick work of checking through the rubble for survivors, and finding none, we begin our journey home.

It is the screams of those inside that echo in my mind as we glide through the clouds.

And it is the sound of shattering glass that pulls me from a deep sleep.

* * *

We are under attack. Protect them. Protect her, the draxilio shouts in my head. I race out of Alussanai's second sleeping room, down the hall, and through the curtain dividing the living area from the eating area, where I find my sister and Kate throwing plates against the wall.

"Niro!" Kate shouts, then looks panicked. "Oh, sorry. Did we wake you?"

"You are smashing plates. Of course, you woke me," I reply, willing my heart to slow its chaotic thumping.

Alussanai giggles, and then Kate joins her.

I notice Kate is no longer wearing her torn leggings. Instead, she dons a pair of loose black pants that are rolled several times at the end to create bulky cuffs around her ankles. "You changed?" I ask.

She looks down and her eyes light up. "Oh, yeah. Alu rewrapped my leg and let me borrow these."

They do not fit her short, voluptuous frame, but they are certainly an improvement from the ratty, blood-covered scraps she had on before.

"So what exactly are you doing?" I ask both of them, gesturing at the pile of yellow and green shards that were once Alussanai's dinnerware. A former lover gave her the plates as a farewell gift when we left Sufoi.

"We say good-bye to the past!" Alussanai gleefully shouts as she tosses another plate against the wall next to me.

"Yesss! To the future!" Kate hurls one right after, and the shards land beside my bare feet.

"This is wasteful and reckless. I thought you cherished these plates from Daukanvi."

"Pfffft. She stepped on my heart," Alussanai spits. "Kate and I have decided the past needs to be destroyed if we are to look ahead. That is what we are doing."

"And how will you eat your meals with no plates?" I ask my sister.

She looks at me as if I've grown a third horn. "With my hands."

"Obviously," Kate adds. "Trust me, Niro. This is good for her. I wish I could destroy something valuable of Dennis's. It's cathartic."

"Were these not many credits to purchase?" I ask Alussanai.

Kate narrows her gaze at me. "She's got that battle dome money. I'm sure she can replace them."

My spine stiffens. She knows? Alussanai told her?

I decide to play dumb, if only to delay this conversation another moment. "What do you speak of?"

"Come on," Kate prods. "Alu told me all about your time as celebrities on Sufoi. The competitions where you guys battled other dragons in a dome, how you guys always won, and how Bexossanai had his own band of groupies." Kate's eyes gleam with excitement. "Can't wait to meet him now."

Alussanai stands there, saying nothing with a shameless grin on her face. Monster.

"That was long, long ago," I tell Kate. Then add, "The moment you meet Bexossanai, you will regret your words. You will also understand why he was so well-known."

She chuckles as if she doesn't believe me. "Is he *that* dreamy?"

Dreamy.

I do not like how that word sounds on her tongue. The soft lilt of it. The tip of her head as her eyes go unfocused. It is as if she is trying to picture a male she has never met and is left breathless by that image.

My blood turns hot. "He is not what you think."

Her trance breaks and her lips flatten into an almost-frown.

"They were enjoyable times, indeed," Alussanai pipes in.

"Yes, your battles were always the most viewed," I say to Alussanai then turn to Kate. "The crowd adored her, mostly because no matter how well-known she became, her opponents would underestimate her. And they would lose, every time."

"I just cannot imagine *you* doing anything in front of a crowd," Kate says to me. "Did you stomp around angrily the whole time until your opponent gave up?"

"Attendees did adore your scowl." My sister throws her head back and laughs. "But no," she says to Kate, "he was brutal and efficient in battle."

"I did not enjoy the experience. Every second was excruciating."

"Then why'd you go along with it?" Kate asks.

There are many reasons why. Most of which I do not care to share with this human, but I will give her the obvious one. "The credits. That is why."

I pin Alussanai with a glare. "What else did you tell her about us?"

"That was all," she replies. Then her eyes light up. "Ooh, we should swim!"

"I'm in," Kate says with an excited hop. Kate looks down at her small bare feet, and gingerly steps around the broken glass until she is at Alussanai's side by the door.

I hop over the plates and follow them out onto the balcony overlooking the waterfall that pours into a pool of clear blue water below. The pool is surrounded by steep cliffs, making it a secluded swimming hole Alussanai spends a lot of time in.

"Alussanai first!" my sister bellows as she leaps off the edge of the balcony and swings over the water by a thick rope tied to a tree that towers above her home. She swings back toward us once, and then jumps off the rope into a backflip before straightening her body and landing feet first into the pool far below. I have seen her do this many times, but it still causes my heart to lodge into my throat.

Mek releases an agitated squawk as he flies in a wide circle above while watching Alussanai splash in the water.

"What the whaaat did she just do?" Kate asks, her eyes wide in bewilderment.

"What she does," I say with a chuckle. "Alussanai is fearless. Also, quite fortunate with her luck."

"I'm jealous," Kate says quietly.

I watch as Kate chews on the inside of her cheek, marveling at Alussanai's light smile as she paddles around the pool. "You should not be," I tell her, my tone hard. "It is not an ideal existence to live without fear."

Kate turns, her copper hair hanging loose around her face. "Wait…what?"

I suppose it is the appropriate time to tell Kate the truth about us. If she is to meet my brother, Bexossanai, she should know why he is the way he is. I shuffle my feet in place, avoiding her gaze. "Roughly translated, Alussanai Dexii iy Gwix means 'Second Version Podling Without Fear.' It is a label, more than a name, given by our handlers. Alussanai is a draxilio podling. We all are, my siblings and I."

Kate nods, her forehead scrunched. "Podling? What's that?"

I clear my throat and continue. "We were created in a laboratory, rather than being carried to term and birthed by a draxilian female. Each of us has endured genetic modification for different and very specific purposes, all of which were to improve our instincts in battle. We served our king as his first line of defense. Whatever he wished for us to handle, any threat to his life or his reign, we eliminated the problem for him."

"So Alu was modified to lack fear," Kate concludes.

"Yes," I reply. "The part of her brain that registers fear was calcified, a surgical procedure that creates lesions in that part of the brain, removing it as an emotion she is capable of feeling."

Kate blows out a breath. "I—"

Her words are interrupted by Alussanai shifting into her draxilio form and flying from the pool up to the balcony, where she shifts back to her flightless form, in midair, and lands on the other side of Kate in her soaked clothes.

"You go, short one!" Alussanai says, nudging Kate in the side with her elbow. Mek lands on Alussanai's shoulder and brushes his beak through her wet hair, as if caring for her.

Kate looks over the railing, down at the water below us, and shoots Alussanai a shy smile. "I think I'll pass, actually." Then she pulls the skin on her forearm up slightly. "Pretty sure I'd shatter like those plates if I did what you did."

Alussanai reaches over and tugs on Kate's forearm skin, but a little too hard. "Oww!" Kate screeches.

Alussanai laughs like Kate is her second little pet. Then she grabs hold of another rope tied to the tree and leaps onto it. Kate watches and shakes her head in wonder.

After a big splash, my sister shifts into her draxilio form once again as she launches out of the pool and shifts back before landing on the balcony.

I look down at Alussanai's foot and notice a slender black vinepus wrapping itself around her ankle like a coil. Kate screams. The vinepus tightens, its scales flecked with gold, and unfurls its long, forked tongue in a hiss. Alussanai stares down at the creature, and then grabs onto its tail, yanking it off.

She holds it up in front of her to examine, and the vinepus's head curls up and hisses at her again, spitting green saliva across her cheeks. My sister hurls it away, toward the water, and wipes her face with her hand, looking slightly annoyed but otherwise amused at the creature's unfavorable response to her.

"I'm not sure what I expected true lack of fear to look like, but it wasn't this," Kate whispers to me.

I smile. "Our handlers described it as a 'lethal abundance of curiosity.'"

Kate holds back a laugh. "Wow, yeah. That's the perfect description."

"That creature could have bacteria in its saliva, Alussanai," I tell her. "You must be more careful. You should cleanse your face with solution."

"*Mukoor*, brother," she chides me as she moves inside. Kate looks puzzled, so I translate. "It means 'calm yourself' in Sufoian."

"You worry more than a jiobleri with a new cub," Alussanai adds as her wet clothes and hair leave wide puddles with each step she takes. Kate and I follow her through the eating room, hopping over the plates, and back into the living area.

As Kate makes herself comfortable on the couch, I return to the eating room. I will not relax until this shamble of broken glass has been properly disposed of. I pull the cleaning receptacle out of its location and face the head toward the mound of yellow and green porcelain. Upon pressing the red button, the receptacle turns on and begins to suck every shard, every crumb of food, and every speck of dust into it. It takes several moments for the floor to be cleared, but once it is, I release a satisfied sigh.

As I return to the living area, my sister exists the washroom. "You cleaned?" she asks accusingly.

"Yes, and I do not apologize."

She scrunches her nose the way she did as a youngling when she was angry with me, and raises a fist, pressing it to her forehead.

"Umm, what is that?" Kate asks, looking between Alussanai and me.

"We were not supposed to threaten to kill each other as children. Our handlers would always tell us to keep that energy on the battle-field," I explain.

Alussanai smiles at the memory. "So instead of saying it with words, we came up with a gesture. Our handlers never knew what it meant." She looks down at the floor. "Though that did not keep you from the occasional *disagreement* with Bexossanai."

Kate's immediately covers her heart with her hands. "Oh my god, that might be the cutest thing I've ever heard."

She thinks children threatening to burn each other alive is cute?

Kate gasps as she leans forward. "Does your brother have your competitions in the dome on tape? Or recorded somewhere?"

"No."

"Aw, man!" she says with an exaggerated pout. "I would give anything to see you guys hamming it up for the cameras."

Why do we still speak of this? The subject must be changed. "Do you think Bexossanai's texts will have information we can use?" I ask Alussanai.

"Yes. There must be something," she says, rubbing her chin. "Or maybe it is not a hex. It could be… a mate signal."

No. No, it cannot be.

Kate stills, her eyes blinking at me. Waiting for one of us to explain.

My mouth drops open, but I find words not forthcoming.

Alussanai does instead. "In draxilio culture, mate bonds are eternal. They do not always form instantly. Some take time. But when two draxilios are meant to come together, they are each given a signal as a way to find one another."

"Are the signals always the same?" Kate asks.

"No," I reply gruffly. "There are many signals. Hundreds. Possibly thousands."

"It could be anything from seeing the same person many times for a full moon cycle, to a draxilio finding a rare pendant and feeling an indescribable urge to return it to the owner, and upon meeting the owner, they feel the belly tingles."

"The belly tingles," Kate repeats.

Alussanai sighs. "I am not explaining it right. It–"

"It is an indication from the gods that your mate is in front of you, and you must open your eyes to see them," I finish.

"So, like a meet cute?" Kate asks with an amused grin.

"I do not know what that is," Alussanai replies.

"It does not matter. If the dream link is a mate signal," I gesture between Kate and me, "clearly it is an error. Podlings are unlike natural-born draxilios. We were not created to take mates. We were made to serve our handlers and our people by protecting them. And our handlers made it clear that our genetic modifications made us incapable of having a mate bond with anyone."

Something flashes across Kate's pale green eyes, but I am not sure what it is. Hurt? Disappointment? I am proven wrong a moment later when she says, "Yes, clearly a fluke."

She coughs and clears her throat as a flush creeps up her neck and pinkens her cheeks. "I mean, there is no way we're supposed to be mates."

"I agree," I reply quickly. Admittedly, spending the rest of my life with Kate at my side would be challenging, and on many occasions, positively infuriating, but hearing her dismiss it as a possibility makes my chest feel tight.

Is it because I am draxilio?

Or because I am a podling, and not a natural-born draxilio?

Is she disgusted by the sight of me?

Is it my horns?

Does my draxilio form scare her?

As the questions cycle through my mind, I realize the reasons Kate might not want this to be a mate signal are many.

She has seen my dreams, and what I am. I am a monster. A killer. In her eyes, I am nothing more.

CHAPTER 7

KATE

I have to suppress the laugh that bubbles up my throat at the suggestion that Niro and I are connected by some kind of dragon fate. Not because I don't believe in magic. I do. But there's just no way in hell we're supposed to be mates. First, we can't stand each other. Second, I'd rather rip off my toenails and eat them before becoming anyone's mate.

Belonging to another person wholly and completely…forever? As in no escape? As in till death do us part? That is not for me.

When I was in my early twenties, discovering that I had an eternal mate would've been a thrill. But I'm no spring chicken. I'm a thirty-nine-year-old woman who just escaped an abusive marriage, and I'm still extremely sleep-deprived. I don't have the energy to give anyone my heart again. I want to sleep soundly every night, take a nap every day, and just be left alone.

"We will examine the texts and determine our strategy from there," Niro says in a strangely eager and shaken tone.

"Sounds great," I reply.

Alu smiles and claps her hands together. "Shall I make more food? Some fuuni noodles for the last meal?"

"We should leave promptly if we are to reach Bexossanai's farm before dark," Niro says, his voice somber. Despite the bickering between him and Alu throughout the day, it seems like he's missed spending time with her. How often do they see each other? And why did she move out of his caves? The more I get to know about this dragon, the more questions I have.

"How long does it take to get to your brother's place?"

"In human time, about three hours," Niro says.

"You are taking the human away from me so soon?" Alu asks as she reaches my side.

"Pshhh, you haven't seen the last of me, girl," I reply, giving her hip a nudge with my elbow. "You should come visit me in the village." I doubt the clan would be happy about the presence of another draxilio, but whatever, I can just step out of the tree line to chat with Alu. Maybe Chloe and Ava would want to join us. I have a feeling they'd like her.

Niro shakes his head. "You already plan your next visit with her, yet I have not seen you in several moon cycles."

"You are much less fun, brother. That is why," Alu quips before trotting down the hall.

He dismisses her comment with a wave of his hand before heading to the front door. I fill my palm with a few chunks of bread and candy before following. Niro sits on a bench next to the door to lace up his boots, and I tuck my travel snacks into my pocket.

As I shove my feet into my boots and pull the zippers up along the side, Alu comes racing toward us with a bundle of fabric in her arms. "Wait!" she shouts.

She separates the items in her hands and wraps one around my body. "A blanket?" I ask.

"Yes! Bexossanai's place is chilly when the sun lowers," she says. "And I imagine being bunched inside Nirossanai's claws while he flies is not the most comfortable experience."

"Yeah, it's not the best," I reply. "But this will certainly help."

"And this," Alu says as she holds up the other item, "is for you, short one."

It's a dress, pale green like my eyes, with short, puffy sleeves and a billowy shape.

"You may need to adjust the length as you did with the pants, but it should fit," Alu adds, looking closely at the hem. She's right. If this is a maxi dress on her seven-foot frame, it will swallow me whole. But shortening the hem is an easy fix, and I'm excited to add another piece to my very limited wardrobe.

"I can't thank you enough for this, Alu," I tell her as she folds the dress and places it in my hands. She goes to hug me, and instinctively I stiffen. She notices this and gives me a subtle nod before taking my hand. She gives it a single squeeze, and I find that I miss her already. Most people don't seem to register my aversion to physical affection, and they hug or touch me however they want until I tell them to stop. Alu, on the other hand, paid attention. Then she acted accordingly, giving me the space I need.

I turn and see Niro watching me intently, and I wonder if he followed the unspoken interaction Alu and I just had.

The silence in the room grows heavy, but before it starts to suffocate us, Alu gives us directions to the tunnel on the other side of the house. She gives Niro a tight hug, and playfully flicks one of his horns before we head outside. With me close on Niro's heel, we stroll around the house to the side where the waterfall and pool are. To the left of Alu's balcony, there's a narrow dirt path that takes us through the newly cleared trees and bushes for about five minutes before a black stone arch is revealed.

This must be the tunnel.

We head inside its mouth, and the darkness envelops us in an instant as a steady drip echoes loud enough that the hum of bugs and nature all but disappear. The lack of visibility inside the tunnel is alarming, but the cooler temperature eases my nerves enough to keep me moving. I have no idea how long this tunnel is, I just know the second we emerge from the other side, the sun is so blinding that I scream obscenities at it until my eyes finally adjust.

"Are you done?" Niro asks, standing with hands folded behind his back a small smirk on his face.

"Yes, just making sure the sun knows where she and I stand, that's all."

He makes a clicking sound with his tongue and says, "Are all human females as vulgar as you?"

I stop mid-stride, releasing a huff from my nostrils. "The more you swear, the clearer your skin. Everyone knows that." Shoving the blanket and dress Alu gave me into Niro's arms, I roll up my sleeves to my elbows, concentrating on folding the cuffs so they are even.

"Truly?"

"No."

"You didn't answer the question."

I pull out the hair ties from my braids and separate the wavy pieces until my hair is a crimped mess hanging down my back. I bend at the waist and flip my hair over, my fingers catching on tangles as I pull it all together. Gliding it through a hair tie, I secure it on top of my head in a floppy bun. I'm certain little red hairs are sticking out in every direction, but I can't bring myself to care. "I suppose that depends."

"On?"

"On how many ridiculous questions a woman has been asked in a day."

The skin around his eyes tightens as he narrows his gaze. "What about that question is ridiculous?"

"Well, what makes you think women being vulgar isn't the norm? Why is that so shocking? Would you ask the same question of a human man?"

His mouth quirks up on one side. "I would if he hurled obscenities at the sky. Then I would ask if he could count how many fingers I was holding up."

"So I'm crazy now?" I say with a scoff as I yank my blanket and dress back from him. "If you're going to insult me, at least come up with something original."

"You are angry," he mutters knowingly, as if he enjoys getting under my skin.

"Please," I reply, my tone dismissive. "I'm just saying the sun is…

a lot. Is it so much to ask that she hits the dimmer switch every once in a while?"

He laughs, the sound raspy and low.

"Especially for those of us with delicate Scottish skin," I add. Wrapping the blanket around my shoulders, I create a hood, my bun keeping it perched above my head and shading my forehead and the back of my neck from the sun. "I'm going to start baking like a chicken out here."

"I'm sure the sun will take your comments into consideration," he says.

"Hey, what happens if we're spotted?" I ask him. "Like if someone from my clan sees us flying around."

"They will not," he replies simply. "Draxilio can bend light around ourselves when we fly. To remain invisible."

I'm not sure if I'm relieved or distraught by this information. If the clan spots a draxilio in the sky, they'd surely follow it, looking for me. But if they can't see us at all, they probably won't have any leads, and it will take longer for them to find me, which means I'll be spending more time with Niro.

Or maybe they haven't even noticed I'm gone.

Regardless, Niro promised to take me back soon, so there's no use dwelling on it.

"This way…" he says.

I follow until we reach a wide patch of dirt surrounded by tall grass and scattered pockets of flowers. Then I ask a question that's been bugging me for hours. "So, if Alu's first name means *second*, does that mean 'Niro' means *first*?"

His eyes widen as if caught off guard, but immediately he softens his features into a neutral expression. "You are correct."

"And what were you genetically altered to do?"

Niro swallows, his throat working hard to push the saliva down to his belly. Is he nervous? Then he sighs with his eyes pinched shut and says, "Nirossanai Dexii iy Prava means First Version Podling without…" he pauses, "without remorse."

Huh.

I suppose a typical reaction to hearing that the guy you've been spending time with has been genetically altered to experience zero guilt would be to run in the opposite direction. I should be afraid of someone who is intimidatingly large and muscled and isn't capable of feeling regret. That's a recipe for a brutal killing machine.

But strangely, I'm not afraid of him at all. I don't know, maybe the smart part of my brain has been calcified without my knowledge. It would certainly explain a lot of my choices over the years. Despite my close relationship with fear, I don't feel anything remotely close to that when I'm around Niro.

Sure, he's a pompous rich boy. And a killer. And he's so hard to read that sometimes I want to rip my hair out. But he's also capable of using his overwhelming strength against me at any time, and he hasn't, despite having several opportunities to do so.

I'm not sure I believe that he's incapable of feeling remorse, either. I remember the pain in Dream Niro's eyes as we watched him burn those people in the cage when he was a child. He's still haunted by that day. Why else would he continue to dream about it?

As I look at him now, standing in the clearing, his gray eyes downcast and his shoulders slumped, he seems genuinely concerned about my reaction to learning the meaning of his name.

"Any response?" he asks me.

I pull a piece of candy from my pocket and pop it in my mouth as his admission washes over me. I realize how chewy it is, having not soaked the soft exterior layers in tibbi first. Eventually, I swallow and ask, "Were you also modified to be a compulsive liar?"

His brow lifts in surprise. "No."

"Great," I reply. "As long as you keep your word and take me back to the village in two days, I don't care how you were made." This type of genetic modification seems cruel, and I have a feeling Niro and his siblings were treated terribly by their handlers in order to hone their battle skills.

"Oh," Niro says quietly. He clears his throat, and his spine straightens. "Good. That is good."

Was he expecting me to mock him for something he didn't choose? I know I'm a bottle of vinegar in human form, but I'm not *that* vicious.

"So how was Bexossanai modified?" I ask. "Give me a heads up on what to expect."

Niro sighs, and his gaze focuses behind me on the sprawling jungle. "Bexossanai was modified to lack trust, which makes him a cold, calculated opponent. He is quite gregarious upon introduction, which is how he won over so many spectators at his battles. He knows how to work a crowd. But beyond those surface interactions, he is not easy to connect with."

What a miserable life that must be. I can see why he lives alone. I can also see why Niro lives alone, but Alu is so bright and cheery, her life of solitude doesn't make sense. Though she does have Mek to keep her company, so she's not completely alone. I wonder what happened between these misfit dragon siblings to make them drift apart.

Before I can ask Niro about this, he holds up a hand, indicating I should stand back.

"Dragon time?" I ask.

Instead of answering, he shifts, and I take a moment to admire this version of him. He's beautiful in his flightless form, and I'm pretty sure he knows it, but this is beyond beauty. His cerulean skin glitters with each subtle movement, the oval scales smooth to the touch. His sharp, ivory teeth are as terrifying as the blue-black pointed ridges that cover his long snout and run down his back, all the way to the tip of his wide tail. The dragon tilts his head slightly as I stare at him, making him look like an airplane-sized puppy, and I can't help but smile.

I know Niro can't talk to me while in this form, and that makes me even more curious as to what he must be thinking right now. Do I look like a tasty treat to him? Is it a struggle to resist eating me?

He uncurls his front foot, and I climb inside his palm. I sit with my back leaning against his middle claw as the rest gently close around me. I feel his foot lift off the ground and my stomach dips like I'm on a roller coaster. Just before Niro leaps into the sky, I notice that he's got me pressed against his chest, and even when his wings begin to flap and I can feel the cold air whip through his fingers, I know that he'll keep me against his beating heart until we land.

A trickle of warmth spreads through my body at the thought, and it catches me completely off guard.

Is that... No. I decide quickly. That part of me is long gone. I will *not* develop feelings for this dream-hijacking, remorseless kidnapper. No, no, no.

Peeking between his claws, I watch the clouds zip past us as Niro darts through the sky. The wind continues to beat against my face, so I duck my head down against Niro's chest. Then I wrap the blanket tightly around my shoulders and let the rhythmic beat of his heart lull me to sleep.

CHAPTER 8

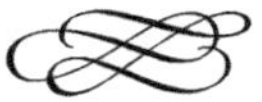

KATE

I tiptoe down the dark, empty halls of the caves inside Niro's mountain, peeking around corners for a flash of blue skin. I see none and let out a sigh of relief. The warm plush carpeting beneath my feet quiets my steps until I arrive at my destination: Niro's workroom.

There are candles lit on the mantle behind his big, mahogany desk, and a single lantern on the far wall reveals all his treasured knick-knacks displayed on high shelves and stacked low in the corners. I take in the books that look like they're about to crumble into dust, the weapons behind locked glass cases, and the gilded sculptures that fill every open space.

Then I find my prize: the vase.

I threatened to break this garish thing the night Niro took me.

But why do I want it now? Had I planned to steal it? Or break it?

I can't remember.

Before I can search my memories for the answer, the door to the room closes, and I whip around to find Niro standing there with his arms crossed over his bare chest, his eyes narrowed at the vase in my hands.

"What are you doing in here, Kate?" he asks, his tone a husky rasp.

I look at him, then down at the vase, then back at him. "I–I don't know."

He approaches me slowly, his hands outstretched. "You do not want to break this."

A loud huff bursts through my lips. "What makes you so sure?"

He pulls it from my hands, gently, and I let him. He places it back on the podium and covers it with a bottomless glass box. "Because it would hurt me if you did."

"Maybe I want to hurt you."

Niro chuckles. "No, you don't."

What the hell does he know?

"But I know what you do want," he says, no louder than a whisper. "And I know I'm the only one who can give it to you." My heart is hammering inside my chest so loud, I'm surprised I heard him at all.

I swallow. "What?"

He leans down so his mouth is next to my ear. "You want to be fucked. Hard."

I scoff and push against his bare chest with my hands. He doesn't budge. It's like trying to shove a building. "You are so cocky. I could go literally anywhere in the universe and get my needs met. You're not special."

"Oh no?"

"No."

"You think every male in the universe would be as accommodating to your specific needs?"

I roll my eyes. "What are you even talking about?"

Niro walks around his desk and pulls two sets of restraints from the bottom drawer. The same bindings he used on me when he brought me here. He slaps one around his ankle, and a cuff from the other set around his wrist. He sits in the same chair he put me in, then loops the chain through the bottom rung of the chair and closes the other cuff around his ankle. "Help?" he asks, gesturing to his free hand.

"Ooh, are we locking you to a chair for the rest of time? I fully

support this." I say, kneeling to pull the chain of his handcuffs through the back of the chair. The cuff closes around the shimmering skin of his wrist, locking in place. "Okay, now what?"

"Now you use me as you wish, and I cannot put my hands on you."

Oh.

"That is what you crave, is it not? The only way you can experience pleasure?"

I'm not entirely sure, because I've never done it before. But I have fantasized about it. The only sex I've had is with my estranged husband, Dennis. I met him in college, he was my first, and then we got married after graduation. Sex with him was...fine. It was fine. It wasn't the toe-curling, brain-melting, full-body orgasms that appeared in my favorite smutty novels, but I figured that wasn't happening in real life for anyone.

Then he changed. He became someone else. Someone whose hands were not kind or gentle when they touched me.

"I will not move from this spot, Kate," Niro vows, pulling me away from the thoughts about my past. "I am yours."

Well.

What an unexpected turn of events.

I dig for a reason not to. A reason to say no. But I find none. What he's offering is something I've craved secretly for a long time. I just didn't think it was possible. I didn't think I'd ever find someone who a) I was physically attracted to, and b) willing to give this to me. Sex, for me, has been a chore. A way to appease Dennis enough to get him to leave me alone for a few days. I developed the ability to shut down, mentally and emotionally, to go numb, until the moment it ended.

The shame from these encounters is piled high in the deep recesses of my mind. Someday I will need to face it, but I refuse to allow that day to be today.

I look down and realize I'm wearing the billowy green dress Alu gave me, and nothing underneath. My nipples are hardened peaks against the soft fabric, but with each step I take toward Niro, they ache, and the dress starts to feel like scratchy wool grazing my skin.

Niro's lips part when I stand in front of him, pushing myself between his thick thighs. I follow his gaze as it slowly trails from my mouth, down my neck, and landing on my breasts. His tongue traces his lips, and my breaths quicken at the sight. I want those lips on me. I want to feel them everywhere.

"May I taste you?" he asks, his gaze heated and his chest heaving.

My mind goes blank, and I can't speak. So I nod once and then he's on me. He's leaning as far forward as the bindings on his wrists will allow, and his mouth is hot as he laves my nipple through my dress.

A sound emerges from my throat, a startled, breathy combination of a gasp and a moan. My head tilts back and I close my eyes, focusing on the feeling of his tongue as it traces circles around my nipple. I hold onto his thick black horns, anchoring myself to him as he worships my chest with his mouth. He releases my nipple with a final hard suck, and moves to the other, paying the same focused attention he paid to the first.

Warmth pools in my belly as goose bumps cover every inch of my skin. My clit pulses between my thighs as I suck in a breath. If I were wearing panties, they'd be soaked right now. At the base of my spine, tension begins to build, and I can't believe how close I am to coming just from this. I never realized how sensitive my nipples are. Or perhaps, this is a testament to how good Niro is at pleasuring me.

My gaze drops to meet his. His gray eyes swirl with need and desire and something else. Something I'm not ready to acknowledge, because if I do, I'll no longer belong to myself.

His lips leave my breast, and he whispers, "Come for me, Kate," and I'm done. My body shakes as I tumble off the edge. My knees buckle as my orgasm rolls through me, and I land straddling his thigh. My arms wrap around his neck instinctively, as if he's my safety net, and his hot breath tickles my ear as he whispers into it.

What he says, I don't know.

I'm too lost in the haze of ecstasy to pay attention to anything but the buck of my body as my pussy weeps and clenches around nothing. I need him inside me. I need to be filled by him.

When I start to come down, I stroke the glimmering scales along his sharp cheekbone, drifting down to his jaw, and let my hand explore his chest, and then his stomach. I lean back to reach for the waist of his pants and then...I pause.

My hand rests against the silky black cloth, and even as I will myself to move it, to uncover the long, thick cock I can feel hardening beneath me, my hand remains still.

"I..." I say with a swallow. "I don't, um, I don't kno–"

"Look at me," he says softly. When I don't, he growls, "Kate. Look. At. Me."

I finally do as he says, and I'm ashamed of the tears that threaten to spill onto my cheeks.

"You're safe. You're here. With me."

"I know," I whisper as the tears fall. "I know, but..."

"And you are in control. If you want to stop, we stop."

He's right. I can get up and walk out of this room and not look back. Nothing will happen to me if I choose to end this.

Yet, I can't. My body won't move from this spot. And more importantly, I don't want to.

Niro notices the moment I decide to stay, and a proud smile curls his lips. He uses the tip of his nose to catch the tear running down my cheek, and then he presses his lips against my hair, breathing me in.

I wiggle my fingers, ensuring they will cooperate with the direction I want to take. Slowly, I lift the waistband off him, pulling down until his cock springs free.

I let out a gasp at the sight. "I–"

This, I was not prepared for. I knew he was big, and I figured he'd be blue down here, but this...

This looks like a giant, curved, blue banana.

It even has the raised seams running down the length of it on three sides. As in, where the skin of the banana separates into peels.

Is this what all alien dicks look like? Am I...Am I supposed to peel his dick?

Suddenly I'm terrified. Because the longer I look at it, the more it looks like a blue banana, and I have no idea what I'm supposed to do with it.

* * *

"Kate!" Niro shouts as he shakes my shoulders.

"Mmm, no banana," I grumble as his face comes into focus. His brow curves up at my words, and that's when I realize what I said, and why I said it. "I'm awake! Yup, I'm...I'm awake. Are we here?" I ask as I sit up and look around, eager to shake off my bizarre dream.

The wind swirls around us in a tame yet refreshing gust. The air here smells of soil and newly plowed land and a hint of something else. A strong herbal fragrance that reminds me of dill. The sky is an inky black with twinkling white stars scattered about. There are various lights on the farm, mostly on the barn on the other side of the crop field. I can't tell what the crop is that we landed next to, but it grows in neat lines with tall brown reeds sprouting up and topped with a slim greenish-beige flower.

"Yes, Bexossanai's home is on the other side of the field," Niro says, pointing toward a pale-yellow structure that looks to be two stories high.

Then, just above the tip of Niro's finger, a blue blob darts across the sky. My eyes follow its path as it grows, coming closer.

This must be Bexossanai.

He lands smoothly about ten feet away, the flutter of his wings causing the tall reeds to blow around us wildly. When his big dragon feet touch the ground, he shifts into his humanoid form.

The fact that he had groupies does not surprise me at all.

He's slightly taller than Niro, or perhaps the confidence emanating from his every pore just makes it look that way. He shakes out his long black hair and it falls in shiny, loose waves around his shoulders. His horns are curled back like Niro's and Alu's, but not as much, making them appear straighter and more dangerous. He's not wearing a shirt, and his baggy gray sweatpants are sloppily tucked into untied combat boots that come up to his calves. His chest and neck are covered in tattoos and his stomach muscles ripple with every step he takes toward us.

"Nirossanai!" he shouts, his voice booming across the quiet stretch of crops.

Niro stands and strides toward him. Bexossanai stumbles a bit before pulling Niro into a tight, swaying hug.

Is he drunk? Can dragons even get drunk?

His glowing yellow eyes land on me and they widen. "Oh! And what do we have here?"

Niro pulls away and gestures toward me. "This is Kate. She is hu–"

"Human! Yes, yes, I see."

"Hi," I mutter, giving him a small wave as I pull myself up to stand.

"Interesting," Niro says, covering his nostrils with the back of his hand, "you have been enjoying this night, I see, brother."

Yup, definitely drunk.

"Well…" He jerks back, his glazed eyes narrowing at Niro. "Farm life is not as thrilling as it sounds."

Bexossanai shoves Niro away from him, jokingly but a little too hard, and he seems eager to get to me. Niro blocks his path for some reason, backing up in front of me as his brother gets closer.

Bexossanai's gaze turns hungry, desperate, as he looks at me over Niro's shoulder. Niro pushes him back, seemingly to protect me, but Bexossanai dips to the left and skirts around Niro's big body as he comes toward me with his arms open. "I wish to say hello," he says. Alarm races through me, freezing me in place. Then he says, "Come here, tasty little one," as he wraps me in his grip, lifting me off the ground and pressing my body against his. I squeak as I feel his length harden against me.

Then three things happen: Niro shouting, "Do not touch her!" as Bexossanai's head is pulled back, Niro's fingers tangled in his hair and pulling hard. Me hitting the ground with a thud as Bexossanai lets go, the wind knocked from my lungs at the unexpected contact between my tailbone and the ground. And then, Niro and Bexossanai becoming a blur of bulky limbs as their fists connect with each other's faces.

I scramble to my feet and yell at them to stop whatever this is, but it's too late. They separate long enough to shift into their draxilio forms, and then they take flight, spewing hot flames across the sky as they attempt to burn each other alive.

CHAPTER 9

NIRO

I notice the aromatic air even before I land on the edge of Bexossanai's nnduli crops. The scent, sweet and heady, drifts into my nostrils and makes my mind hazy. It is much like that of Kate's hair and skin, but this is stronger.

My claws dig into the soft soil the moment I land, and I pull Kate away from my chest so I may inspect her properly. My claws unfold around her, and I discover she is asleep in the center of my palm. The blanket my sister gave her tightly wrapped around her shoulders, and the dress bunched under her head as a makeshift pillow.

Her dry, cracked lips smack together as her body shifts and that's when I see it. Kate's thighs shaking slightly as they press together.

She is aroused.

The scent, sweet and rich like a frosted pastry, comes from her cunt.

She is in need, my draxilio notes. Taste her. Give her the release she craves.

I shake my head, denying my draxilio's commands, and shift into my flightless form. I cannot have his desire for her influencing my actions. My cock pulses against my thigh, the fabric tightening around it as it grows. Roughly running my fingers through my hair, I take a deep breath and try to calm my rapidly beating heart.

Bexossanai will soon know we are on his property, and I cannot have her arousal scent still lingering when he arrives. Frantically waving my hands over her body, I push the scent away, hoping the fragrance of the crops covers it. I am only partially successful, and while her arousal aroma wanes, it does not vanish. I nudge Kate's arm in an effort to wake her. It takes several attempts of shaking her shoulders for her eyes to open.

She mumbles something that does not make sense, and frantically covers herself as she scoots into a seated position. As I show her where Bexossanai's home is located, his draxilio appears in the sky above us. He lands and shifts, and immediately I smell he has been ingurgitating his self-made mead.

I try to engage him in friendly chatter, introducing Kate and teasing him for imbibing, but admittedly, this is not a skill of mine. It would not matter anyway, because the moment he sees her and catches her glorious scent on the wind, he becomes fixated.

Bexossanai is overly affectionate when he drinks, which makes this such a dire situation that I must diffuse. I saw how Kate reacted when Alussanai tried to hug her. I see how she reacts to my nearness and touch as well. She is timid and afraid. I assume it is unfavorable memories of her former mate that consume her mind and leave her as still as a statue.

My draxilio is already feeling particularly possessive of her, having just been exposed to her arousal scent, and knowing Bexossanai's touch will instill fear in her heart makes me want to shatter every bone in his skull. I shove him away from her as he edges closer, but despite his drunken state, he is still quick on his feet, and slips through my grasp.

I watch in horror as he wraps her in his arms and lifts her off the ground, pressing her against his body. A snarl builds from the depths of my chest, rage thickens in my blood at the sight of him touching her. Holding her.

He touches our mate. End him, my draxilio snarls.

My hand shoots out in front of me, and before I realize what I am doing, I give Bexossanai's long hair a hard tug. His pained howl fills me with delight, and I tug again, this time, coming away with several torn strands hanging limp in my hand. He releases Kate and she falls to the ground with a yelp.

I am eager to check her for wounds, but Bexossanai shoves me into a patch of nnduli reeds. My body responds as anger races through me, and I am on my feet and charging him in an instant. I cannot make out his words as he shouts them, and I do not care. He must pay for causing Kate even a sliver of anguish.

We pull apart, and shift into our draxilios at the same time. Battling in our flightless forms can take us only so far. To truly end this, we must take to the skies and let the fire from our lungs provide the solution.

Out of the corner of my eye, I see Kate standing at the edge of the field, her hands cupped around her mouth as she screams at us. I cannot hear her, but I am confident she is calling us children and urging us to stop. That is the kind of thing she would say.

Envisioning her mocking tone takes too much of my focus, because the next thing I know, flames engulf my tail and char the skin at the tip. I send a blast in Bexossanai's direction as a response, and he winces as it hits his neck.

I've grown tired of this game and will do what is necessary for an abrupt end. I dip my chin and aim my fire below, setting a large section of his crops ablaze.

It does the trick, because once the fire catches, Bexossanai is on the ground in his flightless form racing toward the shed where his water drones are kept. I float to the ground and shift at Kate's side as the drones fly out of the shed and dump gallons of water onto the burning field.

"Are you injured?" I ask Kate.

She stares at me blankly. Perhaps surprised by our short battle in the sky. "No, I'm good," she finally replies.

Once the fire is out, the sizzle of the burnt crops fills my ears. It is a peaceful sound; one I have always equated with a job well done. I know it will not last, and right on cue, Bexossanai stomps out of the shed with tension rolling off his body in waves.

"What were you thinking, burning my crops? What is wrong with you, Nirossanai?" he shouts. "Why are you here?"

He approaches until we are nose-to-nose and spittle flies from the corner of his lip, landing on my chin. *Shoving was better*, I decide, so I do just that to create space between us. "You were not paying attention."

He throws his hands up in frustration. "What did I do that warranted such a dramatic reaction from you?"

I would blame his callousness on the mead, but Bexossanai's ability to see nonverbal cues has always been lacking.

"You fail to see how your behavior affects others. If you wish to greet Kate with a touch, you ask her permission to do so," I state simply. I gesture to his crops that, mere moments ago, were swaying in the wind, and are now a barren patch of blackened twigs. "If you try anything like that again, I will turn every single crop to ash, and you will starve."

"Do you know how long it has been since I have seen an unmated female?" he asks, gesturing to Kate as if I should understand that because he was lonely, he acted on impulse, and I should tolerate it.

I do not accept his reaction. Why do I expect more from him? I know this is how he was made to think, to react, but I still do not like it. "Did you not see her eyes widen as you approached? Did you feel her lack of embrace as you lifted her? She did not return your affection. She wanted no part of it. And if you opened your eyes, you would have seen it for yourself."

Bexossanai tries to mask it, but I notice the slight drop of his shoulders and the heaviness in his amber eyes. Bexossanai turns to Kate and lowers his head. "I am sorry for the discomfort I have caused you."

My eyes stray to Kate, and I find she's staring at me with her mouth hanging open. She looks stunned, or perhaps surprised. I cannot tell. It is clear she was not expecting me to defend her. Am I the first to do so?

That thought only causes my anger to grow.

"Her name is Kate," I say.

"Kate," he quickly amends. "I forgot myself. I hope you will forgive me." Then he swings his head in my direction, "But didn't you notice her scen–"

"This is Bexossanai," I say in a rush. I do not want him mentioning her arousal scent. He never should have been close enough to discover it. So I speed through a proper introduction that was absent before. "Bexossanai, this is Kate."

They smile awkwardly at each other as the draxilio inside me is still reeling. *He scented our female. He must die. Burn him.*

It is fortunate I spend most of my time in my flightless form, because my draxilio is a feral being that would get us into much trouble.

"Say, Bexossanai," Kate says, her voice cracking slightly, possibly due to nerves, "this display of your dragon powers has been fun and all, but I don't suppose you have any more of that alcohol left, do you?"

At that request, Bexossanai's entire face lights up. "I do, Kate. I have enough for us all. Come, come!" He gestures at us to follow. "We shall drink, and you may tell me what brought you to my humble farm."

Humble? Without others nearby, his farm spreads as far as the eye can see. He began with a few vlespenium trees, and now tends a vast orchard. His aukiro roots span the same amount of land as Kate's village. The outer edges of his farm are reserved for qirb stalks, as well as dennabona that he soaks, boils, and prepares into a well-preserved mash.

"So do you like living on a farm? It must be hard work," Kate says as we follow my brother inside his home.

"The drones and machines I have acquired handle most of the strenuous labor," he says. "But I inspect the crops as often as I can."

We remove our shoes by the front door and trail him into his small eating area. There is a cold box in the corner that comes up to my hip, some shelving and racks that extend to a red center table with bright lights hanging above it, and a single chair at the end.

"There is enough mash pie for three of us," he says, pulling three bowls from a high shelf. Kate stands on the other side of the table, facing me.

"You want?" Bexossanai asks Kate as he holds a bowl in front of her.

"Yes, please. I'm starving," Kate says as he places it in front of her. She looks at the pile of aukiro and crust and dennabona mash and licks her lips as she waits for Bexossanai to deliver her spoon.

I nod in agreement as he hands me mine. "Thank you, brother."

He returns moments later with utensils, a jug of his tapaya mead, and a bowl of mash for himself.

"Do you not have drink containers for the mead?" I ask when he puts the jug on the table. Then my brows rise as he sits in the only chair available.

"No," he says with a large bite of pie in his mouth. "We can share, yes?"

"I suppose," I reply, still standing. Because we have to.

Really, it is not his fault he is such an inadequate host. He has no interest in entertaining guests because he trusts no one to be inside his home. So why would he need more than one chair? Or a cup to drink from when he can drink straight from the bottle?

Part of me is embarrassed, and I wonder if Kate is silently judging Bexossanai, and me by extension, for his behavior. But when I look up, she's happily munching away on her meal.

The three of us, equally ravenous, eat silently until our bowls are practically clean.

"That was delicious, Bexo. Thank you," Kate says.

"Bexo," he repeats slowly. "Why do you call me this?"

Kate looks at me, her cheeks pink. "Oh, sorry. Do yo–"

"No, it is interesting," he replies, lifting his hand, his tone thoughtful. "Bexo. I like it."

"Oh! Oh phew," she says, sighing in relief. Kate grabs the mead jug and gulps down several large sips before placing it on the table. "Whoa."

"It is a potent mead, Kate," I caution.

"So tasty though. And sweet," she replies.

Bexossanai nods in appreciation, shooting her a wide, toothy smile.

"My friend, Bruvix, makes his own ale," she says. "But it's not nearly as good as this! You should give him some tips."

Bruvix.

I picture the face as soon as the name leaves her mouth. He is the scarred one from her village that lingers too long in her presence. I have seen it happen in her dreams. She does not dream of him often, and I do not get the sense she is attracted to him, but he clearly does not understand that.

My draxilio grunts in annoyance. He is not fond of the male either.

"Tell me, why have you come, brother?" Bexossanai asks.

I lean forward and rest my hands against the cool table. "Kate and I require access to the draxilio historical texts."

"For what?"

I take a moment to determine how much I should reveal to my brother. When I thought this dream link was Alussanai's doing, I had no problem telling her the details of what Kate and I are dealing with. Even upon learning she took no part in it, I did not hold back. I have always been able to trust Alussanai. To tell her everything.

Bexossanai is different, however. Just as he struggles with lack of trust, his motives are almost always self-serving. What would he do with this information about Kate and me? Would he find a way to use it against me?

Ultimately, I decide to share what is necessary for him to know and nothing more. "We must check for curses placed on our kind since the date of our creation."

"Curses? Why?"

"There are witches in my clan…my village. Or Hexrins, as they like to be called," Kate blurts. Her eyes are locked on mine as she takes another swig. She must have seen my apprehension in sharing the truth with Bexossanai. "There have been some strange happenings, lately, and Niro and I are trying to figure out if they're responsible."

"*Niro?*" he says, his tone teasing.

"She has a nickname for us all, it seems," I tell him as I keep my gaze on her. For such a small person, she drinks mead far too quickly. If I am already feeling the effects from a few sips, she must be quite impaired.

My brother nods slowly, taking in Kate's words. "It sounds like these Hexrins pose a threat to you, Nirossanai. Why not be proactive and eliminate them?"

"What?" Kate shouts. "No! No, look, you don't understand." Her eyes dart from Bexossanai's to mine and back to his. "We–we just need to look at your books. Please."

"They are of no threat," I clarify. "We are not at war with the Hexrins. We are…gathering information that could be useful in the future."

Kate grabs the jug again and takes another sip. When he realizes the jug is empty, Bexossanai grabs another from the cabinet.

"Kate, you must slow your drinking," I whisper. "This mead is very strong."

She ignores my warning. "You need to make sure your brother isn't planning an attack on my village now," she says, attempting a whisper but failing.

"Me? This is your fault," I reply. "I was disseminating the amount of information to elicit no further questions."

She rolls her eyes at me. "I was trying to help you!"

Bexossanai returns, and Kate connects her gaze with mine as she takes a big sip from the new jug.

"Kate," I say, warning in my tone strong.

"Here's a free lesson on human women for you, Niro, since you're so obsessed with us," she slurs. "We don't like to be told to calm down, and we really, really don't like being told how much we're allowed to eat or drink."

She takes another long swig, and when she comes up for air, she looks at my brother, her expression sweet and amiable. "Bexo, I would love a tour of this place. Show me around, won't you?"

He stands quickly and offers her his arm.

After they have left the room and are out of earshot, I kick his only chair onto its side and smash it into kindling under my foot. Only after it is destroyed, I realize Kate is now drunk and alone with my brother. I race after them.

CHAPTER 10

KATE

I let Bexo guide me through the halls of his two-story home, and I nod and smile as he tells me the story of how he built it after leaving Niro's caves four years ago. I'm not really paying attention to what he says, because the mead is making my mind all fuzzy and light. Maybe Niro is right, and I should take it easy on the booze. But it's my choice to feel this way, and that power is heady. I've felt powerless for too long.

As we continue on the tour, I notice that there's only one bedroom in this entire house, which isn't a good sign for me and Niro.

"Where will we sleep?" I ask Bexo as we turn the corner from his bedroom on the second floor and head back downstairs.

"There are lounge chairs in the library. That should do just fine," he replies as if expecting anything more than that would be insane.

I hear Niro clear his throat behind us. "Bexossanai does not entertain guests. He much prefers the company of his crops and books to that of living creatures traipsing through his home."

Bexo smirks in amusement. "We don't all have the means to build a palace inside a mountain, brother."

"You do not have the means?" Niro asks incredulously. "The credits you earned on Sufoi built this entire farm. You are saying you could not afford to upgrade your pipes and add heat to your water, or put beds in some of these empty rooms?"

"Why would I do that? Cold water is enough. And no one visits. That would be a complete waste of credits."

We reach the end of the hall on the first floor and Niro and I stand waiting in front of two black wooden doors. Bexo slowly opens them to reveal a large room with floor-to-ceiling bookcases overflowing with books. The room itself is dimly lit, has a single, small diamond-shaped window, and just as Bexo described, three chaise loungers sit in the center of the room, facing each other. Each chaise has a blanket draped across the back, and even though it might be less comfortable than having my own bed, sleeping in this incredible library won't be so bad.

I have to remember to tell Chloe about this place. She'll lose her mind.

Thinking of her sends a wave of sadness through me. I have to get back to the village. Chloe must be worried sick. And she's pregnant. She shouldn't be dealing with any excess stress right now.

Niro promised to take me back in three days, which means, if he keeps his word, I'll be returning the day after tomorrow. Will we have answers by then? Will our dreams still be linked? If we don't find the answer to this problem within the pages of these books, what are our options?

I take the bottle from Bexo and throw back another sip of mead to calm my nerves. Maybe getting drunk with Niro and Bexo isn't the most efficient use of my time, but since I can't read Sufoian anyway, I won't be of much help to them.

Bexo is currently blathering on about where he got all the books that fill the shelves, but I'm not listening. Instead, I watch as Niro closely examines each title, pulling out a book, looking at the cover, and putting it back. I follow the flex of his back muscles beneath his T-shirt. I zero in on the sleeves, stretched taut around his biceps, leading down to his thick forearms. His tendons twitch as he takes another book off the shelves and checks it out. Tracing the length of his veins with my gaze, I realize too late that my mouth is hanging open, and Niro is staring back at me, book still in hand.

I've been caught.

Shit.

I have no idea what to say to him, so I turn to face Bexo and pretend nothing happened. He continues to list the many popular books he has here. Some stories and myths, but mostly nonfiction. His favorites are the ones written by the elder draxilios, recounting their history as a species.

He guides me to that section, which occupies an entire wall of dark wooden shelves. These books look much more weathered and decrepit. I'd be nervous they'd fall apart under my grasp after just pulling them from the shelves. Niro has no such hesitation, however, because he starts pulling multiple books off the shelf and dropping them next to one of the loungers. Once he has about ten books, he plops down in his chaise and starts reading.

Then he looks up at Bexo expectantly. "Will you be helping us?"

"Why would I?" he replies. "This is your predicament, and I am not clear on what that even is."

Bexo sighs and shifts his gaze to me, then down at the half-empty jug in my hand. "Another?"

Do I want another? I look at Niro and hold his gaze defiantly. He certainly wouldn't want me to get another. But truthfully, I'm not sure there's room in my stomach for more. With every step I take, my stomach makes an unpleasant sloshing sound. And I'm trying to blink back the sensation of the room spinning.

"Um, I'll pass, I think," I say to Bexo.

He takes the jug from my hand. I go to sit on the chaise lounge across from Niro, but apparently, my depth perception is hinky because I miss and my butt lands hard on the floor. I feel my bones rattle upon impact, and my vision blurs.

Seconds later, I'm on my knees and heaving, all the mead I just drank covering the floor with an endless splat.

* * *

My hands press into the cool floor, and I crawl off the edge of the carpet to get my cheek in on the action. It's a welcome sensation, because my body feels like it's on fire and I just want to die.

But retching into a bucket for hours, or minutes, I have no idea how long I've been like this, can have that effect on a person. So much for proving Niro wrong. I wanted to show him I can make my own decisions and that he doesn't have to hover over me like a helicopter parent, and all I got was this throbbing headache and a bucket full of vomit.

A soft touch along my spine makes me sit up in a rush, and dizziness causes me to moan.

"Easy, Kate," Niro says in a whisper.

I turn to look at him over my shoulder, expecting a disapproving scowl to be etched across his sharp cheekbones and proud nose, but in its place is a warm gaze. There's pity there, and a bit of judgment, but mostly worry.

"Well, this sucks," I mutter, wiping my nose and watering eyes with my sleeve.

"I–" he starts.

"If you say 'I told you so,' right now, I'm dumping this bucket over your head."

He chuckles. "We will discuss my infallible wisdom another time."

I try to deliver a witty retort, but my mouth fills with saliva and I know my misery is not over yet.

As I cough nothing into the bucket, since my stomach is empty but still angry, I feel Niro's long fingers run through my hair. He pulls loose strands away from my face, then takes out my hair tie and puts it into a cleaner, tighter bun.

How does he know how to do a girl's hair? I wonder as my stomach muscles clench and my throat burns.

I feel him rise to his feet behind me, and my skin tingles, longing for his return. When he does, he reaches around and holds a cool, wet cloth against my forehead. A relieved groan escapes my lips, and I lean into his touch.

Following his breathing, I focus on inhaling slowly and exhaling to match the pace. I keep my eyes closed and force myself not to picture the current contents of the bucket, because I know that'll make me sick all over again. After a few minutes pass, I push the bucket away slightly and sit back, shifting my legs out in front of me.

Niro guides me into his arms, and settles my back against his chest, still holding the cloth to my forehead. "Better?" he asks.

"Yeah, I think I'm all puked out," I say quietly, hoping not to jinx myself by saying the words too loudly. "Thanks for helping me."

"And for cleaning up your mess?"

I giggle. "Yes, that too."

"And for holding back your hair?"

"And that."

He sighs, the sound satisfied. "You owe me quite a few favors now, it seems."

I attempt to roll my eyes, but the pain between them is too intense. So I say, "You can't just do good things to be a good person, can you?"

"I am not a good person, Kate," he says after a loaded silence. "You should know that by now."

Maybe he's not. But how is "good" even defined? Most days I wonder if I'm a good person, and just as often, I don't have an answer. I guess that could be why we ended up in this situation. Two bad eggs, destined to torture each other forever through our shared dreams. Karma just doing its thing.

My stomach grumbles and I decide that grim thoughts are not what I need right now. What I do need is sleep.

Niro walks me to a room down the hall that has water in a basin, and waits outside, even after I tell him he doesn't have to, while I wash my face and rinse my mouth.

Bexo has a crude mirror above the water bowl, and I can't resist looking into it once I'm done. The woman that looks back is certainly a messy little bitch, but she looks surprisingly well-rested. Despite the bloodshot eyes, the bags and dark blotches underneath them are mostly gone, and my complexion is rosy, almost emanating a glow. But that's probably because I exerted myself while puking.

I meet Niro in the hall, and we quietly tiptoe back to the library. He tucks a blanket around me and disappears with my bucket out the door. When he returns, it's empty and clean and I'm relieved the acrid stench is gone.

Snuggling into the chaise lounger, I watch as Niro sits on the one surrounded by books and begins skimming the pages of the opened book at the foot of the chaise. "So you'll stay up, then?" I ask.

"Yes, I will," he replies without looking up.

"Good-night," I mutter, and shut my eyes just as he turns a page.

"Sleep well, Kate," I think I hear him whisper. But I'm already gone, floating away, into a dream that is wholly my own.

* * *

"Okay, Dennis will be home from work soon, so I can't stay long, but thank you all for coming," I tell my parents and brothers. They are seated in a half-circle around me in my parents' living room, their brows furrowed, their eyes full of questions. It's almost seven, and I glance at the phone sticking halfway out of my purse for the fifth time since I arrived, making sure I haven't missed any texts from him. He loses his mind when I don't text back immediately.

"Denny!" my brother, Tim, hollers in a low voice while cupping his hands around his mouth. "How's our boy doing?"

"He's, uh, fine," I reply. "Look, I called you here because I need help," I say, shifting my weight from each foot in a nervous gesture.

"What is it, sweetheart?" my mom asks softly.

I blow out a breath and take off my worn black zip hoodie. The sides of my powder blue tank top dip low, showing off my ribcage, which is precisely why I'm wearing it. I hear a gasp as I turn slowly, lifting the shoulder of my tank on one side and pulling it down to show my ribs on the other side, exposing the bruises.

"Jesus," Tim says in a whisper. "What the hell happened?"

My brother Matt leans forward, inspecting the bruises, but says nothing.

"Dennis," I reply, gritting my teeth to hold back the tears. "He, um. He's been hurting me."

"What?" my dad shouts in a tone that's equally shocked and disbelieving. "Dennis? Your Dennis?"

"Yes, my Dennis," I say, frustrated by his initial reaction but trying to have patience while they process this. "There is no other Dennis."

My mom's bottom lip wobbles as she looks to my father and then each of my brothers. Then she looks down at her hands in her lap and shakes her head.

"Did you call the police?" my other brother, Jason, asks.

"Well, no."

"Why not?" he replies, his tone accusatory.

"Uh, because he's a criminal defense attorney and is friends with all the local cops," I tell him. "They wouldn't help me." Though I shouldn't have to spell this out, since Jason, Matt, and Tim have attended our summer cookouts where several of Dennis's cop friends have been present.

I've thought about reporting him, or getting a restraining order, but what would that do? Give me a few hours of peace while Dennis is held at the station? Then when he gets home, he's even angrier than usual? That would only make things worse.

"Geez, he's always so polite when he's here," my mom says then looks at my dad, "Isn't he, Jeff?"

My dad nods as if this detail is relevant to what I'm trying to share with them. "He's become like a son to us."

"Yeah, okay," I reply. I remind myself that I've been living with this longer than they have. They just need time to adjust, and eventually they'll say the right thing.

"Was he drunk?" my father asks suddenly.

"What, when he hit me?"

"Yeah," he clarifies. "Was he drunk then?"

I throw up my hands, my patience wearing thin. "What does that matter?"

"Well, you know…" he starts, then tilts his head and scratches his chin. "It happens sometimes, you know? When men drink…they forget themselves. They aren't always aware of their strength."

I don't know what to say to this. Are they truly more desperate to find a reason not to believe me than to accept I'm getting abused?

"I mean, I've never hit anyone while drunk. And certainly not the person I love the most," I reply. I grab the stool from the corner of my parents' living room and plop down on it, no longer containing the energy to stand. The thin cushion my mother sewed using my old sheets flattens beneath me, providing no comfort from the hard wooden stool. It feels like the perfect seat for the setting, frankly. Punishing and disappointing.

"I don't know what to say," Jason mumbles quietly, dropping his gaze to his feet.

My mom rises and comes over to me, petting my hair like I'm the family dog. "I'm sorry, sweetie. Marriage is work. Eventually, the honeymoon ends."

That's when I snap. "Are you kidding me?" I yell, dodging her touch. "There is a huge amount of middle ground between the honeymoon phase of a relationship and physical abuse."

"Sis, calm down. We get it," Tim says, holding up his hands in a placating way that makes me want to scream while ripping my hair out. "Did he apologize? Maybe if—"

"Yes, of course, he did!" I holler at Tim. "He apologizes, then he buys me flowers and makes me breakfast in bed, then we have a few days where things are fine, then it happens again. This has been going on for a year!"

Jason sighs, rubbing a hand down his face. "I just can't believe this. Dennis is such a good guy."

I look down at my shaking hands to see if fire is shooting from my fingertips, because it sure feels like it. "To you! And after what I just told you, how can you still think that?"

Jason says nothing. Neither does Tim. Or Matt. My mom and dad just look at each other with a sad, helpless gaze, as if doing anything or saying anything in this moment is not within their capabilities.

My phone buzzes in my purse, and I curse under my breath as I walk over to the end table to grab it. "I have to go," I tell them after checking the time. Dennis will be home in twenty minutes, so I have seven minutes to drive home, two minutes to change, and eleven minutes to throw the rest of last night's lasagna in the oven and make a salad before he walks through the door.

"Okay, sweetie," my mom calls as I throw my purse over my shoulder and head toward the front door. "Call us if you need anything."

I turn to look at them, my family, as they shoot me awkward, loaded glances. They were my only option of getting out of this. My only hope. Now I have nothing. No one.

Somehow, I hit every red light on the drive home, and beads of sweat run down my back as the minutes pass. If dinner isn't basically ready when he gets home... I blink back my tears, trying not to think about it.

I swerve into our driveway, letting out a yelp as the car bumps over the curb, and book it inside. I race upstairs to our bedroom and change into a red, long-sleeve shirt with white polka dots and shove my tank top and hoodie into the hamper. When I come back downstairs, I turn on the oven and throw ingredients from the fridge onto the counter.

I focus on my breath as I chop the lettuce and tomatoes and toss them into the large, green-speckled stoneware bowl my parents bought us from our wedding registry. It's part of a set. With a matching clay serving spoon, oversized spork, and eight salad bowls it's "the perfect set for an intimate meal with those you love under the starry night sky" or so the website said.

"With those you love" pops into my mind, and I start snickering. Just once I'd like to see a product description that's honest. Something like "This salad bowl set will work just fine for the stressed-out wife who's been gaslit by her family and is trying to throw together a medi-ocre meal in under ten minutes so her husband won't throw his shoe at her or stomp on her phone." I don't know. Something relatable.

My phone buzzes, lighting up the screen.

> Dennis: Happy hour with the fellas. Might be home for dinner, might not. You should make something just in case. I'm in the mood for fried chicken.

I look over at the porcelain casserole dish with lasagna and bite my lip, wondering if I should order takeout and whether he'll notice that it wasn't me who cooked it. Then my phone buzzes again.

Don't eat too much though.

We have that dinner with the partners on Saturday, and I don't want to show up with a cow on my arm.

I'd rather look like a cow than your average white supremacist rally attendee. Lost in a sea of inbred, unremarkable faces. Maybe shave your back before you come at me again, mmkay, bitch?

Okay.

I can't express any of the vitriolic thoughts in my head, because it'll only fuel my husband's rage. And that will ultimately come back to bite me in the form of a shove down the stairs, most likely.

These people are important to me. You need to look presentable. You should wear that blue dress that hides your fat rolls.

The oven beeps, indicating that it's preheated. I stare at the knife for a moment before it drops from my shaking hands. Then I cover my mouth with my sleeve as I let out a scream.

A jolt from my body wakes me, bringing me into the present. Blinking several times, I take in my surroundings. When I spot Niro hunched forward on his chaise and squinting as he reads the book in front of him, I relax. Dennis isn't here. My family isn't here. I'm with Niro and I'm safe.

Safe.

With…Niro.

As I weigh the accuracy of this thought, my eyelids get heavy again, and I let them close, knowing Dennis is too far away to hurt me now.

CHAPTER 11

NIRO

*P*age after page, I look for curses and dreams and mating signals that in any way resemble what Kate and I are experiencing, and I find nothing. I curse under my breath as I close another book, placing it on the floor and grabbing another.

This particular text is a documented list of draxilio mates and the signals that brought them together. The most notable pairings, I am very familiar with. My eyes land on the story of Lady Guuvi and Dashk ib Tilknaye, a princess and a warrior from opposite sides of Sufoi. Battles between their rulers brought them together, over and over, with him saving her life each time.

I find the tales of kings, princesses, warriors, hunters, scholars, pirates, cooks, servants, all who were led to the person they were meant to spend eternity with. Draxilios of all classes, from every social standing, were worthy of this gift.

Yet, I am not. Because I was made in a laboratory.

That is what I was told by my handlers, at least.

So why am I even reading this book? I think to myself. What is the point of this search? It's not as if I need a reminder that I am unworthy.

The words of my handlers replay in my head each cycle at full volume. It is not something I've forgotten.

A yawn pushes past my lips, and I rub my eyes. They feel heavy after having squinted at the pages of these old books, trying to decipher the hurried scribbles of our elders' handwriting.

I lean back in the lounger and let my gaze drift to the ceiling. I count the exposed black beams overhead as my eyelids slowly close.

* * *

"Fuck!" Kate shouts, as I am thrust into our dream void. She scurries toward the large screen in front of us, trying to block my view.

It is then that I realize what she is trying, and failing, to hide from me. We are in her dream, but the dream takes place in my caves. Dream Kate is standing in the middle of my workroom, and she's looking down at…me.

She is dreaming of me.

I approach Kate, and though she fights me, I move her away from the dream screen.

"No! Niro, don't look!" she shouts. "It–It's not what you think!"

The dream version of me is seated in front of her, my wrists and ankles bound to the chair in front of my table. It is the same chair I sat her in when I first brought her to my caves.

"Am I your prisoner in this fantasy?" I ask, pleased and confused at the imagery before me.

"Not exactly," she replies, her tone thick with shame.

"Do not be embarrassed, Kate," I tease. "It is perfectly natural to dream of someone you are attracted to."

She shoves my shoulder. She is trying to shift my focus to her, but I cannot. I cannot take my eyes off the dream. The moment my mouth covers her hardened nipple through her dress, the breath leaves my lungs entirely.

Kate makes a pained sound beside me as she holds her face in her hands.

She jumps at my side, trying to cover my eyes, but I block her easily, holding both of her wrists in one hand. She struggles, yelling at me to stop watching, but I ignore her.

Dream Kate is moaning with her head thrown back and her eyes pinched shut, and that is a sight I was not prepared for. Her shoulders shake as I suck harder, leaving a wet circle on her dress where her nipple is hidden from me. She grips my horns, and lowers herself onto my thigh, writhing slowly, the movement subtle, before she gets close to release and rocks harder against me. My mouth works on her other nipple, licking and suckling the pebbled tip.

When Dream Kate comes, I have to suppress the growl that rises in my chest. Her brow is dotted with sweat, her face twisted in sweet agony as my name falls from her parted lips as she rides my thigh. Kate's grip on my horns is so tight, her knuckles are practically translucent.

I cannot feel anything but the blood rushing to my cock, and the tightness of my pants as it lengthens beneath them.

Kate has just had a sex dream…about me.

But why am I bound to the chair? Is this something she prefers? I should've listened more closely to what the dream versions of us were saying. I could only focus on the movement of our bodies, the distance evaporating between us as she leans over me, and then the look of sheer bliss on my face as I took her nipple into my mouth.

I feel Kate tugging on my arm, and it brings me back to myself. "What is it?"

"Can you just…not watch this next part?" she asks, her eyes begging.

"Why, Kate?" I ask with a smirk. "What is about to happen?"

She scoffs, rubbing her forehead. "Please, Niro. Do me this one favor."

"Just one? You are already indebted to me by many favors, if I recall."

"Come on, seriously!" She is panicking now. "Do not look."

Kate steps in front of me and begins jumping again, trying to block my view. It is pointless, just as it was earlier, because her small frame hides nothing.

Dream Kate is reaching for the waist of my pants as her hand starts to shake. I watch as Dream Niro calms her and reminds her that it is just the two of them. That she is safe.

She is comforted by this, and pulls my pants down, allowing my cock to spring free.

But this...is not my cock. This is a strange, bent blue shape with vertical ridges, and a black spot at the tip. "Is this what you think my cock looks like?"

Kate groans and falls to her knees on the floor of our dream void. "Dear god, this is a fucking misery marathon."

"Do not be embarrassed, Kate," I say with a chuckle as I reach for my pants. "We can clear this up in an instant if you'd like."

She glares at me from her spot on the floor. "You don't mean..."

"If you wish to see my cock, I am happy to show it to you."

"Are you kidding me?!" she squeals.

"If only for your edification," I clarify. "You never know when you will have another dream about me."

"Okay, how do we get out of here?" she says, stomping around the void, looking for an exit.

"I would prefer to be represented accurately in your mind."

"No. We're done here," she replies, covering her face with both hands.

"Are there other dreams? Or is that the only one?" I ask.

She crosses her arms over her chest, silently glaring at me.

"Am I always tied up? And seated?" I ask as a blush creeps up her throat, turning her pink cheeks a deep red. "Have I ever bent you over my table—"

"Can you stop?" she pleads. "Look, I would really appreciate it if we could just pretend this never happened."

I rub my chin, considering this. "If the dream had been mine, would you grant me the same courtesy?"

Her eyes dart back and forth before meeting mine. "Of course."

I lean down, scrunching my nose at her, and whisper, "You are a terrible liar."

* * *

A loud, crinkling sound jolts me awake in my brother's library. I scan the room, searching for an intruder to disarm. Then I look down and notice that my feet are resting on top of the book I was reading last night.

Rubbing the sleep from my eyes, I sit up and look over the pages once more.

Nothing. Nothing about curses, or dreams, or mate signals that is useful to us.

I lift my gaze to Kate, curled in on her side across from me, snoring loudly and drooling onto the velvet fabric of the chair. Her hands are pressed against her chest, and suddenly I am reminded of the dream she shared with me.

Of me in the chair with my hands and feet bound as she took her pleasure.

Her body, soft and round as she rubbed against me.

Her expression while in the throes of her orgasm.

Her mouth twisted in a silent scream.

Her copper hair, wild and surrounding us like a curtain as she lowered her face to mine.

I will never forget it. Any of it.

I know it was just a dream but seeing her crave me in that way—it creates a warm, fluttery feeling within my center.

Kate's nose twitches as her eyes open, and she quickly wipes the side of her cheek covered in saliva. Her eyes adjust to the glow of the lanterns scattered throughout the room.

Kate's green eyes land on me and her cheeks flush. "Oh, hi," she says quietly.

She is picturing the dream right now, it seems.

"Hello," I reply. "Sleep well?" I ask. I cannot help myself.

She releases a squawky groan. "Fuck off."

I chuckle.

"You were supposed to stay awake while I was sleeping," she scolds. "That was the deal."

"Yes, well, these texts are dull. And since I am doing all the work here…"

"Whatever," she says, her tone dismissive. She yawns loudly as she stands and drags her feet toward the door. I get up to follow, but she notices and holds up a hand. "I got this. My hangover is gone, thank god."

"Very well," I say and return to the chair. I trade the book I had open for another in the stack and begin skimming through it.

This text is a record of mates who have rejected their signals and chose not to be together. The list is relatively short, including detailed stories of five-hundred pairs over our eight-thousand-year history. Looking through the stories, I am surprised by the sadness that fills my chest. Each of these tales are tragic in their own way, resulting in one or both mates going to desperate lengths to break the bond. The ones that could not find a way to do so chose death.

The few that did find a way spent an overwhelming amount of time and credits to ensure the bond was truly broken. They sought spiritual leaders, engaged in death simulations, took potions, tried hypnosis, or hired trained killers to assassinate their mate.

If this is truly what has brought Kate and me together, would either of us go to these extremes to break the bond? I want to believe we are better than these draxilios who chose violence or death, but I am not so sure.

Kate was able to escape her terrible mate on Earth by careful strategizing, saving the credits she earned, and pretending to be okay. But if she had no path to escape, what would she have done?

And if we have several moon cycles of sharing dreams ahead of us, losing sleep and carrying the stress of each other's emotional burdens, what will become of us?

I am starting to see Kate as less of a problem that needs to be solved and more of a companion with the same goals. But we are not always aligned in our thinking.

I want us to be free, no matter where that freedom takes us.

Shaking my head to rid my mind of these thoughts, I turn the page. It is in the last paragraph of that page that I find what I am looking for. It is not exactly an answer on how to break the link, but it gives me a very good idea.

CHAPTER 12

KATE

*N*iro rushes into the kitchen with a book in his hands. I don't even care if he's here to make fun of me about the sex dream because Bexo will not stop grilling me with questions about the village. He wants to know about Varrek because he's the leader, and why we chose to settle on Oluura of all places, and what we plan to do in the next year, two years, and five years, and I just want to smash his face. I have no answers to any of these questions, really, none that satisfy him anyway. And yet, he keeps asking.

I know he can't help it. But, holy hell, is it irritating.

"I found something!" Niro declares with a smile and holds the book in front of me.

"What?" I ask.

He points to a section at the bottom of the page and begins to translate. "This mated pair rejected their bond and sought an enchantress to break it. And it worked."

Bexo pipes in, "Wait, this is about a mate signal? You two are mates?"

Eek. I forgot we were intentionally keeping it vague with Bexo. Seems Niro did too.

"We do not know," Niro says, his tone resolute. "We are linked by an unusual connection. But we do not know if a mate signal is to blame, or something else."

"So, wait," I say to Niro, desperate to prevent Bexo from asking a million questions, "You think we need to see a witch about breaking the bond?"

"I believe," Niro starts, and then simultaneously, we say, "the Hexrins."

He shoots me an appreciative grin, accentuating that dimple in his left cheek, and it heats my core.

I finish chewing the hard slices of bruna fruit Bexo prepared for breakfast and toss the skin and seeds in the trash bucket next to my foot. It was placed there the moment I walked into the kitchen. I think he assumes humans are constantly puking. I guess I gave our kind a bad name. Oh well.

I'm too intrigued by Niro's idea to care very much.

"We should go then, yeah?" I ask Niro.

"Yes, but we will return to my caves first. Then I will take you to the village this night."

"This visit just flew by," I say more to Bexo than Niro. Though he was clearly not pleased to have us here, he did provide food and shelter, which is what we needed.

Bexo gives me an odd look. "Well, that will happen when you sleep for two cycles."

"What?" I shout. "Two days? We slept for two whole days?"

"Yes," Bexo says simply.

"Okay, yeah, we need to leave," I say, then turn to Niro. "You need to come with me to the village."

"I doubt your clan will be pleased by my presence," he notes.

He's not wrong. "Most of the time, they don't even seem pleased by my presence. But I need you there. What if they need both of us to break the dream link?"

Niro sighs, and then nods. "You are right. We shall remain together." He turns to Bexo, holding the small book in his palm. "I will need to keep this for a time."

Bexo's mouth forms a grim line. "How long will that be?"

"I do not know. As long as we need it," Niro tells him.

I place my hand above Bexo's forearm, not touching him, but hoping to calm him. I know what's going through his mind. "I get it. Lending your books out is a scary thing. He'll return it though. I promise."

Bexo shakes off my almost touch and comes around the kitchen counter to stand in front of Niro. "If you do not return it in four days, I will burn your vaultri gopa."

Niro's eyes widen, his mouth falling open. "You…you have my vaultri gopa? How?"

Bexo smirks. "I stole it from your caves before I moved out."

Niro stiffens and his chest puffs. "You had no right to take that."

"This is true, but I did," Bexo says plainly. "And you have no idea where it is."

"I will—" Niro begins through gritted teeth.

Bexo lifts his hands in surrender. "It will be returned to you as soon as the book is returned to me."

"Anyone care to translate?" I finally ask. I'm starting to learn that if I don't interrupt these two, they will fight for the rest of time.

Bexo smirks at me. "It is a sacred gift all draxilios are given after our first kill. Niro's is a hand-woven wrap his handler Hauvi made for him."

"She was a handler to all of us," Niro retorts.

"But she cared for you the most," Bexo adds.

I turn to Niro, wearing a smile I refuse to hide. "You have a blankie?"

"Blankie? No," he says with a sneer. "Well, I do not know what that is. But it is a warm wrap I have kept for centuries. I thought I had lost it."

"You did not!" Bexo says, beaming. "It is here. And it awaits your return, brother."

The air is thick with tension, and even though I'm no longer hungover, I'm not in the mood to deal with this sibling rivalry nonsense they have going on. "Should we go then?" I ask Niro, dragging him out of the kitchen and into the hallway. He moves reluctantly, as if one word uttered by Bexo is all it would take for them to have a fire fight in the middle of Bexo's house. "The sooner we go, the sooner you can come back for your blankie."

"Why do you say it like that?" he asks, sounding vexed.

"Come on, blue man. Left foot, right foot," I'm pushing his back and guiding him toward the front door. I run inside the library to grab the blanket and the dress Alu gave me, and pop back out into the hall in time to keep Niro moving in the right direction. We sit on the bench by the door to put our boots on, and Bexo appears.

"See you soon," he says with a wink.

Before Niro can respond, I do. "Yep, thanks for the hospitality. Much appreciated." I wave with one hand as I tug Niro's wrist with the other.

We walk silently down the path from Bexo's house, passing drones of various sizes hovering over the crops as they sprinkle water or trim the tops into a uniform height. The wind is warm, but whipping around us, causing my hair to blow in my face every other second. I stop Niro so I can re-do my bun and he obliges as he stares down at the book the whole time.

Once we get to the clearing where we landed two nights before, Niro hands me the book. "Do not damage this," he warns.

"I won't," I reply, wrapping the dress around it as proof.

He raises his hand, and I instantly move back a few steps to give him space to shift. I'm getting used to the movements of his body, his little quirks, and what they all mean.

This strange journey hasn't been the worst, I realize.

Huh.

Niro huffs a breath through his gigantic dragon nostrils, and it tickles my face. I marvel at the sheer size of him compared to how gentle he seems in this form, at least with me. He could swallow me whole or char me like a chicken nugget, but all he does is tilt his head back and forth as his heavy tail wags slowly behind him. Before I climb into his palm, I reach up and pat his muzzle, just as a thank you for not eating me.

I settle myself inside his claws, wrap Alu's blanket around my shoulders, and clutch his book to my chest as he takes off in the direction of home.

I need a scarf or face mask of some kind, I decide, if I continue flying inside Niro's palm, because the wind is just too severe to fully enjoy the experience. I spend most of the ride with my head under the blanket.

By the time we float through the open glass ceiling inside his caves, it's around lunch time. At least, that's what my stomach tells me. The ceiling closes above us as Niro shifts back, and I wait for his heat signature to register and the door to the rest of the caves to open. Once we're inside the tunnels, I let out a sigh.

The moment it's out of my mouth, I place my fingers to my lips in surprise. It was the kind of sigh that falls out of you the moment you return home after a long trip. The way the familiar warm scents wrap around you and welcome you in.

But this isn't my home. It's Niro's. And technically, I'm only here because I'm his captive. I need to remember that.

We're not friends. We're allies, and only because that's our way out of this. As long as we work together, we can break this link and go back to our lives.

I'll be able to sleep.

The idea of that makes me so hopeful, I want to cry.

"Wait!" I shout as we pass by a room I didn't notice before. "What is this?" I slowly step inside, and my eyes are met with colors and textures, and I want to put my hands all over everything. It's a room filled with fabric. Bolts of fabric are hung on the walls and organized by color and type. There's a separate section for printed fabrics, too, and they cover an entire wall on their own.

In the center of the room is a huge machine that reminds me of what the very first computers looked like.

"It is the wardrobe room. Have you never seen one of these?"

"No," I mutter, still in awe. "We have closets, but this doesn't look like a closet."

Niro walks in front of me and gestures to the machine. "This is a digital stitcher. It contains my measurements and chosen silhouettes. I select a fabric from the wall," he points at the plethora of options, "and place the bolt in here." There's an opening that's perfectly bolt-sized, and he pulls one down to show me how it works. The fabric he selects looks like a thick cotton/rayon blend in black. Though it's probably something else since I don't think either of those fibers exist on Oluura.

He presses a button on the side of the screen and the machine hums to life. The screen is a bright blue at first, then switches to a maroon color with alien words and shapes. Niro taps the screen three times in various spots, and I hear cranks begin to turn. He swipes his hand in front of the screen, passing by more design options, it seems, and presses a green button on the screen before stepping back.

Gears turn, lights blink, and I watch as the fabric is pulled from the rotating bolt and disappears into the inner compartments of the machine. It continues to make strange beeps as it works, and after about five minutes, a black crewneck T-shirt rolls toward us on a brown conveyer belt. Niro pulls the shirt off the rollers and shuts the machine down before holding up in front of him.

"See?" he asks, showing me that it's his exact size.

"Can you make additional alterations?" I ask. "Or add details?"

"Of course."

"Wow" is all I can say in response. This machine would save us so much time and effort in the village. Not only that, but it would be an absolute dream to tinker with it myself and make a few custom pieces. I can't believe this is how Niro and his siblings have gained such extensive wardrobes.

"How did you get this here?" I ask, marveling at the sheer size of it. "Did you bring it from Sufoi?"

"No, no," Niro says with a dry laugh. "We could not bring much with us beyond credits and a crate filled with personal items. I acquired this not long after we arrived, through a scrapper who comes to see us every few moons."

"And he just brings you cool, innovative contraptions like this?" I ask incredulously. How convenient to have a digital stitcher just dropped off at your doorstep. Though that does explain why his caves look so luxurious.

"She," Niro corrects. "We tell Zeyda what we are seeking, and she does her best to locate it among her contacts. She makes trades all over the galaxy. As long as we pay her well, she finds whatever we need."

"Well, shit," I reply. I wonder if this scrapper lady could find me a TV and some DVDs to pass the time.

Niro tosses the shirt over his shoulder and gestures for me to follow him into the hall.

"We're leaving?" I ask with a pout.

He scrunches his nose. "I was going to show you where you can bathe. You are in dire need of one."

Oh no. Do I really smell that bad? I lift my arms and sniff, not finding any nasty odors, and then I catch Niro grinning like a fool. I roll my eyes. "You dick."

He throws his head back and bellows his laughter. The sound is loud, but deep and raspy and very Niro. I'm starting to crave that sound.

"A bath does sound nice," I say. "Then maybe I'll curl up with my favorite blankie…"

His laugh dies suddenly, and he smile fades to a grimace.

"Too soon?" I ask.

"Indeed, it is far too soon."

CHAPTER 13

KATE

I've never been much of a bath person. But this? This is no ordinary bath.

Niro spared no expense for his bathroom, which isn't a surprise. It's the size of my bedroom back in the village, and it contains a bronze "toilet" with a beaded flush pulley that hangs from the ceiling behind it. There are two "sinks," like a his and hers situation but are square in shape, in the same deep bronze color, with at least a foot of counter space in between.

Exposed golden pipes emerge from beneath the sink and tub and behind the toilet, running up the walls until they connect to the golden pipes in the hallway.

The "tub" occupies most of the space in here. Like the sinks and toilet, it's bronze in color, and a wide oval in shape. It sits on a raised wooden platform the color of pine. Above the tub is an adjustable waterfall-style shower head that can be moved closer to the ceiling if you choose to stand and take a regular shower. But if not, there's enough room for about four humans to sit and soak, or one, maybe two, draxilios.

And the soaps!

Niro has a ridiculous array of soaps to choose from, and honestly, I admire that. No shame in a solid soap game.

For my bath, I choose the one that smells like a mix of cherry and vanilla. Once I lather my hair and scrub every inch of my skin, I lean back against the edge of the tub with a contented sigh. The water comes up to my chin and is still piping hot, but I can feel the tension leaving my muscles with every passing minute.

Once the water has cooled, I step out and wrap one of Niro's extra-large towels around my hair, squeezing excess water from the ends. Then I pat my skin dry and head back to my room.

I change into Alu's light green dress and twirl around a few times on the plush carpet. She was right, it's a bit too long, but it hangs loose enough on me like a caftan without looking like an unflattering sack. Plus, the color matches my eyes and looks great against my skin. I run my fingers through my drying hair, and quickly put it into a French braid that ends in the middle of my back.

Barefoot, relaxed, and fully refreshed, I carry Niro's book in hand as I go looking for him. And since I didn't get the chance to explore the first night, I take the time to do so now. I pause in front of each open doorway, peeking inside.

This room is a bedroom, but I don't think it's Niro's. It has a black, gold, and white color scheme with no furniture beyond a bed and a side table. I'm guessing this is where Bexo or the other brother used to sleep. I let my hand linger on the soft black velvet comforter, stroking against the grain and then back again.

"Looking for something?" Niro says from behind me.

I squeak in surprise, and whirl around to face him.

"Not really. Just getting all up in your business," I reply. No sense in lying.

"You will not find my business in here, little rivi," he says with a smirk.

Did he just call me… rih-vi? That's weird.

"This room has never been mine. It used to be Kulissanai's," he says.

"Right. The fourth podling," I clarify. "What's his deal again? How was he modified?"

"Come, it is time to eat," he says, gesturing to the door.

I follow, and we walk side by side down the hall, Niro with his hands clasped behind his back. "Kulissanai was made to lack what you call awe."

What an odd choice for an emotion to remove. "How would that benefit your handlers?" I ask.

Niro lifts his chin as his eyes wander along the domed ceiling of the hallway. "He is not impressed by anything. He is not shocked by anything. Kulissanai operates on logic infused with pessimism. His expectations for others are extremely low."

"Huh," I reply, not knowing what else to say. It sounds like a sad existence, much like Bexo's without the capacity to trust anyone, but I don't tell Niro that. He seems fully aware of how upsetting it is to create a living, breathing person who doesn't have a full range of emotions to process things.

"In the battle dome, this made him quite clever," he says, his tone a strange mix of pride and pity. "There was nothing an opponent could do to catch him off guard. He went in ready for the worst, prepared for an enemy to fight without honor."

"I guess that's good, right?" I add, trying to sound optimistic.

"He was very successful, yes," Niro nods. "But it is difficult to connect with him outside of the dome."

"So, seeing Alu simply exist without having an ounce of fear and approaching a threat like it's her new best friend, that didn't impress him?"

Niro chuckles. "No, it did not. He was often hard on our sister. He saw her lack of fear as a hindrance, much like Bexossanai and our handlers did."

We stop in front of a room with a wide arched doorway, and Niro gestures to the long table filling the center of the space.

There are two place settings on the far end of the table—one at the head and one on the corner next to it. I take a seat in the chair Niro pulls out for me, and once I'm settled in the corner seat, he grabs two plates heaped with food from what looks like a retro, industrial-sized oven.

Similar to the digital stitcher, this appliance is massive, and is pushed against the entire length of the back wall. It looks like it's made of steel and painted a soft yellow, with multiple ovens and compartments where food is made. It also has separate sections with touch screens which seems to be where you make food choices.

My stomach growls the moment the plate is set in front of me. Some of the same root vegetables and meat we eat in the village are present, but with different seasoning added. Then there's a pile of white mush that could pass for cottage cheese, but I'm pretty sure that's not what this is. "Um, what—"

"Rofan mash," Niro says. "It is a vegetable that can be mixed with bes cream into a soft consistency."

I get a few long blue beans on my fork and dip the very end into the mash. Rich, buttery goodness explodes on my tongue the moment I take a bite. "This mash is gonna make me pass out."

Niro chuckles, the sound low. "And that is good?"

"Yes, very good. My compliments to the chef," I say, holding up my mash-covered fork in a mock cheers.

"Oh, I did not prepare this food," he says sheepishly. "That did." He points to the appliance along the back wall.

"You just… enter in what you want, and the machine makes it for you?" I ask.

"Not quite," he says. Then he points to the square section on the far left. "That is a cold box that stores meats, bes cream, vegetables, and certain herbs. When you choose an item on the screen next to it, it pulls the food from the cold box, and moves it through the heat box there." He jerks his chin toward the middle section with multiple ovens stacked on top of one another. "Then it comes out there," he says, gesturing toward the rotating lazy Susan under red lights on the far right.

All it needs are some neon colors and honking sound effects and this thing is straight out of *Pee-Wee's Playhouse*. "What's it called?"

Niro pinches one eye closed and says, "I believe you would call it a food dispenser."

As a person who doesn't enjoy cooking, I appreciate Niro's need for convenience. "That's cool. You don't like to cook then? You find no joy in preparing a meal for yourself?"

"No," he replies quickly. "I was never taught how. I suppose had I not had cooks or machines like this to prepare my food for me, I would need to learn. But I am not sure I would enjoy it."

"Well," I begin as I take another bite of the mash, "I didn't have cooks or crazy, decked-out machines to make food for me, and I certainly don't enjoy it."

"No?" he asks.

"Nah. I cooked because it was cheaper than ordering a prepared meal from a restaurant, but it wasn't something I looked forward to. I did it because I had to." I smile as I look at the food dispenser connected to the mini fridge. "But having something like this? I'm envious, that's for sure."

He nods, looking surprised by my comment at first. Then we both go back to eating silently for a while.

Eventually, I take a sip of water to clear my throat and ask, "What made you and your siblings leave Sufoi, if you were so successful in those dome battles?" It still doesn't quite make sense to me why they came here, and why they've remained for so long.

Niro swallows hard, and gulps down half of his water before placing his glass on the table. He sighs, his chin dipped, and slowly closes his eyes. When he opens them, his irises have turned a darker, stormy gray. "We were banished. Forced to leave."

Of all the things I expected him to say, that was not one of them.

"Remember I said that I studied humans for a mission?" he asks.

I nod, saying nothing.

"Well…" he starts, "that mission was not sanctioned by our king and his council. We did it on our own, and the goal was to send a group of podlings to Earth to live among the humans."

"What?" I ask in what sounded like more of a scream than a question. I'm glad I didn't have any water in my mouth because I would've definitely spit it out all over my plate.

Niro sighs, running a rough hand through his black hair. "There have been many podlings since my siblings and me. We were the first, but certainly not the last. And none of us are allowed to take a mate. Ever." He lifts his heavy gaze to me. "You have no idea how lonely life can get when you live as long as I do. And I have been lonely for a very, very long time, Kate."

I nod and reach for his hand across the table. His fingers twitch at the contact, but soon wrap around mine.

He lets go and takes another sip of water. "After my siblings and I were dismissed from protecting the crown in actual battle, we had no way of earning a living. We were free, but not really."

"Wait, why were you dismissed?" I ask.

"Alussanai's lack of fear was not what our handlers predicted, and not what they wanted at all when they created her. She was dismissed first. I was dismissed next because my modification seemed to fade and correct itself every twenty-five years."

"So the part of your brain they messed with would heal on its own?"

"Yes. It would heal, regrets for my kills would flood in, and because I still had my memories, but had processed none of the remorse, it would hit me all at once. There were days I could not move at all because of it."

I inhale, long and deep, trying to make sense of all this, but it feels impossible.

"Ultimately, they would sedate me until they could operate, and then they would manually calcify the part of my brain that feels remorse. It would last another twenty-five years, and it would heal itself once again." Niro recounts the memories, shaking his head in anger. "I had the same procedure done twice more before they gave up and I was dismissed from service."

"What about the others? You said they were good in battle, right?"

"They were frequent victors in the battle dome, which came later. In actual battles to protect the king, however, they were unmotivated and refused to continue fighting. We were the king's army. And my brothers hated the king. So once Alussanai and I were out, the other two requested dismissal and were granted it due to poor performance."

"What happened after your dismissal?" I ask, feeling the anger surge through my blood on his behalf. "Were you just expected to get a new job and suddenly live a normal life after fighting countless wars?"

"Typical draxilio warriors enter retirement and are able to live comfortably on the royal allowance until they die. Podlings have no such rights, though. Or they didn't when we were dismissed."

I push my fork through the small remaining cluster of mash on my plate, my hunger now completely gone.

"We became a bit of a legend, the four of us. Because we were the first podlings, there was always a certain amount of interest into our lives. Once we were dismissed, a story was released about how we lacked the same benefits awarded to draxilio warriors, and there was an outcry from the public to fix that," he says with a warm chuckle. "Strangers. Draxilios we had never met, were demanding our right to live normal lives."

"What happened?" I ask.

"We were granted some rights, but not all that naturally birthed draxilios are given. The king wanted the distinction between us to remain. So, we were given a smaller benefit that would allow us to secure a home and give us time to look for work. We were younger than most warriors when we were dismissed, so none of us were prepared to retire. But because we had gained a level of celebrity, getting the jobs we wanted was simply not possible."

He abruptly stands and takes our empty plates to the wall with the food dispenser, and places them into a brown container beneath it.

Niro grabs a glass jug from a white cabinet next to the dish bin and pours us each a mug. "Tibbi?" I ask with hopeful eyes. He nods and smiles as he puts the half-full jug away.

He takes his seat next to me and picks up where he left off. "We were offered the chance to participate in these battles that took place in a domed arena. They were recorded, and there was a live audience, and the audience would vote on who we would fight each week. Sometimes we fought each other. Sometimes we fought other podlings together. We were paid well, and it was work we could do.

"It was when we started to accrue a large number of credits that we began looking for ways to invest it. We dabbled in many illegal activities that earned us enough to stop fighting in the dome and live comfortably for the rest of our days. And each of us still had many days ahead."

"That's when you started studying humans?" I ask.

"Yes," he replies flatly. "But Earth was not our first choice. We wanted to leave Sufoi, knowing that financially comfortable is all we would ever be there."

"For a lot of people on Earth, that's the best outcome we could envision," I reply. I want Niro to realize how lucky he is.

"It was not enough for us. We had so much taken from us already," he mutters, scratching his chin. "We wanted more. We wanted to see if it was possible to have more."

I take a sip of tibbi and keep the glass in my hand.

"Earth was fourth on our list of planets not yet colonized, but species-compatible for procreation."

Compatible for procreation? "You mean…"

"Your kind and mine can have offspring, yes," he finishes.

Well, okay then. File that one away for later. I'm not ready to unpack it yet.

"Various reasons precluded us from reaching our top three planets, and the mission took a long time to assemble, because we had to do it all in secret. But once we settled on Earth, we knew we needed to blend in, and we needed volunteers to travel there as our test subjects."

Wait. "Are you telling me dragon shifters are living among humans on Earth right now?"

His eyes grow heavy and my stomach drops. "Sadly, no." He takes a long swig of tibbi before continuing. "We had volunteers. It was the thirteenth group of podlings. We called them 'the skins.' They were given physical modifications after countless mental modifications yielded no positive results. This group had the ability to camouflage their skin to any color and hide their horns at will. But they did not survive the journey to Earth."

I swallow the lump in my throat. "How many?"

"Five," Niro answers, his tone somber.

"Did their ship crash or…"

"Yes, we think it exploded upon impact just outside Earth's atmosphere. Their comm screens went blank and their biological indicators stopped sending feedback at the same time," Niro says with a sigh. "They had internal pods within the ship, but from that distance, there is no way they survived a crash with nothing to protect them from impact but the pod's exterior."

"I'm so sorry, Niro." I tell him. "That's awful."

"Yes, it was a tragedy. They were fine males." He drains the rest of his glass and wipes his lips with his napkin. "After that, our mission was no longer a secret. My siblings and I were the most involved in it, having funded the entire thing, and were punished as such."

I'm not following. "Wait, why? Why did this mission need to be a secret?"

"Draxilios are not allowed to leave Sufoi unless for an approved mission, and in those cases, our movement is monitored by the king's council until we return," he explains.

I jerk back, my brow furrowing. "So you were trapped on your planet? Every draxilio. Even though you had the ability to travel through space?"

Niro sighs, nodding at my incredulous tone. "It is a way to prevent interspecies breeding. Our king is aware of how…uncommon our abilities are as draxilios. He believed this advantage would cease if we were to mate outside our species."

I'm appalled at first, but then I try to imagine taking Niro back to Earth and having a baby with him as we attempt to have a normal life. I doubt we'd make it a week before someone snatched him away and started experimenting on him inside a government building.

Wait. Am I really fantasizing about Niro and me having a kid? *What is wrong with me?*

Niro lifts one shoulder in a half shrug as if to say "It is what it is."

"Were you sent to jail? Or whatever your equivalent of that is on Sufoi?" I ask. I can't picture any of them tolerating more than five minutes in a cell without luxe amenities, to be honest.

"In a way, yes. We were sent here," he replies. "Cut off from all contact with anyone from Sufoi. This is our prison."

I look at the grand dining room table we're sitting at, the gold utensils and crystal glasses. I want to laugh, but I hold it back. "How exactly is this your prison?"

"If any of us try to leave this planet, we die."

"What?"

"They placed a device in each of us before we were sent here. It is attached to our hearts and if we breach the atmosphere of Oluura, our hearts stop beating," he says in a tone too frank for the subject.

"You're stuck here? All of you?"

"We were able to take the credits we still had, which is how we have been able to build comfortable homes here, having furniture and devices shipped to us, but we may never leave."

I let my back hit the chair as a breath escapes my lips. I do remember him calling this a "prison planet" when we were on our way to Alu's. I thought it was just his diva-like way of describing Oluura. I didn't realize he meant it literally.

"Jesus" is all I can say. "I had no... I'm so sorry, Niro. You guys really got fucked over."

He chuckles bitterly. "I suppose we did. But the lives of those five podlings were lost because of us. Because we got greedy. Because we sought more than we had. They would still be alive if we had not been so obsessed with relocating to another planet just to find mates. Mates that probably do not exist...for any of us."

"Oh, come on," I say. "Their ship crashing was not your fault. It was a freak accident. Accidents happen all the time."

"Perhaps," he replies. "But we were rushing. Desperate. Had we spent more time checking the ship, making sure the route was safe, creating fail safes in case of the very thing that occurred, they would be living among your kind. Happy, I would assume."

I want to repeat that this isn't his fault. That he can't wallow in guilt forever. That he deserves to live the life he was so passionately seeking for himself and the podlings that died in the crash. But I don't have the right to say any of that. Just hearing his story doesn't mean I know his story. Not truly.

It's like all the times I tried to tell myself to get over the trauma from being with Dennis. You can't just flip a switch and erase trauma. Pain sticks. That's just what it does. The only way past it is through. I offer the only kind of advice I feel comfortable giving. "Tomorrow is a new day. Try to do better than you did today. That's all anybody can do."

Niro glances at me sideways before turning his head in my direction. "I suppose you are right." As I place my empty glass on the table, he says, "So what will we tell the Hexrins?"

I shrug my shoulders as I start mentally preparing for my return to the village. "The truth."

"You think they can help us?" he asks, taking our glasses to the same place he took our plates.

"Who knows? But they're our only shot, so fingers crossed, right?"

"Of course..." he replies, confusion wrinkling his forehead as he twists one of his fingers over the other.

"Time to go then?" I ask with a laugh, standing and pushing my chair in.

"Yes, it is time."

With Bexo's precious book in hand, I follow Niro into the launch room. His black shirt snags on a rough edge on the door frame, leaving a tear the size of my fist on his back. He growls and rips it over his head, tossing it to the floor. He shifts, and by the time I've gotten settled inside his palm after takeoff, clutching the book to my chest and curled in a ball to avoid the bitter lashing of the wind, I feel him getting ready to land. The flight itself is about ten minutes long, and I find myself feeling relieved that Niro's home is close by.

We settle on the ground just outside the tree line, and Niro shifts back. Still shirtless, he straightens his pants, and fiddles with his belt for a second, and I realize he's nervous. This is the first time I've seen him nervous.

It's cute, in a way.

"Ready?" I ask.

He nods and follows me into the forest. I stop about five feet away from my favorite tree, holding a hand up for Niro to pause because I hear footsteps, and suddenly I'm worried coming back here with Niro was a terrible idea. How will they react when they see me? How will they react when they notice I'm not alone?

I haven't missed the constant anxious thoughts that cloud my mind whenever I leave the little house I once shared with the girls. These last few days have been a nice break from that.

A soft giggle catches my ear.

Ava.

She's home. Why is she home? Is Ahlvo healed? Is she home because of me?

Then I continue walking because out of all the people to see me upon my return, I want it to be Ava. She'll understand that I can't give her all the answers right now. That I can't exactly reveal why I was taken or what Niro and I have planned. She has always been understanding and wonderful. There's no reason for her to not have my back this time too.

I hand the book to Niro, and he tucks it in the back of his pants. Readying myself for whatever is to come, I square my shoulders and take a breath before stepping out of the tree line.

But as my shitty luck would have it, Ava is not the first person to see me as I emerge. It's Ahlvo. Then Varrek. And before I can even take a breath, they push Ava and Chloe behind them and hold out their weapons as Niro steps out from behind me.

This is bad. Very, very bad.

CHAPTER 14

NIRO

I am not shocked to see the golden males step into an attack stance the moment they lay eyes on me. Any decent male would do the same, especially with their mate at their side.

The shocking part comes when Kate steps in front of me, blocking my body from their weapons. "Kate, move," I command. I do not want her in the way. As she said, accidents happen, and I do not want her to be involved if one should occur here and now.

Melt their flesh. Destroy them all, my draxilio urges.

No, I send back. *These are Kate's people. I cannot hurt them.*

He growls his disagreement.

Kate keeps her focus trained on the golden males. They, too, shout at her to move, and the females hiding behind them hurl questions at her about her whereabouts over the last few days. The one with the long, gilded sword asks Kate about something on her arm, and the moment she looks down, adrenaline fills my blood, readying for a fight. Kate is distracted long enough for the one with the white hair to pull her away from me, and for the one carrying the sword to leap in my direction.

Time seems to slow as multiple events happen at once. I follow the glint of the blade as the sharpened point sails toward my chest. He may be a skilled warrior, this golden one with the many braids, but I am draxilio. I am faster. I am stronger. I am eternal. I let the bloodthirsty grin spread wide across his face as he comes closer. I enjoy giving my opponent a false sense of security. It is a game I will never tire of playing.

Just before the sword connects with my chest, I roll to the side, twisting toward the ground, and away from harm. Immediately I leap into a crouch, ready for my next move, but it is unnecessary, because the braided one struggles to get back onto his feet. His mate rushes over to help him as Kate stomps on the booted toe of the white-haired one and breaks free of his hold.

She's at my side in a flash, panic in her eyes as she looks me over. "I am uninjured," I tell her. She helps me to my feet and gets in front of me once again, blocking her clan from another attack.

"What the fuck is going on here?" the one with the deep brown skin yells. "Kate, are you okay?"

"Yeah, I'm good," she replies, her tone dazed. She shakes her head and pushes a few wild red strands of hair from her face. "Look, obviously we have a lot to talk about, but I'm not saying another word unless you guys promise not to hurt him. Got it?"

I am…stunned.

I would not expect her to shove me into harm's way upon returning, we still have to break the dream link, after all. But I did not envision her defending me with such ferocity. As if I am a member of her clan, or a trusted friend. Perhaps that is what we have become.

"I do not understand," the braided one says. "He kidnapped you, did he not? And you protect him? Why, Kay-teh?"

"Why do they pronounce your name incorrectly?" I whisper to Kate.

She shrugs and rolls her eyes as if used to it. "It's not that simple," she replies to the braided one. "And I can't go into much detail at the moment, but you guys have to trust me." She puts a hand on my arm. "He didn't hurt me. Plus, the whole kidnapping thing was a miscommunication. And he's not going to hurt anyone here…right?" she asks.

I clear my throat. "Kate speaks truth. I am not here to cause your clan distress."

"Then why *are* you here?" the white-haired male asks. He is the clan's leader, I believe. The way he holds himself and the commanding tone of his voice support my conclusion.

"I made Niro promise to bring me back today so that you guys wouldn't worry," Kate says. Her hands start to shake, and when I look up, I see that more of the golden people have gathered to see what the commotion is. "Can we…can we maybe do this inside? Our place, or Varrek's? I don't really want to have this conversation out here."

"Kay-teh? Is that you?" the golden male with the short white hair and the scarred face calls out as he approaches. I recognize him from her dreams. His eyes are locked on Kate. He looks at her as if she holds his heart in her small, spotted hand.

I find that I hate him. My draxilio concurs.

He runs up to her and grabs her hands in his, sinking to his knees in front of her. He presses her knuckles against his forehead, as if prepared to worship her body right here in front of everyone. "We have been looking for you. Searching. We found nothing. We thought…" he trails off, his voice cracking slightly.

"I'm fine, Bruv," she reassures him, giving his hands a squeeze. "I didn't realize you guys were looking for me. I'm so sorry. I…" Kate chews on her lip, and I notice the wetness in her eyes.

"Let's take this inside, shall we?" the pale female with the dark hair says when she notices Kate's unshed tears. "Varrek, lead the way?"

We follow the white-haired one, Varrek, into his home and away from curious onlookers.

It is abundantly clear to me that Kate does not feel welcome among this clan. She stiffened the moment she noticed them gathering. Tension rolled off her body when they gasped at the sight of me. Her fists tightened at her sides when they continued to gawk and whisper. This is a feeling that Kate has felt before, I gather, and continues to feel it here. A place that is supposed to be her home.

That does not please me.

When we reach the second floor of Varrek's home, I smile. He has taken us into what looks like a makeshift museum for outdated weaponry. He seems proud of this room, if the lift of his chin and the sharp gaze he points in my direction are any indication. I suppress my laughter, because one exhale from my lungs could melt these swords and daggers into a pool of molten metal. Let him think I am intimidated.

We stand in a wide circle with Kate huddled close to me against the wall. "Well? Where do you wish to begin, Kay-teh?" Varrek says.

"Her name is Kate," I correct.

Immediately, Kate cough-laughs, and shoots me a grin that the others cannot see. "That's a good start. Introductions!" she says with a single clap of her hands. "Guys, this is Niro. He's a draxilio, aka the blue dragon that I've mentioned." Then she turns to me and gestures to each one. "Niro, this is Bruvix, Ava, Ahlvo, Chloe, and Varrek. He's our clan's leader. And Ahlvo is his second-in-command."

The one named Ahlvo winces at her words, but I do not understand the reason.

"Um, actually Bruvix is second-in-command right now, but…" Ava says with a wave of her hand, "we can get into all that later."

"Oh," Kate replies with a tilt of her head. "Anyway, now that we've put names to faces, uh, I suppose I'll start with the basics."

Kate gives them a summary of the events that have transpired, leaving out many, many details. The one named Ava keeps narrowing her gaze at Kate, and I surmise she is disturbed by the holes in our story. She is smart, this one. I expect her to take Kate aside later and demand more information. She is not believing this version one bit.

Kate does not reveal the reason we are here together, or exactly why I took her to begin with. She merely tells them that "we are linked in a way that's infuriating as fuck, and we're in the process of breaking that link." And that "the Hexrins will help us." She tells them we journeyed to visit my siblings in various locations across Oluura, but she does not offer descriptions as to these locations. All three golden males perk up at the mention of more draxilios, as well as hearing about the other types of terrain on this planet.

I cannot imagine they are foolish enough to attempt to seek out these locations. Approaching a draxilio's home without warning, particularly if you are not a draxilio yourself, is a quick way to be turned into a pile of ash.

I shall send warning to Bexossanai and Alussanai to be prepared.

There are many questions asked of Kate that she refuses to answer at this time, which causes the human females to look at each other with fretful, worried eyes. They do not understand why Kate keeps secrets from them, but it is clear they assume it is to protect me, and that concerns them greatly.

I am forced to vow that I will remain docile and cooperative three more times during the conversation. And as long as I remain in the village, I am to be watched. There will be at least one warrior always trailing me, and he will be armed.

And I am to sleep in the food shed behind their meal hall.

Wonderful.

Kate bristles at this, offering to let me stay in her home. But they do not trust me to sleep in the same building as another female. They do not trust me at all, that is obvious.

While I will miss the comforts of home, as I assume I will not be given thick, soft sheets made of ornate lunarsota to sleep on, I will survive. As long as we accomplish our goal, I will endure the conditions they force onto me.

It is pointless to argue. They assume I am a threat and may attempt to kill me. That will get messy, because I will shift, attack them in response, and burn their houses down. I really do not want that situation to arise.

Kate needs me to comply with their orders, and for her, I will.

When the conversation circles back to questions about why I took her and what we need from the Hexrins, Kate rubs her eyes, growing tired of the interrogation. I am about to suggest we put an end to this night, but Ava speaks first.

"We've all had a long few days. The important thing is that Kate is home, and she's safe. Why don't we get some sleep, and we can dig into this in the morning, yeah?" Ava says. She reads Kate well, and when I see Kate send her a smile filled with gratitude, I decide that I do not dislike this Ava.

Kate is ushered to her home once we are outside Varrek's, and I am guided by Ahlvo, Varrek, and Bruvix to my temporary quarters. We reach a grand, open structure filled with tables and several fire pits along the front. This is where they must gather to eat.

The shed behind the meal hall, though, is anything but grand. It is a third of the size of my sleeping quarters at home, and no taller than I am. I duck to enter. When I do, I see baskets of spices, dried foods, and various root vegetables along the entire far wall that look to be recently harvested. The other side of the shed has a narrow wooden bench with a hole broken though the middle, and a bucket at the foot of the bench, which has been collecting rainwater that drips from the corner of the roof.

We are in the wet season on this part of Oluura, so this means I most certainly will get rained on during my stay.

"Here," Bruvix says with a growl as he tosses a thin, ratty blanket at my head. "I will be outside this night. There are several daggers hidden beneath my clothes, and this," he says, lifting the rifle in his hands, "will be at my side. You attempt to leave this shed, and I will not hesitate to kill you, draxilio."

If he is trying to provoke me, he will need to do more than confine me in a shed and reduce my identity to my species. "It is 'Nirossanai,' but I thank you for the warning."

I settle on the bench, which creaks beneath my weight, and with my eyes closed, I lean my head back against the wall. "Sleep well, golden ones," I say with a wave as Bruvix slams the shed door closed.

Not off to a good start.

CHAPTER 15

KATE

I put the final pin in my hair and fluff the ends, adding a little volume. My hands are sweaty, and there are so many possible reasons for it, but I try to shove them aside, because today is Ava's wedding day. All that matters is her happiness. My job is to make sure the ceremony and reception go off without a hitch and be ready to cut anyone who gets in the way.

"You won't need to do that," she told me this morning before I left her to start getting ready.

"I know I don't *need* to, but I want to."

"Lemme just clarify… you *want* to be on standby in case I need someone to cut a bitch?" she asked.

"Yes," I told her plainly. "Girl, let me do my job, okay?" She laughed, and the sound warmed my insides.

I've missed her so much. Apparently, her trip to the lake house with Ahlvo was a success, since he can put weight on his leg, and the two of them finally admitted their feelings for each other.

The only thing that surprises me about her news is how long it took them to reach this place. It's been obvious since the first moment they met that they were meant to be mates. I saw it. Chloe did too. But depression is a nasty son of a bitch, and it completely derailed their courtship once Ahlvo was shot.

A wedding is something Ava has always wanted, though, and she refused to have it until I returned. It makes me want to kiss her all over her flawless face, but it also makes me want to punch myself in the gut. Ava is the one person here who knows about my dreams. I haven't told her everything about the ones Niro and I have shared, but she knows that he's been present, and she knows this isn't the first time I've had visitors inside my unconscious mind.

I want to tell her everything. But this isn't just my secret anymore. It's Niro's too. And I don't really see the point in sharing it if the Hexrins can break the link. Today is all about Ava and Ahlvo's wedding, but tomorrow, Niro and I are hoping to visit the Hexrin house and see what they can do. So, if this is all going to be over tomorrow, why get into the nitty gritty today?

I'll tell her everything if the Hexrins can't help us. But until I know for sure that this problem will continue to be a problem, I'm staying tight-lipped.

I give myself a once-over in the mirror before I head upstairs to Ava's room. Chloe, looking gorgeous in her lavender gown with her adorable little baby bump sticking out, is already there when I poke my head in. When she steps aside, Ava turns toward me, and I suck in a breath.

She is glowing. Actually glowing. Maybe it's my wonky brain creating a hallucination, but I swear I see a soft light emanating from the top of her head, and out her fingertips.

"You look incredible," I tell her. "Are you sure he deserves you? Because I can toss some knives and jerky in a bag and we can hightail it out of here and live off the grid if you want."

She chuckles, then pats me on the arm. "I appreciate the offer, but he's mine and I'm his. I'm ready to make it official."

I nod, knowing she'd respond that way, and then the three of us walk arm in arm out of the house and onto the main path.

The moment we're halfway toward the meal hall where the ceremony and reception are taking place, I catch Niro leaning against

Varrek's house. I give him a nod of approval, and he starts to follow us. One of the warriors, Grotahk, I think his name is, follows Niro, an axe in his hand. Niro doesn't pay attention to him though.

All his attention is on me.

I can feel his gray eyes as they travel down my body, taking in my bare arms and my curve-hugging dress. His gaze is hungry and…familiar. It's the same way he looked at me in my sex dream, I realize. My pussy clenches at the memory, and I can feel blood rushing to my cheeks.

He doesn't look so bad himself, if I'm being honest. He didn't bring any clothes with him, so he had to borrow some from Ahlvo, and even though Ahlvo is the biggest guy here, the shirt and vest are extremely tight across his broad chest and bulky arms.

I'm into it though. Not "into it" into it, because I don't have those feelings anymore. Obviously. But I recognize that he looks objectively tasty.

Chloe and I reach Ahlvo at the altar, and I make sure to thank him for looking for me before I let go of Ava's hand. Ava filled me in on Ahlvo's demotion because of his leg, and even though it depresses him to not be able to move how he used to, he's been working on self-acceptance, and even headed the logistical side of the rescue mission to bring me home.

He's starting to grasp what he can and can't do, and I know that's a huge weight off Ava's shoulders. She loves him, but she doesn't want to be responsible for "saving him" and I don't blame her.

I take a seat next to Niro toward the back. I would've liked to sit closer during the ceremony, but this is Niro's assigned seat, according to Varrek, who has assembled a circle of armed warriors to sit around us. And I wasn't about to let him sit alone. He's here because of me, so if he has to deal with the clan's typical bullshit, then so should I.

I'm trying not to be ungrateful. I know Varrek is wary of Niro, and he has every reason to be. Niro kidnapped a female member of his clan and then strolled into his village by her side days later as if it was no big deal. If I were Varrek, I'd probably want to stab Niro too.

On the other hand, they've been so obsessed with getting answers about why Niro's here and what we're doing with the Hexrins that they haven't even stopped to consider that I have information on Niro they can use. Not to deceive him, but to put them more at ease with Niro's presence. They haven't asked me about his draxilio form, or what he's capable of in that form. They haven't asked me where Niro's caves are located. They haven't even asked why I've grown to kinda sorta trust him.

And that tells me they don't really value my take on any of this. They don't see me as someone with something to offer. They see Niro as a problem, and I'm the one who brought him here. So they continue to watch him, follow him, guard him while he sleeps inside that shoddy food shed at night. They don't even try talking to him. And if they did, they might realize he's not truly a threat. He's just a high-maintenance pretty boy who wants to go back to a life of solitude inside his cave palace.

I don't think they even realize how quickly he could destroy them if he chose to. Ahlvo's new sword is nice and all, but it wouldn't hold up against Niro's fire.

So whatever. I'll stick by his side while he's here, and make sure they aren't giving him any unnecessary shit.

I hear a steady growl from behind, and when I turn, I see the source is Bruvix. Should've known. He's the least pleased to have Niro here. I think it might be because of his weird sex invitation he extended before Niro took me. I give him a small smile and a wave and while he doesn't offer either in return, the growl softens to a lower volume.

"You look lovely," Niro whispers to me.

"Thank you," I say, suddenly nervous. I straighten my skirt and dry my sweaty palms on it. "You clean up nice too."

He smirks, and it causes my heart to jump. *The fuck?* Am I catching feelings for a dragon? No. No, couldn't be that. I'm just feeling protective of him. That's all.

Ava yells, "I object!" and gasps fill the air. Ahlvo looks around, his kind eyes concerned, confusion furrowing his brow. I think I know what this is about, and immediately I want to rush down the aisle to check on her.

She pulls him around the back of the food hall, and we can hear them talking, but can't make out what they're saying. But if this is what I think it is, then Ava is telling Ahlvo for the first time, right in the middle of their wedding ceremony, that she doesn't want kids.

Poor Ava.

I know it's something she's uncomfortable discussing, but mainly because of the reactions she tends to get from others. Which makes me want to smash things. She's the best person on this planet, maybe the kindest and most caring person I've ever met, and she deserves to live the life that makes her happy, no matter what it looks like or how it makes others feel.

A few minutes go by, and Niro leans in near my ear. "What is happening?" he asks.

"I think Ava needed a breather before continuing. Promising the rest of your life to another person is scary stuff, you know?" I tell him with a chuckle.

Am I projecting? Possibly.

Ava and Ahlvo jog around to the altar once again with bright smiles and hands clasped. Ava's cheeks are stained with tears, but she doesn't seem to be crying anymore, so I take that as a good sign. The rest of their vows are ridiculously sweet and tender, and I have to brush away a few tears by the end.

Everybody cheers as they have their first kiss as husband and wife, and the band starts playing an upbeat happy tune as the clan rises and the benches are moved back to each side of the tables. Clan members start dancing on the main path, and I see Bruvix filling mugs of his ale.

He looks up in time to catch my eye, and I smile, but he immediately scowls and goes back to making drinks. I feel bad that I haven't had a chance to thank him personally for the rescue mission and the part he played in looking for me. Chloe told me he was particularly distraught when he found out I was missing.

But I don't really know what to say or where to begin. It's not like we were together before I was taken. And he seems jealous of Niro, which is silly because he and I aren't anything now. I don't feel like

I've done anything to lead Bruvix on, yet every time I see him, betrayal swirls in his gaze, and it makes me shrink inside myself.

Niro isn't much of a dancer, or perhaps he's not in the mood, considering the three warriors that are sitting around us, clutching tightly to their blades. So we remain seated at one of the tables and wait for dinner to be served.

Between dinner and dessert, I slip over to where Ava and Ahlvo sit and give her a tight hug, congratulating them and telling her in a whisper how proud I am that she told him the truth. When I return to my seat, I notice Niro's mug of ale is empty, as is mine. Bruvix passes by, and I hold my mug up for him to fill, hoping he won't choose this moment to yell at me or something. He fills it without comment, but when Niro lifts his mug for a refill, a clearly drunk Bruvix yells, "None for you!" in Niro's ear.

"Christ," I mutter as Bruvix stumbles off. Then I take Niro's mug and pour half of mine into his.

"You do not have to do that," he says.

"I know."

An hour passes and pretty much everyone is drunk, or dancing, or both. I even get Niro to his feet. We don't slow dance, but we do sway back and forth while facing each other, and that feels like enough. While we sway, I realize this is the first time I've enjoyed a clan party.

The last one I attended was Maevstra, and I was miserable. Niro had just scared the shit out of me for the first time in his draxilio form, and nobody believed me. And then Chloe and Ava revealed that they wanted to forget finding a way back to Earth because they were happy here and wanted to stay forever.

I felt trapped. Isolated. Utterly alone.

I watch as Niro keeps his head on a swivel while we dance, and even though we have yet to get our lives back to normal, I certainly don't feel alone. He's with me.

As the song ends, the sky opens up and rain starts dumping on us in buckets. The clan scatters. The music grinds to a halt.

But my booted feet remain planted in the mud, and when I look up,

I find Niro's still here too. In fact, it's basically just the two of us out here in the rain. Everyone else has left, even the bride and groom.

We share a knowing laugh and lift our chins toward the sky. Before I close my eyes, I peek at him, and find the muscles in his face are relaxed, his shoulders look loose, and his eyes are closed as he lets the rain cover him. I join in, and we spend several moments like this.

Eventually, a splashing sound catches my attention, and I open my eyes to find Bruvix stomping angrily toward us with a mug that is full but seems to contain more rain than ale. "Shed" is all he says, and Niro and I nod in tandem. Party's over, and it's time for the prisoner to return to his cell.

I wave good-night to Niro as Bruvix nudges him toward the shed.

I'm staying in Ahlvo's old room, just above Kaiva's med room, so the newlyweds can have some privacy. I take off my boots once I'm inside the med room and climb the steps quietly to the second floor.

I should start thinking about a more permanent living situation since Ava and Ahlvo deserve to have the house to themselves, and I can't stay with Ahlvo's parents forever. But that's a task for another day.

I quickly change out of my soaked dress and into a tunic and leggings, checking the scrape on my leg before pulling my pants on. The bruising around the cut on my shin has faded, and it's just a long scab that runs halfway up my thigh. I ring out the rain from my hair with a towel then crawl beneath the covers of Ahlvo's monstrous bed. A minute later, I realize I'm not tired. Not even a little.

When was the last time I wasn't exhausted? Like, painfully exhausted? I can't even remember.

The realization fills me with an exhilarated happiness. I want to tell someone. I want to tell Niro. I wonder if he's feeling more rested lately too.

I wrestle with the thought for a second until I decide this is information that cannot wait to be shared. So I sneak downstairs, quietly slip my boots on by the door, and head back out into the rain. This time though, I have my cloak to keep me dry. And a blanket without a million holes for Niro.

I reach the back of the shed, and peek around the side to find Bruvix passed out on top of a table in the middle of the meal hall.

Some guard he is. But maybe a little shut eye will improve his sour mood.

I creep around to the door like a cartoon detective, and race inside before Bruvix can catch me in the act.

"Kate?" Niro says, his eyes wide in surprise.

"Hey, blue man," I reply. "Gotcha something." I toss the blanket to him, and he catches it in one hand.

"But have you not seen? I already have this cozy blanket to warm me." He holds up the holey one with mock appreciation, and then tosses it aside so he can cover himself with mine. "I thank you."

"No prob."

"How did you sneak past my guard?" he asks.

"Your guard is currently lying on top of the table like a cooked roast," I tell him. "Wasn't hard."

He laughs, the sound throaty and low.

"You doing okay out here?" I ask. "I'm sorry they're keeping you locked in this box."

He brushes a hand through the air. "It is acceptable," he says. "We shall see the Hexrins tomorrow, and this will all be over. I can handle staying in this box until then."

Tomorrow. And it'll all be over. An ending I've been so looking forward to and now have mixed feelings about.

I take a seat next to him on the bench, and it jerks slightly, making me think it's about three seconds away from collapsing beneath us. My shoulder presses lightly against Niro's, and I enjoy the contact.

"You were happy today," he says.

I smile. I really was. "Hard to be cranky while watching your best friend get married to the love of her life."

"Ava seems kind. You trust her, yes? More than the others?"

"Yeah," I reply easily. "I really do. We were kidnapped from Earth and placed in a glass cage around the same time. It was just the two of us for a while, then Chloe arrived. But Ava and I got close in those early days. She knows more about me than anyone here." I turn to look up at him. "I guess…except for you. You know the most."

A muscle in his jaw ticks, and I follow the movement. He dips his chin and says, "I am sorry for the intrusion into your mind."

For the first time, I hadn't meant it as a dig, or even a hindrance. "Oh no, I didn't mean–"

"But the lack of privacy hurts both of us equally, so I suppose that is something."

I nod. "This is true."

Niro and I continue to talk about everything and nothing into the early hours of the morning. I'm not sure when he nods off, just that I follow close behind until we are both asleep.

* * *

The first thing I notice is Niro's broad, bare back. The next is the darkness of our dream void that surrounds him and the screen behind him. We are in his dream. And frankly, I'm relieved it's his turn. We need a break from my brain and visions of his blue banana dick.

A grunt from Dream Niro pulls my focus toward the screen, and that's when I realize I've crashed a sex dream.

He and I are standing in the middle of his workroom, just like in my dream, but his arms are wrapped around me, his long fingers digging into the flesh of my ass as he kisses my neck and jaw. My hands are clutching his back and gripping his hair as my head is thrown back in ecstasy. I'm releasing breathy moans as his lips move down to the neckline of my dress, seeking access to my chest.

When I look at Niro, standing next to me, his gray eyes are glued to the screen, but his chin is dipped to his chest. He's definitely embarrassed that I'm witnessing this, and he's deliberately avoiding making eye contact.

Does he think that if he just pretends I'm not here, that this will all go away? Ha! Tried it, buddy. Doesn't work.

"Well, well, well," I can't help but mutter as I cross my arms over my chest.

"Do. Not." is all he says, his eyes still locked on the screen.

I'm tempted to mock and tease, but truthfully, I'm too intrigued by his fantasy. And specifically, how I look in it.

I look like me, but...better. My skin still has the same paleness and freckles, but there's a radiance that makes it look healthy and supple. Like an Instagram filter, almost. My hair is the same bright red, but it's also way shinier than I know it is in real life. But the most interesting part is my size. I've always been chubby, and on Earth I bounced back and forth between sizes twenty and twenty-two, but in Niro's dream, my rolls and dimples and stretch marks are prominent, as if that's his favorite part of me.

It's in the way his hand massages and grips the soft flesh of my ass, the way his eyes trail down my neck and chest and land on my soft tummy, the way he licks his lips when I drop my left shoulder and the rolls on my side are accentuated.

I never would've imagined my fat body looking so desirable. So sensual. So fuckable.

"This is your fault, you know," Niro mutters bitterly out the side of his mouth.

I laugh. "How do you figure that?"

Dream Niro and Dream Kate separate just long enough to hastily rip off their clothes. Then they're standing naked, facing each other.

"You started this," he adds.

Dream Niro reaches for Dream Kate but pauses and looks down at his cluttered mahogany desk. He uses his thick, veiny forearm to sweep everything aside and onto the floor. Baubles and papers and electronic gadgets clatter to the floor.

"And it looks like you're about to finish it, eh?"

Niro growls beside me in response.

My eyes travel down Dream Niro's body, and I frown when I realize I can only see him from the hips up. "Hey, why can't I see your dick? Are you hiding your banana from me on purpose?"

"Banana? This is a human food, right?"

"Yeah," I reply impatiently. "The version of your dick in my sex dream. It looked like a blue banana."

He chuckles under his breath. "I suppose you have not earned it yet."

"What? The sight of your dick?"

"Yes."

"Wow. You're confident it's that spectacular?" I ask. "Because last time we were here you were desperate to prove how unlike a banana your dick looks. You got my hopes way up, and the last thing you want is for me to finally see it and say, 'Sooo, that's it?'"

"Maybe it is less about the magnificence of my cock and more about your desperation to see it that we should focus on."

He's got me there.

Dream Niro licks a trail from Dream Kate's ear to the base of her throat and says, "I must taste you, Kate. There has never been anything I've wanted more."

Suddenly the temperature in the void rises and I'm wiping the sweat from my brow. As anti-affection as I am, I'm not opposed to receiving a good pussy-licking.

Dream Kate bites her lip and nods as Dream Niro lifts her easily and seats her on top of the desk. He spreads her thighs wide and lowers to his knees. Even kneeling, Dream Niro is so tall that he has to bend down to put his mouth on her. The moment he does, Dream Kate cries out so loud, it echoes throughout the caves.

Am I that loud in real life? It's been so long since I've had sex that I actually enjoyed, I'm not even sure.

Dream Niro doesn't seem to mind though, in fact, he takes a break from his thorough licking to praise Dream Kate for it. "Yes, Kate. Tell me. Tell me how to make you feel good."

Dream Kate spreads her pussy lips, points to her clit, and draws a circle around it with her finger. Dream Niro nods and immediately attacks with his tongue. "Fuuuuck. So good," she shouts.

Then the image on the screen blurs. The colors fade and it looks like another image is trying to break through.

This is new. "What is happening?" I ask.

"I–I don't know," Niro mumbles as he clears his throat.

The image returns to the sex scene on the desk, and for a moment, it seems all is back to normal. But that doesn't last, because the next moment, the sex scene has disappeared entirely, and in its place is an image of Niro and his three siblings, sitting in what looks to be a classroom. They all look young here, maybe pre-teen age, and they are being lectured to by two adult draxilios in long white robes.

The male in the white robe I recognize from Niro's dream about his first shift and first kill. This is the guy who yelled at him for picking up a toy. The other draxilio is one I've never seen before. Though she stands tall and rigid like the male, her eyes are surprisingly kind.

"I don't understand," a young Alu says, sounding defeated. "Why are we prohibited from taking mates? What if we find our mates someday? What then?"

"You are not prohibited, Alussanai," the female says.

"You simply do not have mates. They do not exist for you," the male adds.

"But, why?" Bexossanai asks in a colder tone. He is skeptical of their words, because of course, he is.

"Because you are podlings," the male says as if the explanation is obvious. "You are not full draxilio. Mates are a miraculous gift for our kind. But you are not part of our kind, so they are not for you."

"This is your handler?" I ask Niro. When he doesn't respond, I say, "Because, no offense, but he looks like he deserves a stiletto lodged in his carotid artery."

Niro looks at me then, as if his trance has been broken, and lets out a startled laugh. "I would love to see that," he finally says.

We laugh together, no longer watching the screen, but keeping our eyes on each other. Like, whatever memory or fantasy comes next is irrelevant, because we're on the same team.

"Kate!" a voice calls from beyond the void. Niro and I both turn our heads toward it. "Kate!" it calls again. "Wake up!"

* * *

"Ugh, what?" I groan as mysterious hands continue to nudge my shoulder.

"Kate," Niro whispers, and my eyes blink open.

I turn toward the door and find Chloe on the other side of me, hovering over us with the disapproving look of a mother who just discovered her teenage daughter necking with a boy in the back of his car. "What are you doing in here?" she asks.

I rub my eyes and try to orient myself. I didn't have so much ale that I'm hungover, but enough that my mind is a bit mucky. Sneaking out of Ahlvo's old room and coming here, though? That was a decision I was sober enough to make and fully remember. But falling asleep next to him with my head on his shoulder and my fingers laced with his? That I do not remember.

"Uh, you know. Checking on our food supplies," I mutter with a grin.

Her mouth forms a grim line and it's obvious she's not in the mood for my jokes. Fine. If she doesn't want my sweet, then she's gonna get my sour. "I was making sure our 'prisoner' here has a decent blanket. One without a million fucking holes."

Her eyes soften a bit, and she looks over her shoulder, down the main path. "Okay, just come on. Varrek will lose his shit if he finds you in here."

An incredulous cackle escapes me before I can stop it. "Oh, will he? I'm sorry, am I not old enough to spend the night with a boy? Do I need to get written permission first?"

"Kate, can you just cool it on the sass for a sec?" Chloe says.

But it's early and my back hurts from falling asleep against a hard wall.

"No. Can you tell me, um, just who in the fuck does he think he is?" She doesn't answer, and I don't expect her to. It was a rhetorical question. "Or why he separates Niro and me at night but not during the day? What does he think he's protecting me from, exactly? Or is this just about him having control over what I can and can't do?"

She sighs, her shoulders dropping in exasperation. "This isn't about—"

"Then what's it about, Chlo?" I interrupt. "Because I brought him here. I've spent days and nights with him before coming back here.

And just because Varrek is in charge, he thinks he can keep us apart like two lovesick kids in a Shakespeare play?"

"What do you want me to say? I'm just the messenger here!" Chloe shouts. I don't want to fight with Chloe. I don't even want to fight with Varrek, to be honest. I just want one thing, one fucking thing in my life to be my choice. To feel like I have some semblance of control and autonomy. And it seems like whenever I'm here, that gets taken away.

"I don't want you to say anything. I'm sorry, okay?" I stand and touch her shoulder as I slip past her. "Come on, Niro."

He scrambles off the bench and onto his feet, stretching his arms and neck. He neatly folds the blanket I brought him and places it on the bench.

I see Bruvix scrubbing a hand down his face as he stumbles toward us with his dagger at the ready. "What is going on here? Where are you taking the prisoner?"

"How'd you sleep last night, Bruv?" I ask with a sneer. I'm over this whole scene. "Was the table a comfortable bed for you?"

He straightens his spine, looking at Chloe sheepishly. "I don't know what you are talking about."

I wave my hand, dismissively. "Don't worry about it, bud. You're off-duty now."

"Kate, where are you going?" Chloe asks as I start walking down the path away from them. "To see the Hexrins. I've had enough."

CHAPTER 16

NIRO

Kate leads me to the Hexrin house at the far edge of the village tucked behind a smaller, wide, single-story house. I am told these witches live together inside this home that is the width of the food hall and four stories tall. It is the largest building in the village, by far, so I find it strange for it to be hidden like this in the corner, surrounded by trees and brush.

"What is the purpose of this coven?" I ask Kate. "What role do they serve?"

"I'm not exactly sure, to be honest," she replies. "They lead chants and prayers during seasonal celebrations, but outside of that, the clan doesn't seem to engage with them very much."

What an incredible waste of resources. "The clan has powerful witches living among them and they do not call on them to use their gifts?"

Kate huffs a breath and nods. "They certainly seem like an underestimated bunch, that's for sure."

When we reach the front door, Kate does not knock; she walks right in. "Hello, hi. Good morning!" she calls out once we cross the threshold. "Tibik!" she shouts. "You home?"

We enter through what looks to be the eating room and stand in front of one of two large circular fire pits surrounded by bricks in various shades of gray. There are empty stools around each fire pit, and I imagine this is where they gather to cast spells. Was the spell that links Kate and me together cast right here in this room?

There is a wide opening in the far wall with netting covering it. A vent for the smoke, I would guess.

A thin, short female with rich red hair appears before us. Her posture is hunched, and she looks to be a child with poor self-esteem. The moment her eyes land on Kate, her spine straightens, and her golden eyes widen with excitement. "Hello, Kay-teh. How many I assist you this day?"

"Oh, hi, Jobaki," Kate says with a hint of disappointment in her tone. "Is Tibik up yet? We need his help with something."

"Tibik is at the falls reciting a prayer for the goddess. It is his morning ritual. Then he will be collecting buunit root until the middle meal," the small female says. "But I can help you. I'm certain of it."

Kate gives me a worried look, and then turns back to Jobaki. "Okay, sure, Jo." Then she stops. "Oh! May I call you Jo?"

Jobaki's pointed ears wiggle slightly behind her spiky red hair as a smile spreads across her angular face. "Certainly! Call me whatever you wish. This way," she says, gesturing for us to follow. She leads us up the stairs to the third floor and into an almost empty room. Along the walls, there are lit candles on windowsills and shelves, and in each of the four corners there is an altar with freshly cut flowers, tiny wooden figurines, symbols drawn on the walls, and a wiry branch bent into a hexagonal shape wrapped in ribbons.

There is a single wooden chest against the wall beneath a window from which Jobaki pulls three plush, green cushions, a handheld blade, and a chrome goblet. She places the cushions in a triangular shape in the center of the room, with the blade and goblet in the middle.

"Sit, please," she says as she scurries over to the altar in a back corner and takes the ribbon-covered hexagon, as well as a previously hidden clear bottle filled with a dark substance. She places these with the blade and goblet, and then quickly grabs a lit candle from a low shelf before taking her seat on the remaining cushion.

Kate and I exchange intrigued glances as Jobaki makes fast work of assembling her supplies just so, before crossing her slim legs in front of her and taking a deep breath.

"Now, tell me what plagues you," Jobaki says in a soft, yet authoritative tone.

I start. "I–"

"It bega–" Kate says at the same time.

Jobaki presses a hand to her mouth and releases a light chuckle. "Kay-teh, let us hear from you first."

Kate launches into the long version of the story, this time, leaving out no details. Jobaki nods as she listens, and once Kate's done, the witch's eyes land on the book beside me. "And what is that?" she asks.

"It contains the history of mated draxilio pairs. There is one story where two draxilios refused to become mated, and they had a witch break the bond using a spell," I tell her.

Kate sighs, her shoulders slumping slightly. "We thought it might help to have it, but I know you probably can't read Sufoian–"

"Of course, I can," Jobaki replies with a confident smile.

"Oh," Kate says, her green eyes swirling with hope.

Jobaki holds out her hand, and I place the book in it. "I have a great many talents that are unknown to most," she mutters casually as she flips through the pages.

"It is near the end," I tell her. Immediately, Jobaki lifts her fingers off the page and motions in a sweeping point, and the pages begin to fly on their own. "Ah," she says once she finds the correct passage. She reads it, continues reading through a few more pages, and then flips back to the passage as she reads it again.

Then she closes the book, and nods once. "You are unsure if what connects you is a mating signal as is common amongst your kind, Niro, or something else…a hex perhaps?"

"It is impossible for beings like me," I clarify. "I am a podling, and mating signals do not occur for us. We are not capable of taking mates at all."

"This is what he was told," Kate adds, "by the heartless, weapons-grade scumbags who made him in a laboratory, so…not exactly a trustworthy source."

The side of Jobaki's mouth quirks upward as she stares at Kate, almost in awe of her brutal tongue. "I understand now, yes."

"So you can help us?" Kate asks.

"I believe I can," Jobaki replies. "Let us first see if you are under the power of a hex." She pulls a bundle of da'koi leaves wrapped in wire from her pocket and holds the end of the small clump above the candle. It catches, releasing a spicy-smelling smoke into the room. She waves it in front of us as she closes her eyes and chants under her breath. I cannot make out her words, but the sound becomes lower and grittier as she continues. Then the flame on the bundle is blown out, not by Jobaki's breath, but perhaps from her mind. Her eyes open wide, and her expression changes from concern to relief. "You are under no curse," she tells us.

"You are certain?" I ask.

She nods. "Quite."

"Okay," Kate says with a wistful sigh. "That's one theory debunked. Let's hit the next one."

"The dream link, yes?" Jobaki asks, putting the bundle down and picking up the book in one hand, and the hexagonal branch in the other.

"Yes," I reply.

"Kay-teh, I will need a personal item of yours as well," Jobaki says, looking at the book.

"Oh, right," Kate says, as she pulls one of the stretchy hair bands from her wrist and places it on top of the book.

Jobaki lifts the branch above the book in the middle of us, leaving a good amount of space in between the items. "Kay-teh, Niro, place one hand on this sacred wreath. With your other hand, join together. I ask you to close your eyes, and to keep your hearts and minds open to me."

"Very well," I mutter in response as I reach for the wreath and take Kate's hand.

We settle into this seated pose, Kate and I, our hands joined, and our eyes closed for a few moments before I feel an entity. I was not expecting to feel anything at all, honestly, as the dark arts have never seemed more than a peculiar hobby mostly practiced by females. But when my wrists start to tingle, and a chill rushes down my spine, I am proven wrong.

This is no hobby. This is power. Strong, pure, unexpected power.

I focus on the feeling of Kate's hand in mine because it is the only thing that anchors me to the present. I feel a presence inside my mind, poking and prodding, like a thief rifling through my home in search of items to steal. Paranoia causes my palms to sweat because what will this tiny witch find on her search? Will she steal my secrets? Will she come after my siblings?

Kate's fingers squeeze my thumb, a gesture that is meant to provide comfort. She senses my fear. I squeeze back and focus on the way her smooth skin feels against mine, and it helps to loosen my nerves.

Then a blazing white light fills my vision. My eyes are closed, yet I can see nothing but this light. The heat of it burns my eyes, but I cannot tear myself away from it. I hear Kate gasp from where she sits beside me, and I feel my jaw clenching as it continues its relentless assault on my sight.

"Do not let go!" Jobaki yells. Her voice sounds far away, though I know she is seated close to both of us still.

I grunt as the light fills my body, down through my eye sockets and into my nose, throat, and lungs. I want nothing more than to let go of the wreath and pull away from this little witch, to stop her from using her light on us. But to let go would mean to fight her magic, the very magic we have been seeking for several cycles.

"It hurts, Jo! Stop!" Kate yells, and something inside me surges forward. It is my draxilio. And he is furious for the pain this witch has caused Kate. I picture his face, his long snout filled with sharp teeth, his horns that start between his large dark eyes and trail all the way down his back.

The monster wants out, and I am about to let him when suddenly the light disappears entirely. The burning ceases, and we let go.

I hear Kate flop onto the floor moments before I do the same, all the strength in my body vanquished.

"I understand now," Jobaki says, her voice closer and lacking the exhaustion that pulls at every bone in my body. I look up to see her sitting tall and still and refreshed on her cushion.

"What did you do to us?" I ask through gritted teeth. I crawl over to Kate, who is lying on her back, her chest heaving with short, big breaths. I lift her shoulders and push her up into a seated position before settling myself into one as well.

Jobaki smiles, placing the items on the floor and dropping her hands together in her lap. "I needed to look inside your minds in order to see what created this link, the book provided a personal link into your history, Niro, and further context for this mating signal."

"And?" Kate asks, leaning back on her hands.

"And I believe there are multiple factors that have brought you two together."

"Do not be coy with us. Tell us what you saw," I bark. I do not understand why she hesitates.

Jobaki's gold eyes meet mine. "What allows you to enter each other's dreams *is* a mate signal."

That cannot be, I think to myself. It is not possible. Our handlers told us...

"But it is also because of Kay-teh's power. Her mind acts as an open portal for anyone to enter," Jobaki adds. "Her portal pulled you in, perhaps stronger and quicker than the mating signal would have on its own."

"I'm sorry, what now?" Kate asks. "My...power?"

"Why, yes," Jobaki replies as if her words are not news.

Kate remains still with her mouth hanging open as she stares at Jobaki.

Jobaki looks between Kate and me nervously before letting out a chuckle. "Surely you are aware of the power you hold. Why do you think we have followed you around the village?"

Kate's head jerks back and she shakes her head, frantically. "I don't have powers, Jo. That's insane."

"Kay-teh," Jobaki starts.

"No, no, no," Kate interrupts. "I have...things, sure. Little weird quirks I've always had that make me seem like a freak to some people, but I'd call that more of a flaw than a power."

Jobaki shifts her cushion slightly to face Kate. Her eyes soften. "You have had others in your dreams, have you not?"

Kate looks stunned for a moment before she shakes it off and releases a laugh. "I mean, yeah. I used to dream about my Aunt Milly, but she was dead. I mean, she was dead then and…still is, obviously."

"She was communicating with you, through your portal," Jobaki says. "Your portal is your power. Your magic. Your craft. It is a path for the living and the dead to reach you."

"*That's* my power?" Kate asks, sounding disgusted. "So you're telling me that anyone can contact me when I'm asleep, pass along their messages or whatever, and I'm supposed to be thrilled about that? To exist as a dumping ground for people's unfinished business?"

"Very few have had such a gift, Kay-teh," Jobaki says, her tone earnest. "It is the result of a strong line of witches in your family. You should be proud of it."

"There…there were other witches?" Kate asks. Her voice is less aghast. Less biting now. "I mean, my grandmother told me Aunt Milly was, but I always thought that was just her spouting some ignorant, antifeminist nonsense because my aunt never married or had kids."

Jobaki laughs knowingly. "Females who choose less traditional paths will always be vilified. It is the way of the universe, across many lands and cultures."

Kate tilts her head to the side, and a flash of something crosses her face, a knowing, also as if she is seeing Jobaki for the first time. "How old are you, Jo?"

"I am past the turning of my fifth century," she replies. "My life has been long and tragic. And lovely."

"Jesus Christ," Kate gasps. "I thought you were a child! You're so small. And you seem so…nervous, all the time. No offense."

"I am not offended, Kay-teh," Jobaki replies, shaking her head. "And it is my choice to be perceived that way." Then she leans toward both of us, looking over both shoulders for extra ears, even though there is no one else here but us. "You would never assume that a meager child would be leading the Oluura coven of the Hexrins, would you?"

"Shut the front door!" Kate yells in a whisper. "You're telling me Tibik isn't the leader? It's you?" Kate laughs, poking Jobaki's knee. "Little ol' you?"

Jobaki's cheeks pinken and she shrugs. "It is a brilliant ruse, no?"

"It is! It really is," Kate agrees. After a moment of quiet, Kate lets out a breath and says, "Well, what do I do with this *power* of mine? It seems useless."

"No, no, no!" Jobaki quickly says. "The extent of your power is untapped. Right now, it is just your unconscious mind that is open for communication. Also, the portal is too wide, too open. We must narrow it. But there is so much more to discover. We have not yet seen what you are capable of."

Kate bites into the thick center of her bottom lip, looking bashful. It is the first time I have seen someone offer her genuine praise.

"You think?" Kate asks.

"I do," Jobaki replies. "And we can begin your lessons today!"

"Oh, um, let's press the pause button on that," Kate says.

I nod in agreement. I am happy for Kate, but we are here to break the dream link.

"I'm not saying no, believe me," she tells Jobaki, then gestures between her and me. "We just need to take care of our business first."

"Right, the dream link," Jobaki says. "That is simple, really. Since it is rooted in a mate signal, all I would need to do is go into your mind and turn off the signal. It would take mere moments to accomplish."

"Oh, well. Okay then," Kate says with a chuckle. She holds my gaze and lifts one shoulder as if asking if I am in agreement with this plan.

"Will we feel the burn of the light again?" I ask. That is my only hesitation. If it caused me discomfort, I cannot imagine how much pain Kate was in.

"You will, but for not as long," she tells us. "In fact, I do not even need both of you to turn off the signal. I can hold your hand," she says to me, then turns to Kate "or yours, and the signal will disappear for you both."

"So no more dream link?" Kate asks.

"Correct," Jobaki nods, then tilts her head thoughtfully. "Though, I will want to be careful not to damage Kay-teh's portal, so I should hold her hand to turn off the signal. Yes, that will be better."

I clear my throat. "And then…"

"Then you will connect in dreams no longer," Jobaki adds. "And the intense, magnetic pull from the signal that you have been feeling toward the other person will also dissipate."

Have I felt a pull toward Kate? I suppose my draxilio has become quite fixated on her. And her incessant questions have grown less irritating over time. And I find the brown spots that cover her skin more enticing each time I look at them.

I suppose…I have become fond of her.

Does she feel the same about me? Has she felt an unexplainable pull to be near me? To hear my voice?

No. Surely, she does not. She has been abundantly clear that this dream link between us has caused her stress, and how she cannot wait to be rid of it. She wants nothing more than to be able to sleep soundly without me entering her thoughts.

I am shocked to discover that the moment Jobaki reaches both hands out toward Kate, my heart sinks into my stomach. This will soon be over. I shall go back to my caves, and Kate will remain here in the village.

Kate's hands stretch to meet Jobaki's, but just as they are about to connect, Kate yanks her hands away, and covers her eyes, her head shaking back and forth. My heart jumps inside my chest, hopeful she has changed her mind. But after a moment, Kate's hands drop, and she offers me an apologetic smile. "I'm okay now. Sorry. I don't know what that was."

She reaches out again, and Jobaki raises her open palms to meet Kate's, grasping onto them this time. Jobaki tells her to close her eyes, and when she does, Kate's brow bends down and her nose scrunches up. "No!" she shouts suddenly, pulling her hands back toward her chest.

Jobaki's eyes dart between Kate and me, her expression puzzled. "Do you not want–"

"I just need a moment, okay?" Kate stammers. She rises to her feet and nervously paces around her cushion. She brushes her hands down her tunic frantically. "Can we just take a five?"

"A…five?" Jobaki asks.

"Five-minute break. That's all I need," Kate pleas. "I'll, uh, be right back." She pulls the door shut behind and her, and Jobaki and I share a concerned glance as we hear the front door slam from three floors down.

"What–" Jobaki starts.

I feel as confused as she looks at the moment. "It appears Kate has left."

CHAPTER 17

KATE

What is wrong with me?

I ask myself for the fourteenth time since walking out of the Hexrin house. I was so close, so goddamn close to having my dreams to myself again. To having Niro out of my life completely. And yet…I panicked.

I couldn't go through with it. Jobaki was confident she could turn off the mate signal, and Niro and I would immediately be able to return to our lives. Why did I bail?

I let my feet take me onto the main path as I silently berate myself for being a coward.

I just need a breather, that's all. A huff of that fresh, slightly sticky and heavy *wet season* air and then I'll feel better. I'll be able to think straight, and I'll go back in there and break this bond with the blue dragon. I've wanted nothing else for months, and now that I have it, I'm just a little overwhelmed. That's all.

"Kate!" I hear Niro call from behind me. I stop on the edge of the tree line in an effort to not draw the clan's attention to us. Once we step onto the path, I know there will be stares. I know there will be whispers. That's how it's been since we first got back. I just want to delay it a little longer, if possible. "Wait," he says as he jogs toward me.

"I'm waiting," I say, my tone hard. I'm not in the mood for his teasing right now. Can't he just give me a break for one minute?

"Are you all right?" he asks, his hand hovering above my shoulder, a question in his eyes.

I nod in response, and his hand gently lands on my upper back. I feel his large hand rub small circles and I stifle a groan. He's trying to comfort me. I wasn't expecting that. And I certainly wasn't expecting him to be good at it. "Yeah, I'm fine," I tell him. "I guess I'm just overwhelmed by…all of it."

"The news that you are a witch," Niro concludes.

"Shh! I don't want anyone in the clan to know just yet."

"But why? Are you ashamed of it?" he asks.

Truthfully, I don't know how to answer that. I feel a sense of peace regarding the news, like a lot of things make sense now. The dreams of Aunt Milly make sense now. But it still makes me an *other* among the clan. I see how the Hexrins are treated. The clan avoids them like the plague. They already sort of treat me the same way, but could it get worse if they knew the truth? "No, I'm not ashamed," I finally tell Niro. "I'm surprised is all."

"I'm not," he says with a smirk. "I knew you were made of magic. From the very beginning, I knew."

He did accuse me of being a witch. "But you thought I created the dream link, which I didn't—not intentionally, at least. So no, you weren't totally right."

He sighs but looks more amused than irked. "You never let me win."

"And I probably never will," I tell him.

A familiar voice mumbling something about Niro catches my attention, and I gesture for him to follow me quietly. We step onto the main path and find Varrek and Bruvix joining a few other warriors as they head to the meal hall, directly across the path.

They don't see us walking behind them, and they certainly don't lower the volume of their voices in case others hear.

"Well, we cannot allow him to stay. He is a threat to us all," Varrek says to the group. "Kay-teh has returned, so there is no longer a need for patrols, and I do not want my warriors watching over a draxilio day and night. It is a waste of everyone's time."

"But surely we cannot just let him leave?" Grotahk asks. "We do not know what he is planning. And he has been spying on us through Kay-teh's dreams."

"How do you propose getting an answer from him?" Eduno, another warrior, asks.

Bruvix replies immediately, eagerly. "A bit of force should do the trick. Force that I am happy to apply, Varrek."

Whether it's the fact that I just learned that I'm a witch in a long line of witches, apparently, or that I bailed on breaking the dream link between Niro and me, or that I'm sick of being treated like crap within this group, I don't know. But upon hearing Bruvix gleefully offer to torture Niro, something inside me cracks, and rage, white and hot, pours through.

"Or, hey, maybe you could just fucking ask him?" I yell.

Simultaneously, their heads snap around to face me. We're nearing the meal hall, which is bustling with people eating their breakfast, and other members of the clan are coming and going around us.

I shift my gaze to meet Varrek's. "I'm curious, Varrek, why haven't you asked Niro the questions that you've no doubt lost sleep over?"

"Because we cannot trust that he speaks truth," he replies simply.

He hasn't even tried, so how would he know? "What would a draxilio have to gain from lying to us?" I ask. "You make him seem like this evil genius that's conspiring against us, but you haven't even attempted a conversation with him."

"And why do you defend him so readily, Kay-teh?" he snaps back. "Why defend a male who kidnapped you from your home? You have no idea what he put us through with your disappearance."

I flinch at his words, because I do feel terrible that Chloe and Ava were so worried. And Bruvix too. But was anyone else concerned? I mean, did they actually care that I was gone? Or was a small part of them relieved to finally be rid of me and all my weirdness? I can't help but think the latter.

"Granted, Niro messed up. He knows that. I'm not disputing that,"

I say with my hands over my heart. "But I demanded he bring me back within three days, and he did. He did what I asked of him. And…" I hate that my voice starts to crack, but I continue anyway, "he protected me in ways no one else ever has."

I want to look at Niro, to see his reaction to what I said, but I can't bring myself to do it. So I blink back the tears that threaten to spill and clear my throat. "He doesn't treat me like I'm a constant burden, Varrek. He came back here with me because I asked him to. Because there was something we needed to do. And it's nobody's damn business what that is, by the way. He swore to you that he's not here to hurt anyone. I promised the same. If you can't trust him, why can't you at least trust me?"

Varrek looks stunned. He goes to speak, but I hold up a hand, stopping him. "I know why. It's because you've never really seen me as a member of this clan. Not one you value, anyway. I'm not anyone's mate, and I've struggled to adapt. So you wrote me off. All of you. Except maybe for Zohma, who has been patient and accommodating with my sewing projects. And Chloe and Ava, obviously.

"As the leader of this clan," I continue, "you never once considered that having a draxilio as an ally might be a good thing? Really? That maybe he has resources that could be of use to us?"

"Kay-teh…" he says, then his mouth hangs open and silence stretches on between us.

"You know what? It's fine," I say, waving my hand dismissively. "Maybe this just isn't the place for me. I deserve to go where I'm treated with respect." I turn on my heel and give Niro a nod to follow as I continue down the path. About halfway down, Niro lightly taps my elbow and tells me to wait.

"Where are you going?" he asks.

I'm here making plans and didn't even think to ask. "Oh, I thought we'd go back to the caves. Is that okay with you?"

He gives me a roguish grin, and warmth pools in my belly. "Of course. But you should know…Jobaki looked stricken as she listened to you. Perhaps your words have awoken something within, just as hers did for you."

I peer around Niro's wide frame and catch a glimpse of Jo on the edge of the tree line, Tibik talking to her with his back to us. Despite his focused attention on her, and what seems like harsh words, she watches us, her eyes thoughtful. I gesture for her to come to over, and after politely excusing herself from Tibik's towering presence, she does, taking slow, timid steps.

I meet her halfway. "So, I'm leaving the village for a bit. I'm sure you heard."

She plays with the many silver hoop earrings that dangle from her pointed ear. "Yes. How long will you be away?"

"I'm not sure," I tell her honestly. At least until I calm down, and that may take a few days, or weeks. "But will you be okay?"

She gives me a surprised look. "Me? Why would I not be okay?"

"I just…" I look over at where Tibik stands, glaring at us. I lean closer to Jo so I can whisper, "I've been in a situation where I made myself smaller. I withdrew. There came a point where it even felt authentic to the kind of person I was…" I trail off. "But now I can see that it was purely about survival."

Jo nods.

I place my hand on her shoulder. I long to give her the comfort Niro gave me earlier, in the exact moment I needed it. "You deserve to take up space. To rule a coven openly and proudly. To stomp through the world and knock shit over and use your power unfettered. You won't be too much for the right people."

She puts her hand over mine and squeezes once. "Come back soon, Kayyy-teh." Then she clears her throat and tries again. "Kayyyy-t. Kayt."

"Whoa!" I shout. "You did it! You got my name right! How? I thought it wasn't possible for you guys."

"Perhaps not them," she nods toward the crowd of clan members at the meal hall. Then gives me a proud grin.

"I'll see you soon, Jo," I say with a wave as Niro and I continue on.

The moment Jo is gone from my sight, a wobbly-lipped Chloe steps directly in front of me. She says nothing for a long moment, then hands me a screen pad. "Take this."

Chloe chews on the inside her cheek, clearly holding back tears as she places it in my hands. There are so many things I want to say to her, but I'm not sure where to begin. Though I don't regret what I said, part of me wants to apologize to her. For not being able to fit in here, or for being rude to her mate, or maybe for letting her down. But I hate seeing her upset, and I hate myself for being the cause.

"I don't understand any of this," she says quietly. "But the last thing I want is for you to be unhappy. So just call if you need us. Keep in touch. And come back at some point, okay?"

My hands start to tremble as I give her a quick hug, being careful of her growing belly. "This isn't forever," I tell her.

"Better not be," she replies.

I step around Chloe, and I feel the heat of Niro's body once he reaches my side. "Ready to go home?" he asks.

"Yes," I tell him. And I've never meant it more.

CHAPTER 18

KATE

We arrive at the caves, and instantly, I feel at ease. The faint scent of eucalyptus hits my nose like it did on the first night and I feel my muscles loosen. I didn't realize how comfortable I'd gotten here. Or maybe not here, because I haven't spent that much time here, but with Niro. When it's just the two of us, everything feels easier.

"I am going to wash," he says once we pass his workspace. "Your room is still yours. Make yourself comfortable."

"Okay," I tell him as I watch him walk away. Suddenly, a wave of nervousness washes over me.

What the hell am I doing?

I invited myself to sleep over in a dragon's cave. Not my brightest idea, but when I essentially rejected the only home I've got, that doesn't leave many options.

"Stupid, stupid, stupid," I mumble to myself as I close the bedroom door behind me. I pull off the tunic and leggings I'm wearing and throw on Alu's green dress that I washed back at the village. It's much too long in the front, so I use my hair tie to twist and bunch the dress, creating a hi-low effect with the hem. This way I won't trip and tear the dress apart.

I run a finger along the edges of the screen pad Chloe gave me and place it on the bedside table. Ava is going to lose it when she hears I'm gone again. But it's the day after her wedding, and I didn't want to barge in on her and her new husband just to say, "Hey, I'm having a meltdown and I'm gonna need to bounce for a few more days. Okay thanks, byeee." I'll call her tomorrow. She'll understand. Or she won't and she'll tell me I'm an asshole. I will accept either outcome as long as she forgives me.

Wait, what if she doesn't? I wonder to myself. Is this all my fault? Was I being too dramatic? Should I have stayed out of it?

Before doubt can consume me, I leave the room. I hear the water still going in the bathroom down the hall, so I guess I'll just have to entertain myself.

The door to his workroom is open, and I can't help but step inside. I enter and let my eyes roam along the walls at his collection of trinkets. There's so much to see in here, and it's hard not to want to touch everything.

I don't hear him enter behind me, but suddenly, he's there. "I had a dream that began just like this…" Niro says.

I whirl around and find him in nothing but a towel draped low around his waist. His chest is dappled with water droplets, and his black hair is wet as it falls across his forehead. I swallow the pool of saliva that has filled my mouth.

"Or was that your dream?" he asks with a smirk, then crosses his arms over his chest.

I blink twice and shake myself out of my trance. "Hmm, hard to say. Let me take a seat up here and think about it for a sec," I tell him in a snarky tone as I place my forearm on the edge of the table, mimicking a sweeping motion.

"It is not a good idea to make a mess in a draxilio's home, Kate," he says as he strides toward me. He stops directly in front of me, our bodies mere inches apart. "Have you not learned that by now?"

"Well, making bad decisions is a specialty of mine."

"I have noticed," he replies, lifting his brows at me.

I laugh, nerves fraying at the closeness of him. I could just reach out and touch him right now. Press my hand against those washboard abs and feel them ripple with each breath.

"Do you plan on making any more this night?" he asks.

Oh, dear god. Is he flirting with me? Does he want something to happen between us?

Quick, flirt back, my mind shouts. But I'm drawing a blank. I have no idea how to do this. I haven't flirted with anyone in decades. What are the kids today doing? What are they saying?

It's not like he would know. Just say anything. Something sexy.

I take a shaky breath, but not a deep one that he can see. I don't want him to know how terrified I am. Because I want this. I want him. And I want him to want me too.

"I wanna taste it?" slips out like a question before I can stop the words from coming, and I immediately cringe.

His brow furrows, and then throws back his head and laughs.

My cheeks feel like they're on fire, and I just want the floor to swallow me up. "I'm…not very good at this."

He crooks a finger under my chin, as light as a feather, and lifts until my eyes meet his. "You are better than you think. Trust me."

Trust has never been my thing, but I want more than anything to trust Niro right now.

A drop of water runs down his neck and I follow its path. His chest glistens in the soft light of his workspace, and at certain angles, his scales shimmer in various shades of cerulean, teal, and turquoise. The drop continues down onto his pectoral, and I'm mesmerized. I wonder what he would do if I just leaned in and caught it with my tongue?

Only one way to find out.

I push my self-doubt aside and close the distance between us. The drop hovers just above Niro's nipple, which is slightly above my head. I lift onto tiptoes and press the tip of my tongue against his hardened nipple, slowly dragging it up to meet the drop. When it hits my tongue, I taste the earthy freshness of Niro's scent, along with the warmth of his clean skin, and let out a moan.

He sucks in a breath, and I watch as a muscle in his jaw ticks. "You…continue to surprise me, little witch."

I lean back, giving him a smug grin as I place my hands on his biceps. "You and me both, blue man."

His eyes close at my touch, and he sighs. Niro has always been beautiful, almost frustratingly so. But vulnerable Niro is like nothing I've ever seen. He's a work of art. His parted, pouty lips could inspire a thousand poems. The pained expression he wears as I stroke his cheek could send women everywhere to their damn knees.

I know mine are certainly close to buckling.

He presses a gentle kiss to the pad of my thumb and whispers, "There are many, many ways I've longed to touch you. Please, tell me how. I want nothing more than to make you feel pleasure."

That's when I notice his hands are still at his sides. His knuckles are white as they squeeze into fists, and the sight of it melts me. He knows that touch can be triggering for me. What he doesn't know is how desperate I am to feel his large hands on my body. But will it be too much? Will it send me into a series of flashbacks of Dennis? Will I freeze in place and enter a long phase of paralyzing depression?

It's too much to risk. Maybe next time, but not now. Not until I know how his touch will make me feel. "Where are the restraints?" I ask in a whisper.

He nods toward a nearby shelf. "There."

After I find them, I ask Niro to turn around for me. He does, and I place each cuff around his wrists, fastening them into place behind his back. He turns to face me, leaning against the front of the table and offers me a warm smile. "You are safe, Kate."

I nod, hoping it's the last time he'll have to remind me. Standing in front of him, I wrap my hand around the back of his neck and pull him down, bringing his face close to mine. So close, I can feel his breath fan my cheeks. "Let's start here," I whisper before I press my lips against his.

His mouth remains perfectly still at first, perhaps waiting for me to take the lead. I offer a few soft, smacking kisses at first, and then nibble on his bottom lip. I hear the table creak under his grip as his lips open for me.

His tongue slides along mine and my hands fly into his silky black hair. He groans as I suck on the tip of his tongue, and his hips jerk against me in response. I feel my nipples harden against my dress, and wetness pools between my legs at the friction of our bodies, and I cannot imagine how difficult it must be for him to not touch me. My hands seem to be everywhere, because each part of him is amazing and I want to feel every inch.

The rougher texture of his tongue makes my pussy throb with need. How is he *so good* at kissing?

Podlings may not be able to take mates, but clearly, he's had some practice in the bedroom.

How much practice, though? I wonder.

A lot?

Like, in the hundreds?

I don't realize how possessive this makes me until Niro pulls back and gives me a strange look. "You are a bitey little thing, aren't you?"

"Oh god, I bit you?" I ask, embarrassed that my petty jealousy is ruining the moment. "I'm so sorry, I–"

He slides his tongue over his darkened blue lip, and rasps, "I like it."

I giggle as I press my face into his neck, relieved he's not turned off. "Really?" I ask.

"Yes. Mark me as yours, Kate. That is all I wish to be."

I pull back to take him in. His gray eyes, lidded and swirling with heat. His soft mouth. His sharp cheekbones and proud nose. I want to taste all of him. To feel all of him.

"I want you inside me," I tell him. I can't flirt, but I can be blunt.

His eyes widen for a second, and a loud *crrrunnnch* sounds from behind him. I look down and see the front edge of his desk torn off, broken into several sharp wooden fragments in his hands. He looks panicked as he drops them to the floor and waits for my reaction. "Kate, I am sorry. I–"

"No, it's okay," I reassure him. "Kinda hot, actually." The thought of sex with me brought him such intense delight that he crushed his own desk. Perhaps it should be alarming. Perhaps this is precisely why I cuffed him in the first place. The brutal power and strength he possesses. But fear is not what I'm feeling in this moment. Fear is completely absent.

All I want is him. To feel him, and for him to feel me too. So, I remove the cuffs from his wrists because I know he would never hurt me, and he looks at me with complete astonishment as he leans in to kiss me again. "You're certain?" he says against my mouth.

"Mm hmm," I moan in response. I place his hands on my lower back and nod as he watches me, triple checking for consent. Then he lifts me off my feet and walks out of the room. I wrap my legs around his middle as he carries me down the hall. I squeal, worried he's about to drop me. "I have you," he says.

"Where are you taking me?" I ask, my voice shaky with anticipation.

"To my bed, where you belong."

The authority in his voice makes my pussy gush like a river, and I moan as I kiss his jawline and trail down the thick column of his throat.

I quickly decide that I'm not as close as I want to be, so I press myself against him while sliding a hand between us to the top of his towel. He stops in the middle of the hallway the moment I tug it loose, and I hear the muted thud of the towel as it falls in a pile at his feet. Then my back hits the wall and his hips are grinding against me. "Too far," he growls. "Need you now."

"Ooh, you feel so good," I mutter as I slam my head back against the wall. I can't see it, but I can feel the thick length of him as it rubs against my core, the fabric of my dress the only thing that separates us.

"Your scent, Kate. I will never get enough," he growls against my neck. He's licking and sucking and I'm certain leaving red marks in his wake, but I don't care. I want everything he has to give. Then he sticks his nose into my hair behind my ear and breathes in. "It is perfect."

"Yes, yes," I reply as he pulls the hem of my dress up and rests his hand above my core. His eyes lock on mine, pleading. I nod once, and then I feel him. He traces a single finger up and down my slit then lifts it to his mouth, sucking it clean. I mewl at the sight, once again blown away by how a single action can be so fucking hot. But I think I know the answer…because it's Niro.

"I knew you would taste exquisite," he says with a proud grin.

I laugh through panting breaths.

He lowers me onto my feet against the wall and nudges my legs apart, as wide as I can make them. He hands me the hem of my dress, and grunts, "Off. Now."

I do as he commands, and before it's even over my head, I feel his mouth on my breast. He sucks and laves and releases it with a pop as he moves to the other and repeats the sequence. When he's done, he places soft kisses down my stomach, pausing to caress the roundness below my belly button. For a moment, I feel self-conscious about the attention to that area, an area that I've always considered a "problem." But in Niro's eyes, I see that it's anything but, as he kisses over to one hip, and then back to the other.

On his knees, Niro's horns come up to my chest, so he has to shimmy down a bit to press a kiss to my pussy. He nuzzles against my pubic hair, and a chuckle escapes me. It's an odd sight to watch a dragon get ready to go down on you, but also, it tickles.

I watch his fingers spread my lips, and he growls softly at the sight of my pussy on full display. The breath leaves my lungs a second later when he leans in and his tongue flicks against my clit. My nerve-endings erupt. My eyes pinch shut and I scream, the sound bouncing off the walls of the caves. He moans as he continues his assault, swiping quick circles around the engorged bud. "Your fingers," I cry out. "Fuck me with your fingers."

His eyes meet mine and he smiles against my core, adjusting his hand so he can lick me and finger me at the same time. He enters slowly, inch by inch, as I adjust to the thickness of his finger. "So tight," he growls, and then his tongue becomes a frenzy of licks and flicks and at one point blackness enters my vision.

I'm grinding against his face as he adds another finger and surges in and out of me. My hand is tangled in his hair. The other holds onto his horn for dear life as I chase the tension that slowly grows within the pit of my stomach, unfurling into my limbs and down my spine.

"I feel you, Kate. Your grip tightens. Come for me," he demands as I let out another moan. My body moves of its own accord, riding and sinking and shaking as he continues to eat me and fuck me with his hand. He sucks on my clit, hard, and I'm gone. Words and sounds escape my mouth, none of which I can identify, and stars dance behind my eyelids as I continue to fall.

When the haze begins to fade, I see Niro still licking and kissing my pussy, and I'm so sensitive there that I feel like I'm about to collapse. He gets to his feet, towering above me, and I finally get a good look at what he's packing. It's blue, like I assumed it would be, but a darker shade than the rest of his body. And where I pictured a deep curve and a banana like shape, is nothing but straight, long, thick, veiny, male perfection. Swirling ridges rise from tip to root that I'm certain are going to wreck me in the best possible way.

He wraps me in his arms. I press my face against his warm chest as my breathing returns to normal. He kisses my hair as he pushes wild strands from my face.

Niro leans down to lift me, but I stop him. "What are you doing?" I ask.

"You are tired. I am taking you to your bed," he says simply.

"No."

"No?"

"I just needed a minute. I'm not done with you yet," I say.

His lip quirks up on one side, and an arrogant twinkle forms in his eyes. I lower myself to the narrow plush carpet and get onto my hands and knees. I look over my shoulder at him, and say, "I'm ready for you."

His smile is immediately replaced by a feral, heated look as he drops behind me and places his hands on my ass. "This is how you want it then?" he asks.

"Yes," I reply in a breathy moan as he spreads my cheeks and guides himself between them.

I feel the head of him nudging at my entrance, and holy shit is he big. I'm not surprised, obviously, having seen his dick only seconds ago, but looking at it and feeling it about to stretch my insides are two very different things.

"Tell me if I should stop. It does not matter when. I will do what you need," he vows, and this is precisely why I removed the cuffs. Because he checks to make sure I'm still present. That I'm still in this with him. He cares. It's such a simple thing, really, but it makes all the difference.

It also makes me incredibly wet.

"I will go slow," he says as he inches his way in. I moan in response, because even though it's been a long-ass time for me and it's a tight squeeze, the pain is also so delicious. It signifies my body's reawakening, something I didn't think would ever come. One I didn't think I even wanted.

How foolish I was.

"Breathe, Kate," he commands. "You will take all of me, but you must relax."

I close my eyes and focus on my breath as he continues to move, and after my third inhale, he's seated all the way in.

"Yes, my rivi," he croons against the shell of my ear.

There's that word again, but it's in one ear and out the other, because I can only focus on what I'm feeling. And I feel... many things. I feel raw. I feel pain. I feel him pressed against parts of me that I didn't know existed. And I feel so, so full. Of him.

"I'm going to move," he warns as he pulls almost all the way out. I hate the emptiness he leaves behind. But before I can focus on it, he slams back in, and I cry out as I grip the carpet, the soft fibers pinched tightly between my fingers.

Niro gets into a rhythm, and I shove my hips back to meet him each time. Soon the sounds of our sex echo throughout the caves, the slap of his thighs against my ass chasing each moan. He starts to pick up speed, and I reach between my legs to play with my clit. I want us to come together, and I think he might be close.

The moment I finish tracing a circle around my clit, my hand is batted away, and he picks up right where I left off. "Let me learn you. I want to give you the pleasure you crave," he says as he sucks my earlobe between his teeth.

I scream as he continues to relentlessly pound into me. He adds pressure against my clit, and rubs back and forth, instead of the circle. "More. Like that. Yes, don't stop!"

With a primal roar that rips through the mountain, we come together. My body falls limp against the floor, my cheek pressed into the carpet as Niro presses kisses along my spine between heavy breaths.

Eventually, we fall in a heap on our sides, and he pulls my back against his chest as his arms wrap around me. I rest my face on the inside of his bicep, marveling at how wide it is.

I must drift off at some point because the next thing I know, Niro is lifting me into his arms and I'm protesting through a series of grumbles. Then I'm draped atop smooth sheets that feel cool to the touch. I sigh as I sink into the bed and Niro climbs in beside me.

He pulls me toward him until my head rests on his chest. He kisses my forehead, and whispers something I can't make out as sleep pulls me under.

CHAPTER 19

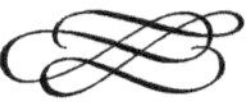

NIRO

I wake up to see the fur blankets raised in a heap above my body, no longer touching my skin at all. I find this troubling, but when a small hand wraps around my cock, the tension leaves my body completely. It is Kate, giving me a splendid gift to start the morning.

Lifting the blankets, I peer down at her and smile. Her wild red hair is a mess of tangles around her face. Her eyes are heavy from sleep, but bright and alert. She is glorious, this one.

"Morning, lover," she says, her voice a breathy rasp that sends blood rushing to the tip of my cock. I watch as her small hand strokes my length as her other cups and massages my sac.

"What a sight you are, little witch," I tell her, tucking a wayward strand behind her rounded ear.

She winks, and then feeds the tip of me into her hot, wet mouth. My mouth drops open, a groan escaping me as she guides me deeper behind her lips. Her mouth is not large, but her lips are plush and pink like her cheeks. And they feel like paradise as they wrap tightly around my cockhead. She sucks as her hand moves up and down, and then she releases me with a swirl of her tongue around the tip.

Kate takes a moment to look at my cock, really study it, and when she notices pre-come pooling at the tip, she licks it off before shoving me back inside her mouth. I throw myself back on the bed with a growl as her tongue slides around me. The only thing better than the feel of her mouth is the feel of her cunt, I am sure of it. There is nothing else in the galaxy that will ever compare.

"You're so big," she says as she runs her tongue along the underside of my cock before moving to my sac. "I knew you would be, but I didn't realize how fucking pretty your dick would be."

"Pretty?" I ask her through huffed breaths, surprised by her word choice.

"Yeah," she replies, "most dicks are fine. They do the job, you know? But yours is just…whew. I love it." Then she takes me back into her mouth, so deep that I feel her gag briefly. I sit up quickly to check on her, but then she begins a rapid stroking motion with her hand as her head bobs up and down, and all the breath leaves my lungs.

It does not take long for me to feel my sac tighten against me, and then erupt inside her mouth. She cannot take all my seed, but she tries. As it runs down her chin, I realize that mating signal or no mating signal, Kate *is* mine. And not because she sucks me so well. That is indeed a plus, but not what draws me to her.

It is her spirit. The fire in her eyes when she defends herself or someone she cares for. It is her softness in the shape of her body and in the depths of her heart. She was made for me. I will accept no other outcome than Kate and me, side by side.

She crawls up my body, a proud smile on her face, and plops herself on top of me. "Mmm, that was fun," she says, her voice dreamy.

"It was indeed," I reply, running a hand up and down her back. "Your mouth is divine." Little bumps rise from her skin the longer I touch her. She lets out a quiet chuckle and kisses the spot on my chest where my heart beats.

Then she lifts her head and drops her chin to my chest. "I'm hungry," she says with a pout.

"Let us feed you then, my rivi."

"What does that mean?" she asks, stopping in the middle of the room.

I hesitate to tell her at first, though I am not sure why. Maybe because knowing she did not understand the word gave me a sense of safety in using it freely. "It means *dream* in Sufoian," I finally say.

Her eyes soften and she takes my hand, lacing her fingers through mine. "I love that." And we continue on.

I do not bother with clothing, and as I stride out of the room toward the eating room. I notice Kate's skin is bare as well. This makes me happy. I have spent far too many cycles deprived of her beauty. Her heavy breasts shaking and bouncing with each step. Her round stomach jiggling and taking new shapes depending on her posture. Her smooth, translucent skin, dappled with those brown spots. All the way to her delicate ankles and small feet, and the–

"Why are your toes black?" I ask, worry filling my chest, tightening it. "Are you ill?"

"Hmm?" she looks down and smiles knowingly. "It's nail polish. I painted them the night before I was taken from Earth. Months ago. This stuff lasts forever."

"Humans are so very amusing," I mutter as I program our meals into the food dispenser.

"What, so dragons never put on war paint or dye their hair or anything?"

"We do those things, yes. But it is typically to signify an event or honor a memory. Every color has meaning," I tell her. "Why did you choose black?"

She flattens her lips and tilts her head. "Matches my heart."

I hold her defiant, yet playful, gaze for a long moment. "You are a terrible liar," I finally reply.

She pokes my stomach with her finger and starts peppering me with questions on the meal I chose for us. Kate prefers to choose her own meals, she tells me with a scowl, and it is "rude of me" to assume I know what she is in the mood for.

After we finish our tea and plates of yunfa oats with cream and berries, which she very much enjoys, she has me show her how to use the food dispenser. The settings are in Sufoian, which she cannot read, but I show her the basic groupings of food choices (meat, bread, noodles, root vegetables, pastries), and I see her mumbling them quietly under her breath over and over in an effort to memorize them.

"We can label them," I offer, pleased she is looking for ways to become more settled here in the caves. I am hoping she will stay forever, but it has to be her idea, otherwise, she will refuse, so I keep this thought to myself.

We bathe together, and I make her come twice more in the water with my mouth and tongue. Once our skin is dry and we dress, Kate is eager to play with the digital stitcher. As with the food dispenser, I tell her what the Sufoian words and symbols mean in English. She takes copious notes on her screen pad, pausing to ask clarifying questions about each step in the process.

I guide her to the center of the room so the machine can scan her body for measurements. She laughs excitedly each time the machine stops and commands that she turn to the side or lift her arms. She begins selecting fabric for the pieces she intends to create when her screen pad starts making a loud beeping noise.

"Uh-oh, it's Ava," Kate says. "She's gonna rip me a new one for leaving." She presses her fingers to her lips, signaling me to be quiet before she answers the call.

"Are you goddamn kidding me, Red?" Ava shouts, her voice angry. "I spend one day in bed getting thoroughly fucked by my husband and you just leave? For real?"

Kate's cheeks pinken and she grits her teeth. "I know. I know. I'm sorry I didn't come tell you. But like you said, you were busy…so."

"Chloe couldn't even explain it to me," Ava says. "So? Spill."

I catch Kate's eye and point in the direction of my workroom down the hall. She nods and I leave, so she may have privacy.

Kate closes the door to the wardrobe room behind me but does not lower the volume of her voice at all. If anything, she talks louder, and her words carry throughout the caves. I do not try to listen. But I also do not try to *not* listen.

I hear her go over the events of the morning prior, when we woke together in the shed, followed by the encounter with Varrek and Bruvix. She leaves out some details, including what happened at the Hexrin house, and I assume that is information she is not ready to share. Ava's voice is too low for me to hear, but her soft tone each time she speaks tells me she understands Kate's position.

She is kind, this Ava. I am grateful Kate has her.

I hear Kate vow to return to the village soon, and it deflates my good mood. I do not want her to leave my caves. Ever. But I know she cares deeply for the humans in the village and will inevitably want to see them again.

You shall go with her. Protect her. Protect our mate, my draxilio commands. I like this idea. I will have to carry her back to the village since she cannot traverse the mountain alone, so I will remain at her side. Then we will return home when she is ready. Together.

There will not come another moment when I am without my mate.

CHAPTER 20

KATE

A wailing cry in the distance pulls me forward, my feet digging into the mushy, wet soil of the forest with every step. I keep my hands by my face as I run, preventing branches and tall brush from lashing at my skin.

"I'm coming!" I yell, though I'm not sure to whom.

The skies are dark and the air is thick, so it must be the middle of the night, between downpours, most likely.

No one responds, but the cry continues, getting louder and angrier. As I cross through the tree line onto the main path of the village, I find the path eerily empty, even for this time of night. Or perhaps it's not the emptiness that feels off, but the silence of the village that doesn't sit right.

Why isn't anyone responding to this cry? Does no one else hear it? It's so loud that it sounds like it's right next to me, but that doesn't make sense.

I race into the house I share with Ava. "Ava! You home? Ahlvo?" I call out, but all is quiet here. I almost trip as I come back down the stairs from my room but quickly recover before I burst through the front door and run toward Chloe and Varrek's.

Once I'm inside, I hear whispers. Dozens of them.

I take the steps two at a time until I reach Chloe and Varrek's bedroom on the top floor. They're here. The entire clan. They're all standing in this room.

"'Scuse me. Sorry," I mutter as I slide past them. Stares, pointed fingers, and hushed comments swirl around my head. When I hear "she missed it," my heart starts to race. "What? What did I miss?" I ask, turning in a circle to look at the others.

"Kate?" Ava calls, and I ignore the faces of pity and shock as I make my way to the corner of the room. "Finally made it, huh?" Ava asks in a dry, judgmental tone that I've never heard from her.

Then I see it.

In the bed lies Varrek with his arms wrapped protectively around a sweaty and sobbing Chloe, who has her arms wrapped around a tiny squealing newborn.

"You gave birth?" I ask, then cringe at the unnecessary question. "I thought you weren't due for another four or five months?"

Chloe ignores me completely, and keeps her eyes trained on the half-Trovilian baby in her arms.

Varrek answers instead. "That is how long you have been gone, Kay-teh. Or have you forgotten the day you yelled at us and left the village?"

"Because we haven't," Chloe adds without looking up.

* * *

I wake with a gasp and realize instantly that my hair is soaked in sweat.

That was a terrible dream, I think to myself. But was it just a dream? Or a warning? I've never had a dream that took place in the future. Is this part of my so-called *powers*? Are they growing and now allowing me to see glimpses of the future?

Ugh, of course, I would get stuck with that ability. It sucks and is ultimately a huge burden.

Or maybe it was just a dream, but I can't shake the feeling of guilt that hangs on me like a cloak. Ava and Chloe are going through such massive changes in their lives. Ava just got married, and Chloe is pregnant with an alien baby. I shouldn't be away from them right now. They need me. Just as much as I need them.

I've been at Niro's for four days now, and it's been a blissfully repetitive loop of sex, food, baths, sex in the bath, more food, making clothes, and more sex. We've been alternating our sleep schedules too, so I'm incredibly rested. But I know I can't stay here forever, and that dream has me worried I've already been away too long.

Niro's side of the bed is empty, and the sheets are no longer warm, so he's clearly been up for a while. I throw on a new caftan I made, stop in the bathroom to splash water on my face and pull my hair into a bun, and then head toward Niro's workspace.

I find him there, tucked in the far corner of the room at a smaller table, looking intently at some squiggly lines and green blinking lights on a screen. "What's all this?" I ask as I saunter in.

"It is what you call a security system," he says with an easy grin as he looks me up and down. "I have not updated the programming in some time, so I am making sure it does not remove my file of previous perimeter scans."

"This is quite the setup," I reply. He has at least six large screen pads lined up that cycle through old heat scans, night vision footage, and other trackers I can't make sense of.

He and Bruvix could geek out on this for hours. If only Bruvix didn't hate Niro with the fire of a thousand suns. Such a shame.

I wrap my arms around his neck and press a kiss to his throat. "Hey, so...I had an awful dream about Chloe. She gave birth and I missed it, and everyone was mad at me."

Worry flashes across his face but is quickly replaced with a mix of warmth and pity. "Could this be due to the guilt you feel for leaving?"

That's entirely possible, but whether it's guilt because of how I left or guilt because the dream might be real and I feel like an asshole for missing the birth of my best friend's baby, either way, guilt is consuming me and I hate it. "Maybe, but it doesn't matter. I need to go back to the village for a few days. To be with the girls, and to start honing my...power, I suppose." It feels weird to acknowledge it. Especially with the sense of excitement that fills my belly. I have power. A skill that's actually useful, once I figure out how to properly wield it.

"Very well," he says as he stands. He pulls me against his chest and rubs my back. "I shall gather a few things for us. And you can take your clothing gifts."

Oh.

This is awkward. "I was, um, thinking that you could drop me off…at the village. I was going to spend some time there alone."

He pulls back and looks down at me like I've lost my mind. "No. I will be at your side. Then we will come home."

Okay, that's a little pushy. I don't love it, but I'll let it slide. Just this once. "I was just thinking, since things are still a bit tense with Varrek and Bruvix, it might be best for you to come back here."

"I do not like it." Niro's jaw ticks and I can tell he's doing his best to conceal his rage. "I will not get to taste you. To touch you. To feel your cunt tighten around me as you come."

A shiver runs down my spine and I can feel myself getting wetter with each word. "I'm going to miss that too. Desperately." I place a hand on his chest and trace his hardened nipple through his shirt. "But just think about all the ways you'll get to fuck me the second I come back."

A growl hums inside his chest and then his mouth is on mine. "How about a quickie before we leave?" I ask against his lips. He growls again, and I take it as a yes, because the next thing I know, he tosses me over his shoulder and smacks my ass as he takes long strides toward our room.

* * *

We land outside the tree line and Niro gently sets me on my feet. I give his dragon's long snout a kiss and whisper, "Don't think I won't miss you too, big guy." He huffs a breath through his nostrils that blows my hair off my face before baring his fangs. But since I know Niro's dragon is crushing on me hard, I'm guessing this is a dragon version of a smile. It's terrifying, but also sweet.

Niro shifts into his flightless form and places the bag I packed in my hands. "I shall return in three days. No later."

"But?" I interject.

"But no sooner," he says with a sigh.

"Thank you," I say as I lean up to kiss him. He smells so good, crisp and earthy and warm. I already miss him. Who knew I'd get so addicted to a kidnapping dragon? "Okay, if you don't leave now, I'm going to rip off your clothes and ride you right here in the grass."

"That is a fantastic idea. Let us do that," he replies with an enthusiastic nod.

"Yeah," I say, shaking my head. "I don't know why I thought that would sound like a threat."

"You should have threatened to ask an endless stream of questions."

That does it. I swing my foot up, pretending to kick his ass, and he sidesteps me with a wide, magnificent grin. I turn and head inside the tree line, refusing to look back. Because if I do, I'll never make it to the village.

Hours later, I'm sitting in Ava's bedroom with her and Chloe and they're going through the pieces I made them with Niro's digital stitcher.

"Are these maternity booty shorts?" Chloe squeals with delight.

I laugh. "Indeed. For those hot nights when you're about to pop but still want to give Varrek a show."

Ava holds hers up. "A head wrap?" She looks astonished.

"Of course," I reply. "You keep saying how you miss wearing them. You like it?"

She holds it against her chest with her eyes closed. "I love it."

"Great!" I say with clasped hands. "Now that I've softened you up with presents, maybe you can help me figure out a way to make amends with Varrek and…everyone."

"You wanna apologize to them? Why?" Ava asks, sounding shocked.

"Well, I feel bad. Like maybe I overreacted," I reply. I don't want Varrek to hate me. I don't want anyone to hate me. I was just so tired of having to defend myself and explain myself and grit my teeth when I hear people whispering about me. It felt like I was destined to relive high school, but with aliens.

On the other hand, the mean girls and dumb guys from high school wouldn't have provided me a home and a place to start fresh. And they definitely wouldn't have lost sleep if I went missing. An apology, whether they deserve one or not, feels like the right thing to do. "I want to move past this," I tell the girls.

"Well," Chloe says, her eyes lighting up as if she has several suggestions locked and loaded. "If you were willing to share a bit more with them, Varrek, in particular, about Niro and what his deal is, I think it might shed some light on why you defended him so fiercely." Her gaze goes to Ava before shifting back to me. "I know it would certainly help us understand."

She's right.

They deserve to know the truth. I'm not sure how much I'm willing to share with Varrek, or the rest of the clan, but Ava and Chloe should know.

Letting out a deep breath, I launch into the entire confusing and messy tale. I tell Chloe about my dreams about Aunt Milly, and how they stopped once I was taken, and how Niro took her place, and all the dreams he and I shared. I tell them about how I threatened to break his fancy vase if he didn't bring me back in three days, and they cackle at what a reckless choice that was. They ask question after question about Alu and Bexo, and what their homes looked like.

Ava refuses to let me continue until I've shared absolutely every-thing I know about the genetic modification process Niro and his siblings went through, and how they each lack certain emotions. I imagine her therapist brain is buzzing right now.

I tell them about his dragon, and how it adores me, and how it isn't all that scary up close. They ask how it feels to fly in his palm, and I'm pretty sure I bum them out when I tell them it feels like being inside an airplane, just without a seatbelt and all the windows down.

When I tell them about how we've been having sex, they shriek.

"Dragon. Dick." Chloe shouts. "I want every detail."

"Wait, did you use protection?" Ava asks, suddenly serious.

Oh.

"Well, no," I reply, feeling the blood rush to my cheeks.

She gives me a stern look. "So you were just…what, hoping your eggs wouldn't be compatible with dragon sperm?"

"I didn't think about it," I tell her honestly. Niro did say we were compatible with his kind for procreation, but I guess I forgot. I wasn't thinking about anything, really. And it was amazing. To not think and just feel. I haven't done that in so long.

"Well, as long as you weren't ovulating, I'm sure it's fine. We can check with Kaiva to see if she has more of these," Ava says, pointing to the gold birth control band around her upper arm.

"Guys, it's fine. I'm not pregnant, and we're just having some fun. It's just sex. I, Kate McNabb, am actually enjoying having sex!" I shout with my arms up. "Can you believe it?"

They nod and smile, and I know they're excited for me. I've told them a bit about Dennis, and how he made my entire existence miserable. They know how big of a deal this is.

"Let's focus on the fact that we're all finally getting the top-notch orgasms we deserve, okay?" I ask.

"Here, here," Ava says, lifting her glass of water.

"To us," Chloe says, doing the same.

We clink our waters together and enjoy some crisp Oluura hydration. "Okay," I say, getting to my feet. "I have a few more stops on the apology/gift tour, so I'll see you beautiful broads later."

I sling my bag over my shoulder and head out into the rain. I decide to take the back way to Bruvix's house, mainly because I'm a little nervous to show my face again after my blow-up with Varrek, but also because there's no easy way to get to Bruvix's house.

He lives alone in a three-story wooden house that's slightly tilted to the left and is tucked deep inside the tree line. I'm not sure if he picked the location because he was expecting at least two other homes to be built directly in front of his, between him and the meal hall, or if it was intentional so he'd be hard to find. When it comes to that eternal grump, I'm guessing it's the latter.

But I want to make amends with him before anyone else, because we somehow ended up in a wildly baffling miscommunication and I want to set the record straight. I don't understand why he's jealous of Niro, or why Niro is jealous of him, because Bruvix and I have never been anything more than friends. There was that time he offered his dick up for my use, but other than being the funniest pick-up line I've ever heard, I didn't read anything into it.

I knock on his door a few times and wait for an answer. When I try again and get no response, I start to worry that he's at the meal hall or somewhere else public I want to avoid. Then I see a flash of gold skin and a tuft of wavy silver hair peek over the roof-top balcony and let out a sigh of relief.

"Kay-teh?" he hollers down.

"Hey, Bruv," I reply. I hold up my bag. "I have a present in here for you. You want to let me in?"

"That depends," he says, wiping his hands on a rag. "Where is your kidnapper? Will he be joining us?"

My eyes roll straight back. Really? More of this?

Although, what was I expecting? For Bruvix to be in a good mood? I let it slide and shoot him an unbothered grin. "It'll just be the two of us. Do I have to climb up there or are you going to meet me down here?"

He stands there, staring down at me, his lips pursed. "I shall be right down," he finally mutters. Bruvix opens the door a minute later. When he comes out, I'm forced to take a step back before the door closes behind him.

"What are you doing?" I ask. "You're not letting me in?"

"I do not want you poking around my house and then running back to your draxilio and telling him about the flaws in our protection system."

"Okay, first of all," I drop the bag at my feet so I can properly and dramatically list these things off while counting my fingers. "I know nothing about security systems, so there's no way in hell I'd be able to detect a flaw. Second, he breached our perimeter, easily, I might add, to kidnap me, so he doesn't really need info on our shoddy security," I say as Bruvix scoffs and crosses his arms over his chest. "And third, I've seen his security system, and it's lightyears ahead of yours. So maybe, the next time I see him, I'll let him know you're interested in hearing all about it. How does that sound?"

"Did you come here for a particular reason? Or was it just to yell at me again?" is his only response. What a giant cranky baby.

"Yes, actually, I do have a reason," I crouch to dig through my bag and pull out a maroon nylon poncho I made for him. He gives me a blank stare, so I hold it up against him. "It's for the rain. Next time you decide to pass out in the middle of the meal hall, on top of a table, you'll stay dry, somewhat."

"I have a cloak. I do not need your filmy sack."

I drop the poncho to my side. "You seriously don't want this? I made it for you."

"Why are you making me things when you have a mate? That does not seem proper."

"I thought we were friends, Bruv," I say, letting my shoulders sag. I don't know how we got to this weird place, but it's the worst. "I'm sorry if I gave you the wrong impression, or if I missed some kind of signal you were giving me, but I don't want to stop being friends."

His chin dips to his chest and he runs a rough hand through his short, silver strands. "I…enjoy you, Kay-teh. I thought that we could be pleasure mates, at first. And then we would see what came next. Maybe someday…we would become mates."

I rub my forehead, feeling bad I didn't see it until now. Of course, he had a thing for me. Maybe what I mistook for flirting—him offering his dick so I could sleep—was more than that. For Bruvix, was that more like a declaration of love? I could've asked. But he also could've made his interest more known.

"I'm sorry. I didn't know you felt that way," I tell him.

"I know," he finally says. "I suppose the goddess has other plans for both of us. I am still your friend, no matter what." He gently pulls the poncho over his head and gives me a questioning look, seeking approval.

I laugh and give him a thumbs up. "Well, it's on backwards, but the color is great on you."

I leave Bruvix's house feeling much better about my place in the clan. Mainly because things feel okay between us now. I swing by the sewing circle to drop off a tunic with embroidered stars on the sleeves I made for Zohma, and they all "ooh" and "ahh" when I tell him about Niro's digital stitcher. I promise them I'll bring back more pieces and some supplies so they can play with different fabrics and threads.

As I'm heading back to Chloe and Ava, I run into Varrek. The nod he gives me is curt, but then he says, "Walk with me, Kay-teh," and while I'm nervous to do so, I know we need to air out our issues. Might as well happen now.

"Look, I'm sor–"

"I do apol–"

We give each other a knowing glance and then laugh. "Sorry, Varrek," I say.

"I am as well," he replies. "I feel I have failed you as leader of the clan."

"No, no," I begin, but he stops me.

"While my focus will remain on the physical safety of the clan, I should also pay attention to everyone's general well-being. Their happiness," he says, his tone somber. "I have never been good at that, but I would like to improve."

I nod, not expecting this admission from him, and not knowing what to say in response.

"I am to begin ther-ah-pee with Aye-vah soon, and I believe it will help me accomplish this goal."

The secret prince of Trovilia is willingly doing therapy? Color me impressed. "That's great, Varrek. I'm happy for you. Ava's brilliant."

"She is," Varrek says thoughtfully. Then he turns to face me, and we stop in the middle of the path. "My Cloh-ee was a mess when you were taken, Kay-teh. She thought the worst had happened," he says, his emerald eyes swirling with distress. "You must understand what that does to me. To see my mate in pain and not be able to help her. I was in agony."

"I know," I tell him, biting my lip with shame.

"But more importantly, Kay-teh, *I* wanted to know that you were safe. I was prepared to do anything to bring you home."

I guess I didn't realize how much I meant to him. It didn't seem like he cared whether I was around or not, only how my presence would affect Chloe.

"You are a member of this clan," he continues. "I value you, and I wish for you to feel at peace among us."

I swallow, holding back a surprising rush of emotion rising in my throat. "Thank you," I say with a cough. "I wasn't expecting that. But I really do appreciate it."

He nods, pleased by my response. "Now, you will tell me about this draxilio, and how we make him an ally to our clan, yes?"

Back to business. I chuckle, admiring his bluntness. "Where should I begin?"

The moment our little chat ends, I spot Jo peeking out of the tree line at me. She gestures for me to follow her as she scampers through the brush toward the Hexrin house. She moves like a fox, fast and impressively nimble. She leads me to the small clearing on the side of the house and asks me to stand in the center with my eyes closed.

"Is this witch practice?" I ask, smirking as I peek one eye open.

"It is," she replies. "Now, focus on all the sounds you hear." Then she lists each sound that surrounds us. "The flutter of bird wings as they fly through the trees. The hum of insects. The drip of this morning's rain falling off the leaves. The heavy feet of the clan as they move through the village."

I focus on each sound as Jo points them out. And damn, the clan is pretty loud.

"Do you hear my foot?" she asks after she starts tapping her boot on a rock.

"Yes."

"Hold onto that sound. Let it fill your round ears," she instructs, and I have to hold back a laugh. "Push the rest away."

I take a deep inhale, and zero in on the clap of her boot against the solid rock. The cadence of it. I picture her tiny foot stomping on it as she watches me, and it helps drown out the other sounds.

"You hear only my foot, Kayyyyt," she replies, dragging out my name in an adorable way. "Nothing else."

She's right. I can't hear the bugs or the birds or even the clan as they clomp around on the main path.

"Very good!" she claps. The moment she stops tapping her foot, the noises of the forest and village flood back in. I open my eyes to find her smiling brightly.

"That's it?" I ask, feeling slightly disappointed. Couldn't anyone do that? I don't want to be anyone anymore. I'm a witch. I want to do menacing witchy things.

"You are not pleased?" Jo asks. Then she nods her head, knowingly. "O fah, you will not be able to use your powers yet, Kayyt," she says, shortening my name a bit more. "This is very new to you."

My shoulders sag. "I know. I just want to start doing the fun stuff. When can we practice jolting someone with electricity? Or levitation?"

She jerks back, incredulous, but shoots me a smirk. "You are not ready for such things. First, you must practice isolating your focus."

"What do you mean?"

"With the sounds, you were able to decide which one was loudest, which one you wanted to hear. In the same way, we will train you to only allow certain beings access to your dreams."

"So I'll be able to shut people out if I want?" I ask.

"Yes."

I like the sound of that.

"You must practice this on your own. Close your eyes, noting the sounds, and focus on only one. And test your scent and sight this way too."

"You're giving me homework?"

Jo looks toward the Hexrin house and scrunches her nose. "You need not work on your home to practice this skill."

I'm not sure why I expected her to know what homework is. "Right. I'll practice this. What will our next lesson be on?"

She straightens her spine and lifts her chin. "That is for you to find out, Kayt."

And just like that, I'm no longer surprised that Jo is head witch.

CHAPTER 21

NIRO

I have been restless since I said good-bye to Kate three cycles ago, and the time has finally come for me to see her face again. It has been awful without her. Too quiet.

I thought she talked too much when we first met, and now her chatter soothes me. Her voice is rich and vibrant, and hearing it reminds me I am no longer alone.

I pace outside the tree line, waiting for her to emerge. This is the place we said we would meet and I would take her home, back to my caves. According to the placement of the sun behind the clouds, this is also the time we said we would meet. But she is not here.

She is in trouble. Find her. Protect her, my draxilio says with a snarl.

She is probably saying her good-byes, I reason.

That is what keeps her from me, yes? Nothing more?

My draxilio has a theory. Perhaps the scarred one is begging her to stay. Destroy him.

No. I shoot back. I cannot let my fear of losing her to Bruvix guide my decisions. It is mere paranoia. And I can best it. Besides, Kate has said she wants no one else but me. I have no reason to worry.

As I count my paces across the clearing and back, worry settles inside my center, supporting my fears, feeding my anxious thoughts. By the time Kate is officially late, I have lost any scrap of patience I have ever possessed, which is not much. I storm through the tree line, my muscles tightening, my body preparing for a fight.

The moment I view the main path through the trees, I see her.

But not just her. *Him* too.

Bruvix stands facing Kate, his face slightly amused as he watches her throw her head back in laughter. Ava and Chloe are present too, but there is distance between them and Kate and Bruvix. My mate talks only to him while the human females carry on their own conversation.

Has she changed her mind? Does she prefer to stay here? With them? *Him?*

She would not choose them over us. Get her. Take her home, my draxilio commands.

When Kate pokes Bruvix in the bicep, I see red. How easy it would be to bust these trees into kindling with my shift and set that treacherous male ablaze with one breath.

I hold back the urge to shift, but I do not wait another heartbeat to stake my claim on my female.

I step onto the path and stalk toward the scarred one slowly. Kate does not see me, as her back is turned, but Bruvix certainly does. The male chooses this moment to glare at me, which is a surprisingly foolish decision on his part. Does he not know what I am capable of?

When Kate waves a hand in front of his eyes, to get his attention, he has the nerve to smile at me, before wrapping a hand in her hair and gliding it through her long, red strands. Rage breaks through my remaining control, and I charge. I give Kate's side a light nudge so she moves out of the way, and I tackle him to the ground.

We are rolling and growling and punching each other for what feels like eternity before I hear Kate screeching in my ear to stop. I feel a pinch at my side before Varrek pulls Bruvix off me. When I look down, blood seeps through my shirt between my ribs.

Kate gasps as she crouches at my side, pinching her eyes closed. "Did he fucking stab you?" she shouts as she lifts her angry gaze to

Bruvix. When I see the small blade in his hand, I lift my shirt to inspect the wound, and thankfully, find it is not deep.

"I will be fine. It will heal by tomorrow." I reassure her. I have had much worse injuries in battle, and then in the dome. This does not worry me.

He made you bleed. Melt the flesh off his bones, my draxilio roars. It is difficult to disagree with him in this instance. But slaughtering Bruvix, as satisfying as that would be, would not help me with Kate, so I grit my teeth as I fight off the urge to shift and kill. It is not easy though, and requires all of my strength.

"He attacked me!" Bruvix shouts. "I was merely defending myself against a violent beast."

I haul myself to my feet, wiping the soil and moss from my clothes. Checking the wound again, I see the bleeding has already slowed. It shall begin to scab in no time. "He dared to put his hands on you. You do not like being touched by others. And…and he did it to antagonize me. I saw it with my own eyes. The look of sheer joy as I watched him touch your hair."

"She seemed to enjoy my touch," Bruvix shouts as he struggles to free himself from Varrek's grip on his arms. Then he spits at me, his saliva landing on the toe of my boot.

"Bruvix, enough." Kate says with a furious edge to her tone. "I don't know what the fuck that was, but it wasn't cool. And you know it. I don't care who started it. You're lucky he heals quickly."

Then she turns to me. "Okay," she says in a softer voice as she places her hands on my chest. "I appreciate how important consent is to you. Really, that's an extremely hot quality that I *will* show my gratitude for later. But," she says, her tone raised, "this whole jealousy thing is the opposite of hot."

"But you are mine," I tell her simply. "No one touches what is mine."

"Yeah, see, Dennis was the same way in the beginning," Kate tells me. "I thought it was cute. Then it reached a point where it was terrifying…and violent."

Being compared to the lowly Earth male who frequently put bruises all over her body sickens me.

"I can't…I can't go through that again, Niro. Do you understand?"

I sigh, nodding and bending down so I can press my forehead to hers. "I understand. I am sorry. You will see. I will prove worthy of you."

Her lip quirks up one side just before she kisses me. I lift her into my arms, never wanting the kiss to end.

Finally, she pulls back and says, "I forgive you. Now let's get out of here."

Kate and I leave the village, hand in hand, and say nothing as we stroll through the forest and out to the clearing. I shift, take her into my palm, and press her small, soft body against my chest before I launch into the air.

I will make this up to her, I decide. The moment we get home, I will worship her body so well that she will never want to leave my side.

* * *

"Niro! I'm clo–" Kate screams as her body writhes against my tongue. I do not stop. I continue to press my mouth against her wet heat, showing her with my tongue precisely how I plan to use my cock once her orgasm subsides.

Her lovely white skin glistens with a layer of sweat as she shakes on top of the table. We are in my workroom, fulfilling one of the many fantasies I have had about her. But instead of bending her over the top of it, I lift her legs, tossing her feet over each shoulder as I coat the tip of my cock with her come. My eyes are glued to her entrance, the slickness of her swollen pink folds, in the same dark pink shade as her nipples and mouth. It is my favorite color, I decide.

Kate's mouth opens wide in a silent, breathless scream as her eyes roll back, and she stays that way until I am fully seated inside her. She raises herself on her forearms, and her large breasts shake as she moans with pleasure. I wish she would remain unclothed all the time, so I could watch as they jiggle and bounce with each movement.

I quicken my pace, pounding into her soft body, and I know I will not be able to hold out for long. I have missed Kate far too much. I have imagined this moment too often in the time she has been gone. "I am close, my rivi."

"Yes," she gasps. "N-need to feel you."

Then I am roaring my release as Kate's cunt squeezes me tightly, her body quaking in time with mine. I pull up and wrap my hands around her back, pressing my nose to hers.

She smiles through heavy breaths, stroking the line of my jaw with warmth in her eyes.

Reluctantly, I pull out of her and reach for my crumpled shirt on the floor and clean my seed from her thighs. I wipe myself off quickly and toss the shirt back where it was. I will deal with it later.

For now, I shall carry my mate to bed and bring her plates of food. She is usually quite ravenous after we mate. She sighs happily as I tuck her under the covers on my bed and pulls me in for a quick kiss before I leave.

Carefully, I juggle the plates of bread, the root vegetable mash that she likes, and polai steak with a salty glaze and place them on a tray in front of her. She smiles brightly, like a child draxilio preparing for their first flight, and starts digging into her meal.

We share the food, and once she starts picking at it with less vigor, I know she is full, and I eat the rest. We are lounging in bed, the covers whirled around us in a messy heap, when I decide to ask a question that has been haunting my mind incessantly. "Have you decided what you would like to do about the dream link?"

Her eyes drop to the inside of her mug before she takes a long sip of tea.

If she will not talk, I will continue. "Clearly, we are mates, but we have not discussed–"

"Um," she says quickly as she puts the mug on the side table. "I…I would love to not rush this if that's okay with you. I mean, I know the mate signal has sort of thrown a wrench into things," she trails off.

I am confused. The mate signal is what brought us together. If not for the shared dreams, she would not be in my bed right now.

"Don't get me wrong, I'm having so much fun with you, Niro," she says, sounding genuine but also a little placating. "It's just been a lifetime since I had this kind of fun with another person, and honestly, I didn't think I'd have this ever again. I was prepared to die alone. I was fine with it. And then…you came along and started tormenting my mind."

She chuckles and I smile in response. I brush a hair off her forehead, and continue to stroke her soft, pink cheeks, enjoying the feel of her.

"I didn't expect you," she adds.

"I did not expect you either, Kate," I reply.

She nods and looks down at her hands in her lap. "I know we have to decide what to do about the dream link. I just don't know what my decision is yet. And I'm not exactly ready to become someone's mate."

I try to keep my face neutral, but it is a struggle to do so. She does not want the gift we have been given. It is disappointing.

"Someone's fuck buddy, someone's girlfriend—those are concepts I can wrap my head around," she continues.

I stare at her, wondering if she has more she wishes to tell me. When I say nothing, she asks, "How do *you* feel about the dream link? This isn't just up to me. It's your life too."

Truthfully, I do not want to break the dream link. It is disruptive to share dreams with another person, yes, and it does not provide the most restful sleep, but this is a part of Kate that is only mine. It is something intimate we share. I have her when we are awake as well, but if she is not ready to accept me as her mate, I want to hold onto the dream link.

But how will she react if I tell her this? I envision her waving a hand through the air and telling me I have nothing to fret over. That she is still mine in all ways without the dream link, even if she is not ready to take me as her mate.

I am ready for every eventuality. I am ready to give myself to her, wholly and completely, and remain hers until our dying breath. My past is complicated as well, but no part of it decreases my desire to be with her. Since she is working through residual anguish, I will let her decide how we handle the dream link as I will wait for her to be ready to become my mate. All of this must be her choice.

"I shall follow your lead," I tell her. "Whatever you decide, I am with you."

Her pupils dilate as she pushes me back on the bed. She throws a leg over me and settles her wet cunt over my cock. "Damn, you really know how to get a woman off." She takes my hardening cock in hand and impales herself on it.

"I shall keep this in mind, little witch," I say as I thrust up into her. I will never tire of this feeling. Never.

* * *

The afternoon passes, and while my Kate is fast asleep in our bed, I creep out of the room quietly with empty plates and mugs in hand. I place them on the eating room table and make my way toward the workroom.

I am in the middle of checking the most recent perimeter scans when a face pops up on my screen. It is a familiar face, one I was not expecting, and one that I am not at all pleased to see.

Bruvix.

"What is this?" I demand.

"Ah. Greetings, draxilio," Bruvix says with a smirk that tugs at the scarred corner of his mouth.

"Again, I will ask, what is this?" I grit my teeth. "How did you reach me on this system?"

He sits up taller in his seat, and I want nothing more than to reach through the screen and give his face several more scars. "Kay-teh babbled on and on about how impressive your security system was, so I decided to examine it myself."

That should not be possible. I am well versed in complex programs like this, and I have added several backup functions in case of breach. And Bruvix just tore through them all.

He narrows his gaze when I remain silent. "Are you not curious as to how I was able to achieve this?"

If he is trying to goad me into getting angry, let him try. I can play this game too. "I suppose it is not high on my list of priorities when I have a lush female waiting for me to satisfy her needs."

He tries to mask it, but I see his face fall when I say it. "That brings me to the reason for this unpleasant chat."

"She is mine," I say, my jaw ticking and my fists balling on the table in front of me.

"It is about her day of birth," Bruvix clarifies.

"What about it?"

Bruvix rubs his chin as if trying to remember the message he was sent to deliver. "Aye-vah and Cloh-ee have calculated their days of birth and determined that Kay-teh's is soon. They wish to throw her a day of birth party in two days' time. You must return Kay-teh to the village at sundown." Then his eyes light up. "Ah! And I am supposed to tell you not to say anything to Kay-teh about this. Apparently, humans enjoy scaring each other with large gatherings that begin with a coordinated shout."

That sounds terrible. "Why do they do this?" I ask, genuinely curious.

He shakes his head and shrugs. "I do not know. They are humans. I understand nothing about them."

"And you were chosen to pass along my invitation?" I ask with a smirk. "Are you being punished for something? The wound in my side, perhaps?"

His mouth forms a hard line. "I am simply the only one skilled enough to find a way to reach you without climbing a mountain."

I am loath to admit it, but his hacking abilities are impressive. "Is there anything else?"

"Yes," he replies. "You are to invite your sister. I do not remember her name. Cloh-ee and Aye-vah are excited to meet her."

"Very well," I tell him. Alussanai will be happy for the opportunity to see Kate again. "Two days, yes?"

He nods.
I nod back.
Then his face disappears.
It seems I have a party for which to prepare.

CHAPTER 22

KATE

I have no idea what Niro's deal is, but he's been acting funny the last two days. Since he picked me up from the village after that brawl with Bruvix, something has been off. Could it be that? He's jealous?

I don't know how many times I need to tell him that there's nothing going on between me and Bruvix for him to believe it. It shouldn't matter how Bruvix acts. I don't flirt with him, I'm not having sex with him, and I certainly don't share dreams with him. Niro has seen parts of me that no one else ever has. What we have is a level of intimacy that goes beyond just sex. Can't he see that?

Or is male pride a flaw among all species?

He's been asking me strange questions, too, about human ceremonies and traditions and holidays. I'm guessing he's trying to find ways to make me feel more at home here, which is sweet, but I secretly wonder if it's a ploy to keep me here in his caves, all to himself. Which wouldn't be a hardship.

His caves are always dimly lit and surprisingly temperate, despite the lack of airflow. There are a few small openings in the cave walls for air to circulate, but I can't imagine that does much. And due to lack of windows, there's no chance for the sun to blast you in the eyes first thing in the morning when you're in the middle of a solid REM cycle. I appreciate that very much.

But no matter what happens between us, I will still want to split my time between the caves and the village. I'd miss Chloe and Ava too much to just hide away here with Niro forever. I'm already looking forward to seeing them, and the rest of the clan tonight when Niro flies me down.

I wasn't expecting a visit this soon, but Niro is meeting with Varrek, apparently, to discuss ways the draxilios and the clan can work together to protect Oluura. I'm relieved that he's willing to speak to Varrek at all, because with his security system, his ability to fly, and a belly full of fire to unleash on trespassers, I'm not entirely sure what he would get out of this alliance.

Maybe it's just for me. So that my worlds can collide without a dramatic explosion every time. That would be nice.

I want Niro to get along with the clan, or the people who matter to me, at least. Because if he can't get along with my friends—my family, really—then this thing between us won't last. It can't.

Tonight has to go well. I cross my fingers in an attempt to summon some luck, and send a prayer to the goddess of darkness, the true Queen of Goth, Wednesday Addams. Who would very much approve of my outfit choice for tonight, if I do say so myself. It's a black empire-waisted midi dress that I made from a breathable cotton-like fabric I found in Niro's wardrobe room. The sleeves are fluttery and short, and the neck is a high ruffled collar worthy of a Victorian ghost. I added a hand-stitched white skull and crossbones design to either side of the top of the neckline, giving it a sweet, menacing pop.

Perhaps if Niro weren't acting so jittery, I wouldn't be as nervous as I am. But even now, he pulls shirt after shirt from his closet before muttering *no* and tossing them to the floor.

"What's wrong with this one?" I ask as I hold up the last discarded shirt on top of the pile.

He turns and gives it a quick look before shaking his head. "It is not right for this night."

I don't understand. It's just a meeting with Varrek. The first time they met, Niro wasn't even wearing a shirt. Is he really that nervous? "I think they're all perfect for this night. Besides, they're all either gray or black anyway," I realize as I scan the pile. "You need some color in your closet, blue man."

He chuckles, the sound low and guttural, making me clench my thighs together. I saunter over to him and run a finger down his back. "Think Varrek will mind if you reschedule? I'd rather you wore nothing at all tonight."

His gaze falls to my lips and a growl rips from his throat. He drops the shirt in his hands and pulls me toward him, crushing my lips with his. His tongue pushes between my lips and I moan as it tangles with mine. This is not a soft, sweet kiss. This is full of hunger and need. And I plan to show him just how much I need him right now. I drop to my knees and my hands go to the waist of his pants.

But he places his hands over mine, stopping me. "We cannot reschedule this meeting. It is very important."

I pout as I stand. "Your loss. I was ready to die choking on that pretty dick of yours."

"Well, you may still die on it later if you wish."

I laugh at his unexpected sense of humor. Is he getting funnier? Or am I starting to fall for him?

"Ah, this one will do!" he exclaims, holding up a black shirt with gray buttons that stop at his pecs.

"You're right, that black shirt is much better than all the other black shirts," I tease.

But my sarcasm doesn't register. "I agree," he says sincerely.

When we reach the edge of the tree line, the main path is too quiet and too empty, especially since it's dinnertime. There should be dozens of golden bodies wandering around the village at this time. It reminds me of my dream where Chloe gave birth and I missed it. Unease settles in my stomach as I force the anxious thoughts away.

Niro emerges onto the path in front of me and takes my hand. But I don't even make it four steps before I grind to a halt. "Let's go see if Chloe and Ava are home," I tell him. I don't know why it looks like a ghost town around here, but I do know I'll be a lot less freaked out if they're by my side.

"No," Niro replies, and his firm tone gives me pause.

"No?"

"I must…I told Varrek I would meet him at the meal hall," he says. "Let us go there first."

"Okay, yeah," I reply. I'm sure if he's there, Chloe is too.

The smell of smoky meat and Waldric's signature sauces hit my nose and my fears instantly subside.

We pass Kaiva's and the meal hall comes into view. As do several bodies hunched beneath the tables and behind benches.

What in the world?

I spot Chloe crouching down next to Varrek in front of the group. She holds up three fingers behind her, then two, then one.

"Surprise!" she and a few others yell, while several clan members yell "Birthday!" at the same time, and Ahlvo just screams "Rahhh" at the top of his lungs with his hands raised above his head.

Laughter is all I can manage to get out, because while I'm confused, I find whatever this is to be extremely entertaining.

"Guys, we practiced this," Ava mutters with exasperation as she looks around the hall. Then she looks at her mate. "And what was that?"

"I wanted her to be surprised," Ahlvo says with a shrug.

"Oh, I am," I reply.

"Well, anyway, happy birthday!" Chloe says, hopping up and down.

Huh. "It's my birthday? Wait, how do you even know what day it is?" I ask. Because even though we determined early on that the measure of time here is similar to that of Earth, I have totally lost track of days and months. And since there are only three seasons on Oluura, I really have no idea where we are in the current year.

"Well, we know you're a Scorpio," Ava explains, "and we figured we're still in that window."

"So we picked a day for your birthday and that's today!" Chloe shouts.

"Wow, thank you, guys. I truly was not expecting this," I say, blood rushing to my cheeks. I kind of assumed birthdays were an Earth tradition we left behind, but I'm touched that they not only remembered, but also wanted to celebrate with me.

"You," I point my finger at a smirking Ava, who is clearly behind all of this.

"Me!" she yells as she opens her arms wide.

I run into them and squeeze her tight. "Thank you, Doc."

"Not a doctor, but you're welcome, Red," she replies, patting my hair.

Chloe runs over and wraps her arms around both of us. At some point, Bruvix comes by and places a mug of ale in my hand and in Ava's. I take a sip and spot Niro, holding his own full mug, as he stands alone at the edge of the group. But not for long, because a tall, blue blur with long black hair runs up to him and says, "Hello! I am here for the yelling!"

Alu.

Alu is here. She sees me and her mouth opens in a silent, happy scream. She holds out a hand for me to grab, but instead, I pull her toward me and give her a hug. She's not a stranger. She's one of my people now. And therefore, I trust her with touch.

"Happy day of birth, little human!" she says. "I am so delighted to be here with you."

I pull back and look between her and Niro. "Did you invite her? This was all a ruse, wasn't it? There was no meeting with Varrek…"

He clears his throat and one side of his mouth quirks up. "That is correct. I am responsible for the trickery." Then he turns to Alu. "Though I am surprised you received the message—"

"I read all of your messages, Nirossanai," she replies. "I just choose to ignore most of them."

He gives her the stink eye and then his lips form a wide smile as he looks at me. "I did well, did I not?"

"You did very, very well," I say. I lean up on my toes to kiss his chin.

"Ah, so it *was* a mating signal," Alu says with a teasing nod.

Niro and I share a look of amusement before I reply, "A little of this and a little of that."

"And you have decided to keep the dream link then?" she asks.

"We have made no decisions yet," Niro helpfully adds. I had forgotten Alu knew all about our situation. That's another person who will be curious about our status and asking questions about it. Luckily, she doesn't live close, so those questions won't be tossed at us daily.

Hours pass, and the night grows dark. Bruvix continues to do his typical party job: refilling everyone's mugs with his ale. But unlike at Ava and Ahlvo's wedding, he happily keeps Niro's mug full. And whether he's nervous or finally feeling comfortable around the clan, Niro gets visibly buzzed. Alu does as well, but at a slower pace.

I do my best to mingle so I can thank every member of the clan who helped put my party together. This feels like an opportunity for a fresh start with everyone, and I want to make sure I make the effort. Making small talk goes against all that I am, but it's easier to do with my mug full of ale. Anytime I run out of things to say to one person, I take a slow sip and walk toward the next.

The clan has been wonderful tonight as well. They all offer me smiles and warm greetings as I approach. A few of them even pronounced my name correctly, which is as good a birthday gift as any.

Out of the corner of my eye, I spot Alu and Jobaki seated on a bench, whispering animatedly into each other's ears. I know Alu's ex-girlfriend was a witch of some kind on Sufoi, so I guess she has a type. They would be super cute together.

I go to find Niro so I can tell him, but Bruvix appears in front of me and I'm so surprised by it that I practically run into him. "Oh hey there, Bruv. Having fun?"

"It is a fine time, yes," he says with a nod. That's high praise coming from him. "But it is not my day of birth party. Are *youuu* having fun, Kay-teh?" he asks as he swirls his finger in front of my face before giving my forehead a poke.

I chuckle. "I am indeed." I'm relieved to see him having fun, and for things to feel normal between us. I hated the awkward tension from before, especially since there was no reason for it.

Bruvix empties his mug and opens his arms wide. "Well, I just wanted to say that I am glad your human mother pushed you out of her body and into the world." Then he pulls me in for a big hug.

I stiffen at first, not expecting it, but then I relax against him and wrap my arms around his back. Bruvix is not an affectionate person, as far as I can tell, so a hug from him means a lot. And because we've become close, it doesn't cause prickles of discomfort to appear on the back of my neck.

Suddenly, Bruvix lets go of me and falls onto his back in the dirt. Panicked, I back away quickly and land on my butt, spilling my ale all over my dress. When I look up, I see Niro standing above Bruvix, breathing heavily, teeth bared, and muscles tensed.

Oh no.

While Bruvix moves a bit slower than usual because of the ale, he drops his empty mug and leaps into a crouch facing Niro. The clan gasps and backs away, giving them space.

This cannot be happening.

"You dare put your hands on my mate?" Niro shouts. The air around his body is crackling like he's about to shift into his draxilio but barely holding himself back.

I can't see the expression on Bruvix's face, but his arrogant tone gives it away. "She did not pull away. You saw it with your very own eyes, draxilio."

Why is he antagonizing Niro? He's not even into me. Is this just a fun little game for him?

"Guys, enough," I yell, but my words go ignored.

"She is mine," Niro growls as he pounds his chest with his fist. "No male will touch her but me."

Red flags start popping up in my head. The moment possessiveness stops being sexy is when it morphs into jealousy and starts impacting my other relationships. This is what Dennis did before he started slowly forcing me into an isolated bubble of abuse. I will not let that happen again. This isn't what I want.

"And what does *she* say about that?" Bruvix adds, pointing at me. Ah. I get it now. He wanted to draw this insecure side out of Niro because he knows I'll be disgusted by it. But he's only successful because that part of Niro exists.

"*She* answers to fucking no one," I yell, stepping between them and facing Niro. "Bruvix is a friend and was giving me a birthday hug. That's it."

"I saw your face. You did not want him touching you." Niro says, his eyes glassy from the ale.

I sigh, stress killing my buzz. "I was surprised but it wasn't unwanted."

"I do not care if you think I am being unreasonable. You are my mate. *Mine*. No one touches what is mine," Niro yells back.

"Hey," I say to him, softening my tone and putting my hands on his biceps. "You've had a lot of ale. Let's discuss this another time, okay?"

He brushes my hands off with a frustrated look and scoffs. "I will do no such thing. You are being reckless allowing this wretched male to put his hands on you. Giving him thoughts that you approve."

So now I'm getting scolded at my own birthday party? Uh-uh. "This *wretched male* is my friend, and I've told you countless times that there's nothing between us." My fists clench at my sides and my blood runs hot through my veins. This conversation is taking me to a dark, but familiar place, and if he wants to do this now, in front of everyone, we will. "My words don't seem to matter to you though. I'm not doing that again. So here's the deal…" I trail off.

I feel the eyes of the entire clan on my back, but I shake it off. I'm disappointed that all the progress I've made with them tonight has probably been obliterated by this dramatic little outburst, but one problem at a time.

"I'm gonna make this really easy for both of us. This?" I point between us, "it's over." I scan the crowd until my eyes land on a crop of spiky maroon hair. "Jo, there you are." The crowd parts as I make my way over to her. I give her my hand, palm up. "Break the link."

Jo sucks in a breath, but holds her hand out, above mine, not touching it. "Kayyyt," she says in a slight slur, "you are certain? Do you not want to think on this decision a bit more befor–"

"No," I interrupt, my hand shaking and my vision blurring from the tears. "Do it now. I'm done."

She looks nervously at Niro, and he stands there with his mouth hanging open and his hard gaze locked on my wrist. Maybe he doesn't think I have the gall to go through with it. That's where he's wrong.

Jo nods slowly and takes my hand in hers. I close my eyes and feel her spark seeping into my skin. That electric feel of static cling, but lighter, and in a steady stream. Then it gets hot. Everywhere. Everything is hot. My blood, my skin, my bones, it all feels like it's on fire, burning me from the inside. I grit my teeth, trying to hold back a scream.

The last thing I want to show right now is any sort of vulnerability. Niro doesn't deserve to see it.

I hear Jo whispering an incantation under her breath, and the fire inside me grows. It spreads to my fingers and toes, and I'm squeezing Jo's hand so hard, I wonder if I'm about to break it.

Then it's gone. As if the fire was a lit candle that has been blown out. I feel the lingering tingle of Jo's magic, but the pain has disappeared.

I let out a breath and blink my eyes open. Everyone remains crowded around us, their expressions ranging from awe, to excitement, to fear. I find Niro's gaze and it drops the moment we connect. He turns his face to the side, and I catch a wet trail running down his cheek.

"It is done," Jo says quietly as she lets go of my hand.

"So that's…that's it." I clear my throat, and reply, "Thanks," as I try to mask my sniffle.

Niro looks as murderous as he does heartbroken, and my chest tightens at the sight of him. Before he can shove his way through the crowd, the clan scuttles aside, giving him plenty of room.

Alu is at his side in an instant, draping an arm over his shoulder. "Come, brother. It is time to go," she says. She gives me a small wave and I hope this hasn't ruined our budding friendship. But something tells me it has.

I watch as they slowly walk down the path, Niro's shoulders hunched over, his steps carrying him away from me. My dream guy is finally gone. This is what I wanted, wasn't it?

So why do I feel so gutted?

CHAPTER 23

NIRO

"**B**rother, it is time to rise." Alussanai says as she pokes her head into the darkness of my bedroom. She thinks I have been asleep this whole time. I have not. Sleep evades me since I lost Kate. The sun has risen and set several times—I do not know how many—since she tore my heart from my chest in front of my sister and her entire clan, breaking our dream link, effectively turning off our mate signal.

She is no longer my mate. She is just a human female I will love for the rest of time, and I will be a monster she hates for the rest of hers.

"Give me a reason to rise," I reply, my throat scratchy from lack of use. Also, a lack of water and food, I suspect. I cannot eat, either. The food I used to enjoy does not have the same flavor. It has no flavor at all.

Alussanai pushes the door so hard that it swings open and smacks against the wall. "Very well," she says. "We have a visitor. Is that reason enough?"

Kate? She is here? I throw the furs off my body and race down the hall toward the clinking sound in the eating room. Perhaps she regrets her decision to break our dream link. Perhaps she has missed me just as fiercely as I have missed her. Perhaps she is here to apologize and put this all behind us.

I skid to a stop just inside the door, where my brother Bexossanai sips tea from a mug and proceeds to dip his bread into it before taking a bite. "Oh, Bexossanai."

"Such a chilly greeting," he says with his mouth full. "Do I deserve this?"

"Why are you here?" I ask, genuinely curious. He has not returned to the caves since he left. He was the first to set out on his own. His bouts of paranoia made for an unpleasant living arrangement for the rest of us. I have not missed his presence.

"I was summoned by our sister and her annoyingly soft heart."

"This is true!" Alussanai shouts excitedly from behind me. She saunters into the room and takes a bite of Bexossanai's bread, earning a frightening glare from the male. "It is important for us to be together in the caves while Nirossanai mends himself. He is shattered from within," she says with an exaggerated frown.

"The human's doing?" he says with a laugh. "This is why it is foolish to trust humans."

"But you think it is foolish to trust anyone," my sister replies.

"Because it is!" he shouts with his hands up.

Then he pulls something from the spot next to him in the chair and tosses it toward me. I catch it, and the familiar scent briefly settles the storm inside my mind. "My vaultri gopa. I assumed you had burned it by now."

He waves his hand through the air and purses his lips. "It would be a waste of my fire to burn that rag."

I offer him a dip of my head, an expression of gratitude, before dropping the wrap to my side. "I do not need anyone here. And I am not shattered," I state. Then I try to search for a word that does not represent the whole of my pain, but just enough that will not lead to additional prodding. "I am disappointed, but that is the way of life. I shall be fine. You may leave."

Just as I gesture to the launch room, the door to it whooshes open, and in walks Kulissanai, his long black hair tied into a wild knot at the nape of his neck. "Why have I been called here?" he hollers, knowing that the other two are here and within earshot.

Alussanai pushes past me and charges into him before tackling him to the ground. "Because we are podlings! A unit! We must care for our brother in his time of need."

"I am not in need!" I yell back, getting increasingly angry that no one is listening to me.

The two draxilios wrestle with each other on the floor a moment longer before separating and leaning against opposite sides of the hall. "Welcome home, Kulissanai," Alussanai says with a wide grin as she kicks the side of his boot.

"This is not home, sister." He looks around the halls as if his mouth has a bitter taste, "My home is much nicer than this."

His insult does not shock or offend me. He has always been the most pompous of the four of us. I tell him, "That is bound to happen when you have Zeyda the scrapper making deliveries every moon. I am surprised she has not retired yet with the number of credits you pay her."

He narrows his gaze at me, and his mouth forms a flat line. "Zeyda does her job. She does it well. And I compensate her accordingly."

I shake my head at him. He is infatuated with the female scrapper and has spent years refusing to admit it.

"Well? What is the purpose of this meeting?" Kulissanai asks as he folds his hands in his lap.

"It is not a meeting," Alussanai replies. "It is a visit. We gather for Nirossanai."

"To watch him wallow?" Bexossanai asks, popping his head into the hallway with another piece of bread in his hand. "I would prefer to do anything else."

"No," she says, amused by the stiff tone of her brothers. She has always been completely unaffected by their biting remarks. "Brother," she says, turning to look at me. "You are in great pain. You have lost your mate. But this is not forever. You *have* a mate! Kate is your mate! This is a miracle!"

"You have a mate? And she is human?" Kulissanai asks, his eyes flickering slightly with curiosity. "When did this occur?"

Alussanai is still smiling as she places her hand over her heart, wistfully. "They were brought together by a mate signal. They shared dreams. Is that not lovely?"

"It sounds the opposite of lovely," Bexossanai replies. "What shall we do with her? Would you like us to kill her?"

"Kill her?" Alussanai and I shout simultaneously.

Bexossanai looks at us as if we have gone mad. "She has seen your dreams, your past. She has information on all of us that could destroy the peace we have built here."

I sigh and rub a hand down my face. Part of me wonders if Bruvix's potent ale still lingers in my blood, making me feel weary and impatient. "She is a human female who lives in a small village among Trovilians. They all know who I am and where I came from. They will not report our location to anyone. It is information they have no need for and would not know how to use if they did."

"The question we should be asking is how you will win her back," Alussanai says.

"Win her back?" I ask. "She does not want me. She made that clear in front of her entire clan."

"She was upset because you behaved like a fool," she replies.

"What did you do?" Kulissanai asks, his tone mocking.

Our sister perks up and offers a summary of the events from Kate's day of birth celebration. Then she comes to the end and recounts my anger toward Bruvix. "He is her friend. He was no threat."

"And you say her former mate was evil?" Kulissanai asks.

Alussanai nods, and he shoots a look of exasperation in my direction. "Of course, she would break the dream link after that. She will not allow herself to be harmed by the one person she should be able to trust."

"Why am I not surprised?" Bexossanai says with a chuckle. "It sounds like a quintessential Nirossanai reaction."

"What are you saying?" I ask, suddenly confused. The way I reacted seeing Bruvix and Kate was an entirely new feeling. I have never experienced such primal fear that I would lose her. No one has ever mattered to me as much as she does. So how can this be something they have seen from me before?

"You love through control. Through protection. That is what he is saying," Kulissanai says simply. "You have an idea of how someone should be cared for. How they should live in order to remain safe and happy. And you do whatever is in your ability to provide that, whether or not they have asked you to do so."

"I—I do not…" I trail off. I am not sure what to say to this.

"Why do you think we all left the caves?" Bexossanai adds. "We grew tired of your meddling and unsolicited advice."

"Your incessant tidying," my sister adds.

"We wanted to exist in our own way," Bexossanai continues. "We could not do that here."

I slump against the wall, my back sliding down until I am seated on the floor in the hallway, like my fearless sister and dispassionate brother. They left because of me? It is my fault we are spread out across this planet that we can never leave.

Alussanai crawls on her hands and knees and sits next to me against the wall. Then she slaps a comforting hand on my knee. "It is not your fault, Nirossanai. Our upbringing traumatized us all in different ways. You were the first podling. We became all you had. You felt responsible for us. You still do."

I look at the hand on my knee, my head shaking at the damage I have done to our family. "I never intended to push you away."

"Ugh, we know," Bexossanai says, throwing his hands up. "We are here now, are we not?"

"Must you be so churlish?" Kulissanai says to Bexossanai. "He is clearly suffering, and you are making it worse."

Bexossanai levels Kulissanai with a dark glare. "This is how I was made. Just as you were made to look bored at everything you witness. Just as Alussanai was made to jump head-first into danger with a smile on her face." He looks at each of them carefully as he notes their modifications. "Then there is Nirossanai, who was made to brutally kill and keep killing, never to process the pain he caused. That is not who sits before us now."

"Your point?" I ask, unsure where this leads.

"We were not made to fit in," Bexossanai continues. "We were not made to be what anyone expects. We were not made to do the right thing. But we were also not supposed to live beyond our time in battle, and here we are."

Alussanai nods, smiling.

"What is the conclusion you are trying to reach?" Kulissanai asks as he picks at his nails.

"My point, *brother*," he sneers, "is that Nirossanai is clearly tormented by his actions. How he pushed his mate away and has pushed us away. He is in the thick of an emotion he was never meant to feel in the first place."

"This is true," Kulissanai notes, tilting his head thoughtfully.

Bexossanai smiles at the slight interest in Kulissanai's voice and continues. "His brain has repaired itself over and over, healing the lesions that our handlers intentionally constructed in his tissue. He has rejected the limited purpose of his existence and has sought more. We all have. The fact that we are still alive, be it on a planet where we are forced to remain, is a direct result of our capability to adapt and change."

"But the skins…" I say with a wince, remembering our Earth mission and the podlings we lost. "I failed them. I let them die."

"The very fact that their deaths still haunt you proves my point," Bexossanai says. His tone sounds surprisingly hopeful, but I am still feeling anything but. "You now know how your actions have affected others, us, and your mate. I believe that you can change, because you have changed, many times over," Bexossanai says. "But only if you really want to change."

Alussanai sits up, looking excited. "And we will help you!"

At the same time, my brothers reply, "No, we will not."

Alussanai's shoulders slump in disappointment.

I nod at my brothers with a fresh sense of purpose, and then turn my gaze to Alussanai. "This is my duty, and mine alone. I will make it right between us," I vow as my eyes land on each of them, "but I must first find a way to win back my mate."

"You know," Kulissanai begins, "Zeyda mentioned that she had come across an assortment of human items, though I cannot remember what. She asked if I was interested in them to continue our research. I declined, of course, since we did not need them, but perhaps your mate would enjoy them."

In my head, I hear Kate's voice and the warmth it holds when she discusses food or entertainment she misses from Earth. She may have nothing she wishes to return to back there, but she does miss the everyday comforts she had access to. I am certain even a torn, filthy towel would make her green eyes sparkle with joy. If I can give that to her, even if she refuses to forgive me, I will. "Yes, tell Zeyda to find anything she can from Earth for me. She may name her price. I will take it all."

* * *

I pace outside the tree line, back and forth, back and forth. I am waiting for Kate to come near. Knowing that her fierce heart is close eases the ache in my gut. Since her day of birth celebration, I have thought of nothing but her. Kate and her bright smile, her small nose that ends in a rounded point, her brown spots that cover her skin, and her soft, ample frame that constantly shakes and sways.

And so, I come here each cycle, just to be close by, in case she needs me. Or wishes to see me. Or even chooses to yell at me. Any acknowledgment would be welcomed.

We have not spoken, and the absence of our dream link means that my dreams of her are just memories of the time we spent together. She has not been present in them, teasing me in our black void about things I say or the way she is perceived. My dreams feel flat, lacking dimension, empty without her snide remarks. I long to answer her silly, pointless questions, and I am certain I would cut off a limb if she would only look in my direction.

I have become a pitiful, lovesick sack of bones.

She is still our mate. She will come back to us, my draxilio says.

Perhaps. If she gives us a chance to win her heart, that is, I send back to him.

"You are here again?" I hear a voice call from the trees. Bruvix steps into the clearing, crossing his arms over his chest and eyeing me warily.

I don't wish to tell him how desperate I am for Kate to forgive me, but I cannot think of a logical explanation for my presence either. "Yes," I tell him.

"Why?" he asks as he strides toward me, his tone stern. "Your repeated visits are becoming a security concern, you know."

I hang my head and run my fingers through my rumpled messy hair. I am so tired. Even after the conversation I had with my siblings, I have not been able to sleep through the night. Their encouragement comforted me, as did their presence in the caves in the cycles that followed, but it brought me no closer to reuniting with my mate. And her absence has broken my soul. She may no longer be in my dreams, but she has full ownership over the heart that beats inside my chest.

I do not realize I have fallen to my knees until Bruvix places a hand on my shoulder. My muscles immediately tense, but when I lift my gaze, I see the look in his eyes holds no challenge or contempt. There is only pity. "Come," he says with a pat on my arm as he strides back toward the tree line.

For a moment, I am confused, and I wonder if this is a trap.

He looks back, noticing I have not followed and yells, "Well? My ale will not last forever."

"You wish for me to share a drink with you?" I ask, still unsure if I should follow or shift and fly back to my caves. "And you expect me to trust you?"

His chin drops and the corner of his mouth quirks up into a slight grin. "You are not my enemy, nor my competition, draxilio. I am... sorry that I interfered with you and Kay-teh. I enjoyed antagonizing you. I enjoyed it immensely. But it was not right. And though I wished to have her in my bed at one time, that desire has faded."

My jaw tightens at the mention of Kate in his bed, but I try to focus on the breath leaving my chest and entering though my nose. I must remain calm in this moment.

Bruvix closes his eyes for a few heartbeats before opening them. "I am tired of watching a mated pair deny the gift they have been given," he says with a sigh. "You have no idea how lucky you are to have someone to miss."

He is right. Though my mind is consumed with thoughts of Kate, I can still remember the emptiness in the life I lived before her arrival. It lacked depth and color. It was a fine life, but quiet. Too quiet. "This is true," I finally say.

"So? Come," he says with a wave of his arm to follow. "We shall drink ale and find a way to fix this."

I nod, looking around the clearing. Should I rely on this scarred Trovilian? The one who put his hands on my mate just to make me angry? The one who shoved his blade into my side?

Bruvix holds his hands up, as if to say, "Well?" and ultimately, I follow. It is not like anyone else is offering to help me reunite with my little witch.

"And how do you plan on fixing my problem?" I ask.

He looks over his shoulder and shoots me a sinister grin. "I have many ideas."

CHAPTER 24

KATE

"You are not focusing," Jo scolds me as she lets go of my hands. We're in the same spell room where she first told me I was a witch and that she could break the dream link between me and Niro.

Maybe that's why I can't focus, because I keep picturing Niro sitting next to me, his big body crushing the tiny cushion beneath him, looking distinctly uncomfortable to be in the presence of Jo's magic.

"I know," I tell her, tired and frustrated with myself. "I haven't been sleeping much lately."

She takes a sip of water from the mug at her side and gives me a curious glance. "You are not still dreaming of him, are you? Was my spell ineffective?"

Am I still dreaming of Niro? Yes, constantly.

But it's not the way it was, and frankly, I miss it. I miss him. I know it's probably best for both of us to go our separate ways, but that doesn't make it any easier to live without him. We bickered constantly, we didn't agree on a lot of things, and clearly Niro has some anger issues to work through, and I can't be his punching bag while he tries to figure that shit out.

I won't. Not again.

"No, it worked. The dream link is definitely gone," I tell Jo. She smiles, looking relieved.

I might not be as kind as Chloe, or as smart and generous as Ava, but I deserve someone who treats me like an equal. Someone who doesn't try to control every aspect of my life.

And maybe that person is me. Maybe I'm all I need.

"Let us try again," Jo says, holding out her hands expectantly.

I place mine in hers, and we close our eyes. She tells me to picture a bright light hovering just above my head. When I see it appear, I lock onto it, gritting my teeth as I attempt to pull it closer with my gaze.

"Watch as it gets brighter. Feel the heat of it on your face," she says.

This beam of light is her pathway into my mind. She is trying to place a thought into it for me to see. If I can read the thought she sends me, then we're going to move onto multiple thoughts, and we'll see how many I can decipher in her mind. Her ultimate goal for me is to become a mind reader. I just need to work on strengthening the portal and opening it to specific people at will, rather than it being an open door that anyone can enter while I'm asleep.

It's an attractive concept, I'll admit. Here I thought I was just a freak who had fucked up dreams and would for the rest of my life. But if what Jo says is right, then I can become a witch with a legitimately useful power. I like the idea of being able to protect my clan with this skill.

This is the story I tell myself, at least, when thoughts of Niro invade my mind, which happens a lot. Constantly. But when they arrive, I push them away by going to sewing circle each morning and listening to the chatter between Zohma and the others. I eat each meal with Ava and Chloe, and sometimes their mates, or Bruvix. And whenever I'm not sewing or eating, I'm at the Hexrin house with Jo, learning the basics of witchcraft.

"Do you feel it, Kayt?" she asks, and in that moment, I realize the hot beam of light has faded to a white speck.

"Ugh, no," I groan as I drop my hands in my lap. I rub small circles into my temples, trying to fight the sadness and exhaustion that threaten to swallow me. "What the fuck, Jo?" I finally snap.

Jo stares at me, bewildered. "You are angry."

"Yeah, I'm angry. I'm a lot angry, actually," I shout. I feel the lack of sleep and stress and depression from missing Niro bubbling up my throat, ready to spill. "You broke the dream link. That worked. We know that. So why do I miss him? Why am I this miserable?"

Jo blinks several times, saying nothing, before finally replying, "I do not understand your question."

"If the mate signal was turned off, why…why do I still want him?" I say through a choked sob. Tears run down my cheeks, and I feel like I was just turned inside out, my feelings and insecurities on display for all to see. "I shouldn't want him. I–I can't."

She nods slowly, her eyes closed, a look of knowing on her face. "I see." Then she puts her hand on top of mine and gives it a single squeeze. "Oh, Kayt. I am sorry you are in such pain. But breaking the dream link was never going to keep you from missing him."

What? I thought that was the whole deal. That if the dream link was broken, the mate signal turned off, that we would no longer feel that pull toward each other. I assumed I would still have the memories of us together, but it would be like memories of my first boyfriend in middle school. Like, "Oh yeah, that was cute. We held hands in math class. I remember how sweaty my palm was. But wait, what was his name again?" I want the warm nostalgia of my time with Niro without the gut-wrenching pain of knowing I'll never feel his arms around me again.

"Well," I start, panic pooling in my belly, "is there a spell you can cast to make me forget him? Or to get over him?"

"Kayt, the dream link was just one of many ways mates of his kind have been brought together," Jo says softly. "It amplifies the bond between two beings that already exists, it does not create the bond itself."

I don't like where this is going. "So you're saying…"

"That you miss Niro because you love him. And love is not something I have the power to erase," she says. "I would not do that, even if I could."

Well, that's unfortunate.

We sit in heavy silence, Jo and I, for what feels like an hour, but may only be ten minutes. Finally, she pats my hand and her eyes light up. "Ah! Let us try something different."

"Like what?" I ask, wiping the stray tears from my eyes.

Jo pulls something out of the pocket of her tunic and holds it over the candle flame. It looks like an oversized sewing needle. She holds out her hand and widens her eyes. I place my palm in hers hesitantly and ask, "Are you going to kill me, one poke at a time?"

She chuckles, the sound like a tinkling bell. "There are many ways I could kill you, Kayt, but this would not be one of them."

I'm surprisingly relieved. I've felt her power and I'm well aware she could kick my ass with just a point of her finger.

"A drop of your blood will clear a path from my mind to yours," she says. "It is a shortcut, which we do not like to use, especially with a new Hexrin, but I think it will create a helpful distraction for you."

"Okay," I say with a nod. I can do this. I can totally do this. It's just blood. Just thick, sticky fruit punch that's pumping throughout my skin sack all day long. I just won't look at it. It's fine.

I feel the quick pinch of the needle sticking into my pointer finger, and before I can stop them, my eyes fly open, zeroing in on the drop of blood pooling at the tip.

"Like, fruit pun–" I don't even finish my thought before my head hits the floor.

* * *

I moan as my body is shifted around, multiple hands beneath me as I'm placed on a cushioned surface. When my eyes open, I realize I'm inside a med tube. Ava's peering down at me, her brow furrowed. Kaiva is looking at a screen pad in her hands, and Jo is off to the side, hands clasped together and pressed against her mouth.

"What's going on?" I ask as the room spins.

"You're okay, Kate," Ava says, grabbing my hand. "You passed out at the sight of your own blood."

A harsh laugh escapes my lips. "Yep, that tracks."

"We are just going to make sure your brain is not damaged, Kay-teh," Kaiva croons in a soft voice. "You hit your head on the floor and a bruise is already starting to form."

I give them a thumbs up as the glass top of the tube closes with a hiss. I try to mimic all the beeps and boops the machine makes while I'm in it but get too tired and give up immediately. Once it's done, Ava helps me climb out and leads me to one of the med beds lined up at the front of the room. Jo comes to stand at my other side, and whispers, "I am sorry I made you faint. It was not my intention."

I wave away her apology. "No big, Jo. I should've kept my damn eyes closed."

Kaiva continues to stare at her screen pad, brow furrowed as she makes her way over to us.

"Everything okay, Doc?" I ask. "Should I wear a helmet from now on?"

She doesn't answer, and my throat suddenly feels dry.

"Kaiva?" Ava says.

Finally, Kaiva looks up from the screen and gives me a strange smile. "Your brain is perfectly fine, Kay-teh, but...well..."

"Just tell me, please," I reply quickly.

"It seems you are with child."

My eyes dart between Kaiva and Ava, and I can't seem to form thoughts or words. I'm completely blank.

"Kate, you good?" Ava asks, dropping into her therapist voice. "It's okay if you're feeling overwhelmed right now. That's natural."

"I'm sorry," I finally say. "I'm...pregnant. With a...dragon baby?"

Kaiva looks down at the image on the screen pad. "It appears to be a normal fetus, from what I can tell. Was the draxilio your only pleasure mate?"

"Niro," I say. "His name is Niro. And yes."

"Nee-roh, of course," Kaiva replies. "Then I would say that yes, your baby is part-draxilio."

Before I'm conscious of what's happening, tears start pouring from my eyes at an almost alarming rate. I've never been much of a crier, but that has changed lately. I guess now I know why. But it's more than just baby hormones that are causing these tears to fall.

It's also fear.

Snot streams out of my nose as I shout, "Am I going to hatch an egg?"

Kaiva looks at Ava nervously and starts showing her the image on the screen. They talk between themselves as the thought takes root in my mind. I have no idea how draxilios are born, but didn't Niro say something about hatching? Or…what did he say about naturally birthed draxilios? I don't remember. I can't carry a fucking egg in my stomach, I know that much. I'm human. What if it is an egg and as it's hatching, the cracked eggshell scrapes the inside of my uterus and I bleed out and die? Is that a possibility?

Is Kaiva going to have to cut me open and then put my baby under one of those weird lights they keep in chicken coops? I don't think we have a light like that. Where am I supposed to get a chicken light for my baby in the middle of deep space?

Oh god. I wish Niro were here.

CHAPTER 25

NIRO

"That board is uneven, Nee-roh," Bruvix comments from across the room. "Did you not learn how to build a home on Sufoi?"

"No," I admit, straightening it and pounding the screws into the sides with my fist. "I grew up in a laboratory."

"And then what?" he asks.

"And then housing was provided for us during battle missions."

"Surely you must have built your home here?" Varrek asks, strolling in with a stack of at least fifty wooden boards the size of the one I am hammering into place now.

"No, the caves were made before I arrived," I tell them. "My podlings and I found them empty and made changes, but all with machinery that does most of the work for you."

"So that is why you are soft," Ahlvo says with an arrogant nod. He leans on his cane with one hand as he sands down the curved arch of what will soon be the front door to this home. Kate's home.

When I followed Bruvix into the village the previous cycle, I was skeptical he would help me. He has no reason to do so, other than decency, but I was not convinced he contained any of that based on his past behavior.

However, I was wrong. He has shared his ale with me, offered a comfortable stack of cushions to sleep on in his home, and has given me a way to make peace with the clan. I have agreed to assist Bruvix in a full assessment of the clan's security equipment and provide upgraded parts where needed. But more importantly, I have agreed to help build Kate's new home by hand alongside several others, including Bruvix.

Kate has made it clear she no longer wishes to be mine. If that is how our story ends, at least I will know she is safe in the shelter I helped build. If I am lucky enough to someday make her mine, then we will have a place to stay when we come to visit the clan.

Bruvix is a male of few words, but the words he spoke last night, after several mugs of ale, shook me. "If you wish to have Kay-teh as your mate, you must allow her to have the family she never had before."

"Would I not be enough of a family to her? As her mate?" I asked him. "I am eager to provide all that she could ever need."

"No," he said, "because her life cannot revolve around only one male. She tried it, and it only brought her pain. She needs her human females. She needs the clan. She will deny it, but it is true."

And even though my mind was fluffy from the ale, I knew he was right. It angered me at first, because this male should not know more about my mate than I do, but I could not argue with him. I have seen Kate's face light up the moment she sees Ava or Chloe. They are home to her. The rest of the clan, she is still warming up to, but I know she longs for that same closeness with each member.

If there is a chance I can spend my life with her, I must support her bond with the clan. Encourage it, even. I know now it does not take away from the bond we have as mates. If anything, it strengthens it because Kate has several people who love and care for her. And that is what she deserves.

"Oh, Ahlvo," I say, remembering something. "I must apologize for frightening you." He looks at me sideways as if confused. "That night in the clearing. You were walking toward me on your crutch. I was in my draxilio form."

His eyes widen as his mouth drops open. "That was…that was real? Yo– Varrek!" he shouts. The leader of the clan strolls into the open room from the outside. "Did you hear what Nee-roh just said!"

"I did not."

"He *was* in the clearing that night. It was not an illusion after all!"

Varrek's brow lifts, and his mouth forms a slight grin. "Huh," he says. "That is a surprising revelation. I am sorry for doubting you, brother," he tells Ahlvo.

Ahlvo hops on his good leg, bristling with relief. "I am so grateful you shared this," he says as he pats me on the shoulder.

"Let us hope your surprises continue to be welcomed," Bruvix says as we hear footsteps shuffling toward the house.

"Okay, keep 'em closed," I hear Chloe say moments before she ushers Kate in through the entrance. Kate takes careful steps inside the house with her hands covering her eyes as Ava and Chloe hold each arm.

Bruvix and Varrek share panicked looks before they guide me behind the tall stack of boards and push me into a crouched position.

What is she doing here? Why would they bring her this early? We have barely finished assembling the doorframe and floorboards of the first level. I did not want her to see it until it was much closer to being done. I wanted her to be able to move her things inside. I wanted her to marvel at the detail in the décor chosen for her bedroom—items I would hand select.

I peek around the corner and watch Varrek and Chloe gesturing wildly with their hands. Neither of them looks particularly happy.

Ava shakes her head and rubs her temple. She clearly agrees this is not a great idea.

Chloe shrugs at Varrek and Ava and says, "Okay, you can look now."

Kate's small hands drop from her face as she takes in her surroundings. I do my best to remain hidden, but I cannot resist seeing her reaction to the place. She smiles, but it is a tight smile, and her eyes flicker with uncertainty. She looks at Ava, and then Chloe and says, "I'm not sure what I'm looking at."

Chloe raises her arms wide. "It's your home."

"Mine?" Kate asks, looking at each of them. "You're building me a house?"

Bruvix clears his throat. "Yes. It is important to us that you have a home of your own here. We are all working together on it," he says as he pounds his fist on the stack of wood I'm hiding behind.

What is he doing? Is he suggesting I make my presence known? That does not seem wise.

"All of us," he says again, kicking me in the side. When I look up at him, he's gesturing for me to stand. And since it seems pointless to continue this game, I do.

I hear Kate suck in a breath the moment her eyes land on me. I come around the wood stack, my body pushing me toward her, but I stop a short distance away, as I am not sure how she would react to my closeness. Her eyes dart back and forth between mine for a moment before tears spill onto her cheeks and she lets out a pained sob. Her hands cover her face as she cries into them, her shoulders heaving with each loud inhale she tries to take.

"Kate, I–" I start, rushing toward her.

"What is he doing here?" Chloe says to Varrek through gritted teeth.

"This was a terrible idea," Ava adds. "Why did you need her to see it today?" she asks Chloe.

"You knew he was helping us. I told you," Varrek says to Chloe.

"I'm sorry that I've developed an aversion to keeping life-changing secrets," she says to Ava while she pins Varrek with a glare.

"But could you not have waited until we at least completed the washroom? Or secured the front door?" Bruvix asks the females. "This is not much more than a neat pile of wood."

"Guys!" Kate shouts. She wipes her tears from her eyes and breathes in through her clogged nose. "Everyone out, please."

I follow the others, but she puts her hand on my arm and I freeze. "Not you."

I nod, resisting the urge to lean into her touch and beg her to keep her hand where it is until my final breath leaves my body.

"Thank you all, by the way," Kate yells as the others file out. "I love my house and I love you all for building it."

"Love you!" "Our pleasure!" and "You're welcome!" are shouted back, but I cannot tell who says what.

We stand there facing each other in the entryway of what will someday be Kate's house, and the words begin to fall from my lips in a rush. "I am sorry, Kate. I am truly sorry for the hurt I have caused. I should not have reacted the way I did to seeing Bruvix hug you. It was immature and unnecessary, and I am deeply remorseful."

She watches me, sniffling occasionally as I continue. "You see, I was told repeatedly I was not worthy of having a mate. That this eternal bond was above me because I am a podling, built for battle and nothing more. I believed it. For centuries, I thought this was true. There are parts of me that still believe it."

Kate's face is red and her eyes are puffy from crying, but I have never found her more dazzling. She is vulnerable in this moment, which is a state she abhors, and yet, she nods as she listens, letting me know she is here with me.

"I am not worthy of your love, I know this," I tell her. The breath leaves my lungs as she takes my hand in hers. She nods once again, silently telling me to continue. "But I will spend the rest of my time trying to make you smile. I will keep you safe while respecting your boundaries. I will be what you need, not what I think you need. I promise you, I will."

"You're wrong, Niro," she says, and my heart sinks.

This is the moment she rejects me. The moment I must begin my solitary life, haunted by the memory of her. It is what I deserve. I should expect nothing more, reall–

"You are worthy of so much more than you realize," she says, looking down and tracing my knuckles with her finger. "Your handlers lied to you when they said you weren't meant to have a mate. That you weren't worthy of it. You are."

I say nothing, just watching her soft lips as comforting words escape them.

"I know you've been through some seriously dark shit. So have I," she says with a dry chuckle. "And that dark shit causes us to react in certain ways that might not be ideal. We'll need to work on that. We won't be able to fix it in a day, or fundamentally change who we are, but we can communicate. We can do the hard work and process the trauma and cry all the tears if that's what it takes to stay together and treat each other the way we deserve to be treated."

She looks up at me then, her green eyes glistening. "Well, I know I can." Kate releases my hand then and takes a step back. "Can you?"

"Yes," I reply immediately, taking her hand back and pulling her toward me. "I can. I can do it all. I will. For you."

I hold her small hand between mine and kiss the tip of her thumb.

Kate smiles, and tugs on the front of my shirt. I lean down as she lifts onto her toes and press my mouth to hers. Wrapping my arms around her, I groan against her mouth as her scent circles my head in a cloud.

I keep the kiss soft and tender at first, but Kate becomes greedy. She nips at my bottom lip and licks at my seam, seeking entry. I let her in as I lift her in my arms, pressing her body securely against mine. She wraps her legs around me, crossing her feet at my lower back.

She moans as I cup the back of her neck, pulling her back slightly. "But wait," I say through short, panting breaths, "how do we do this?"

"What do you mean?" she asks, covering my neck and jaw with quick kisses.

"We have broken our link. I have not heard of another mated pair that has done this and continued their lives together."

She slides down my body until her feet touch the floor. "We'll have to love each other the way humans do."

Humans famously leave their mates and choose new ones at an alarming rate. I am not inclined to do anything the way they do.

Kate sways slowly in my arms and continues. "There's no outside force ensuring we stay together, so we'll have to choose each other, every day. It'll be hard and sometimes we'll argue."

"Sometimes?" I ask with a smile.

"Okay, we'll argue *often*," she clarifies.

I brush a stray hair behind her ear and kiss the tip of her nose. She is perfect, this human.

"So, today I choose you, Niro."

"I choose you back."

She chuckles, pulling me down for another kiss. Then she whispers against my lips, "That's good, because I'm pregnant with your dragon baby."

EPILOGUE

KATE

"**I** don't think you fully understand just how horned up I am," I tell Niro as we walk from the clearing in front of Kuli's house up the stone steps to his door. "This pregnancy has my pussy running like a faucet."

He pulls me against his chest and into his arms, placing his hands on my protruding bump. "I know, my rivi, I promise to suck on your clit the moment we have some privacy," he says, his voice raspy and heated as he licks the spot just behind my earlobe.

"Mmm," I moan as Niro knocks on Kuli's front door. "I really don't think you want your brother to meet me while I'm in the middle of an orgasm. Seems slightly inappropriate."

"Hello, brother," Kuli says in a flat tone as he swings the door open. "Human," he says with a nod down at me. This is the youngest of Niro's siblings, and apparently the most peculiar. He's very private and is never happy or sad or excited about anything. He was modified to lack awe, so he's in a constant state of emotional neutrality.

"Hello, Kuli!" I say with a wave, eager to somehow get him to smile. "May I call you Kuli, by the way?"

He grunts in response as he steps aside and gestures for us to enter. I guess that's a yes.

"I'm Kate. Lovely to finally meet you." I say. He remains silent and stone-faced.

Kuli lives on an island off the western coast of Oluura. The beach on the edge of his property is bright pink and the water a pale blue color. Flying over it, it looked more like an elaborate gender reveal party than a beach, but nothing surprises me about space anymore.

His house is a ranch-style building made of beige stone, surrounded by several layers of tall dark green trees that look like pines. If you landed on this island, you'd see forest, and nothing else. Niro tells me this was an intentional design choice, so Kuli could keep his home hidden.

Niro and I remove our shoes at the door and follow him into a large living room with a sunken seating area much like Alu's, and floor-to-ceiling windows that look out into the trees. Seated on the circular black velvet couch is a purple-skinned alien, a female, I think, in a form-fitting white jumpsuit that tucks into black, platform combat boots.

She smiles and stands when she sees us. "Nirossanai," she says with a cheerful nod. "And you must be Kate, the human," she says to me. "I am Zeyda."

"Yes, though, just 'Kate' is fine," I reply, taking a seat next to her. "Nice to meet you."

Kuli watches as I lean back into the couch, adjusting my position to better accommodate my bump. "Ah, so you have won her back and now you are carrying a hybrid, I see."

That's quite the ice breaker. But I've always appreciated bluntness, so I roll with it. "Yup, the dragon bun is in the oven." And not in egg form like I was worried about. Niro has assured me that draxilio females birth their children in a similar way to humans, and it was one of the reasons humans were determined a compatible race for procreation.

Kuli looks at Niro, confused.

Niro smiles. "It is a human reference for pregnancy. We are expecting a child together." The reverence in his voice makes my heart jump inside my chest. "We do not know when she will deliver, but with draxilio gestation being five moon cycles, and the human cycle at nine, we are guessing she will deliver somewhere in between. You are welcome, of course, to be present at the birth."

"Well, you can come to the village, but I'm gonna insist you wait outside while I push this little fire-breather out of my vagina," I clarify.

"Ah," Kuli replies, not committing to anything. "Well, Zeyda is here with what you requested, brother. Feel free to complete your transaction so you may return home with your mate."

I stifle a gasp at Kuli's lack of hospitality. I try not to be shocked by it. Niro did warn me, several times, in fact. But I've just never seen someone less interested in socializing with new people.

Zeyda just smiles at Kuli as if she finds his coldness adorable. Then she unwraps a large item in the middle of the seating area, and reveals…not one item, but several.

"Oh my god…" I trail off. I spread the items out as I touch each one, squealing as more are revealed. It's a small DVD player along with a pile of DVDs and CDs and books from Earth. And they're all in English, it seems. "How? How did you find all this stuff?"

Zeyda chuckles, a proud grin on her lips. "I am a scrapper. I can find anything."

The final item is revealed, and I let out a scream. "Are you serious? *A League of Their Own*? This was my favorite movie growing up!" Then I look at Niro. "Did you arrange this?"

He nods, his lips forming a sly grin.

"Is it possible to reduce your volume?" Kuli asks me. "The shouting is not ideal."

Before I can answer, Zeyda pulls something out of her bag on the floor and hands it to Kuli. "Found something for you too, boss."

Boss, eh? I am dying to dig deeper into their dynamic. I'm even tempted to test my mind reader skills on these two, but I haven't been able to snoop without Jo saying she can feel me, so I need more practice.

He takes it and unwraps the tissue paper slowly, methodically. Then he pulls out what looks like a USB drive but with four stubby red wires sticking out both ends. "You found it?" he asks, and I could swear I hear a hint of surprise in his voice.

"What is it?" Niro asks.

"It is a collection of ancient instrumental Sufoian melodies," she says. "I've been hunting all over the galaxy for it. Finally found it in the desk of a kilmani guard on a trash planet."

Kuli clears his throat. "This is an item I will thoroughly enjoy. I thank you, Zeyda."

She holds his gaze, her chin dipping slightly in acknowledgement. The air feels heavy in here, thick with sexual tension. Or maybe it's coming from me. Whatever the source, I'm ready to leave.

"Well," I say as I pat Niro's knee, "we should probably get these goodies back home where they belong, yeah?" I get to my feet and wobble a bit as Niro clutches my arm. "It was so wonderful to meet you both," I say to Zeyda and Kuli as we put our boots back on at the door.

"Yes, you as well, Kate," Zeyda replies warmly.

"Safe travels, brother," Kuli says to Niro.

Niro nods and we head outside. I say, "So that's Kuli."

"That is Kuli," he repeats.

We make it home to the caves within three hours or so, and I'm squirming in Niro's palm by the time he lands in the launch room. I need that pretty, blue dick inside me *now*. I crawl away to give him just enough room to shift back. "Love you, drax," I say to his dragon form before the beast fades. It's important to acknowledge my love for the other part of my mate too.

Once Niro is in his flightless form, I toss the bag of human things aside and start clawing at his clothes. "Now? Here?" he asks as his lips blaze a hot trail down my neck.

"Yes, need you," I say with a moan as I tug his shirt over his head. We push apart long enough to strip down completely, and then we're standing naked in front of each other. Niro immediately sinks to his knees, pressing gentle kisses on my belly. I run my fingers through his hair, reveling in the sight of him. The brutality, the hard lines, the monster within, but also, the softness of his heart, the pain he is still trying to atone for, and the innate desire to protect those he loves. I find him utterly breathtaking.

Just as he finishes kissing a line across the lower part of my stomach, he nudges my legs wide, and parts my pussy lips with his hands as he drags his tongue up my slit. I cry out as a shiver rips through my body, knowing the best is yet to come.

"Your taste gets sweeter each cycle," he notes with another tantalizing lick. He mentioned this the first time we had sex after I revealed the pregnancy. I have no idea if it's true, but he swears it is. As long as he enjoys how I taste, I don't care if I'm sweet, salty, or as spicy as hot sauce.

I grip his horns as I writhe against his mouth. He sucks on my clit, and my knees buckle, but he holds me up, keeping me steady. Niro continues his assault on my pussy until I come twice, one right after the other, then he helps me drop onto my hands and knees. He kneels behind me, massaging my ass before he parts my cheeks and glides his tip along my seam, coating it in my wetness.

He growls as he pushes himself into me. "Fuck, rivi. You feel so good," he says, his voice low and gritty. He pulls out slightly before thrusting himself all the way in, the ridges lining his cock stroking me deeply.

"Yes, like that," I moan as he sets a brutal, quick pace. The sound of our sex echoes throughout the launch room as his heavy balls slap my ass each time he fills me.

Suddenly, I'm right on the edge, and as if sensing it, Niro leans over me and presses his thumb into the side of my clit, and I'm frozen in place as I ride the wave of pleasure crashing through my body. He roars into my back as he chases his release. As I come down, I feel him still pumping inside me, his seed dripping down my thighs.

Niro cleans me up using his shirt, and then carries me to our room, gently depositing me on our bed. I pull back the covers for him and once settled, he wraps his arms around me, and I tuck my head against his chest. He kisses my hair and whispers, "I choose you, Kate."

"I choose you back, blue man."

"Do you?" he asks in mock surprise.

"I do!" I reply. It's a little game we've started to play. I'm not sure when it started or why, but it adds to our daily vows in a way that makes me smile.

"That is very good news," he says as he reaches down and places his hand against my stomach. "Did you hear that? Your mother has chosen me today."

I put my hand over his. "Yes, little one. I'm keeping him, for now. We'll see how things go tomorrow."

He laughs as he guides my hand up to his mouth and presses a kiss against my palm. "I plan to make you fall in love with me tomorrow as well."

He'll succeed. I have no doubt about that. Not just tomorrow, but all of the tomorrows that follow. My dream guy is nothing if not persistent.

* * *

Thank you for reading STEALING HIS MATE! I hope you loved Kate and Niro's story. Many of you have asked, "What about Bruvix?! When is he getting his Happily Ever After?" Well, I've got good news, because his story is here!

KEEPING HIS MATE is available now!

"These aliens are so attractive to readers for a reason - this is exactly the type of personality we'd love to see in reality, and it's gorgeous. We're drawn to it. I dive into every Ivy Knox book knowing that not only will I get a beautiful romance, but I'll also see the best of humanity in the most unlikely of places - on an alien planet, with an alien man who knows how to keep his woman happy in all the right ways." - 5-star reader review

Stealing a med tube containing a human female outside the slaver's brothel, Bruvix takes her back to Oluura, where he finds out the ring she wears means her heart belongs to another.

How can that be when he feels the tether connecting his soul to hers? How can his eternal mate be taken?

Eleanor Santos wakes for the third time since being abducted from Earth. The second time, she'd attacked the alien who touched her, thus getting herself shipped back in the white tube to her abductor. Now seeing human females, she knows she's safe, but her heart cries out to the love of her life still on Earth.

Bruvix knows the deeps scars on his body from being attacked by a vicious beast years ago make him too ugly for his mate to look at, but he's discovering that his inara is unique. She has a love of the wild, in more ways than one.

When the slaver who took Eleanor finds her on Oluura, his army comes to take her and the other females back. Bruvix comes face to face with his greatest fear—he can save either Eleanor or himself.

He almost died once, but this time his luck isn't so good.

Want to find out what happens next? Start reading Keeping His Mate now!

ALSO FROM IVY

<u>ALIENS OF OLUURA</u>

Saving His Mate

Charming His Mate

Stealing His Mate

Keeping His Mate

Healing His Mate

Enchanting Her Mate

(This series isn't finished. There's plenty more to come!)

<u>STRANDED ON EARTH</u>

Her Alien Bodyguard

Her Alien Neighbor

Her Alien Librarian

Her Alien Student

Her Alien Boss

ENJOY THIS BOOK?

If you liked this book, please leave a review here! It helps others find my work, and as long as people still love what I write, I'll keep writing! Thank you for reading.

Stay up-to-date on bonus chapters, new releases, cover reveals, giveaways, and general smutty shenanigans by subscribing to my newsletter.

FROM IVY

The moment I began writing *Saving His Mate* (book 1), Kate appeared in my mind as this wonderfully strange, antisocial, mysterious, goth goddess. I didn't know what her deal was, but I was eager to uncover all her secrets and get to the bottom of what makes her so special. It turns out that thing is grit.

Kate is a survivor, but not a picture-perfect inspiring survivor. She's not about to give a TED Talk on perseverance or the power of positive thinking. That's just not who she is. She still harbors a lot of anger for the abuse she endured and struggles with her willingness to face that. Her unprocessed trauma causes her to push people away with dark humor, isolate herself from others, and to lack trust.

Originally, I had her paired up with Bruvix, because I thought her bitterness with his grumpiness would make for a hilariously adorable tale of love and growth. But the more I got to know both of them, the less that made sense to me.

Niro showed up at a time when Kate felt both lost and trapped within the village, and he provided her an escape. That time away from the clan helped her see how much they mean to her, and how desperately she wanted to belong to this group of people. And belonging is not something Kate has ever sought, so that moment of clarity was huge.

Also, since Kate abhorred the idea of falling in love, I knew her story would be enemies-to-lovers. Any mate of hers would need to match her wit while also pushing her to grow, and Niro's arrogance and backstory made him the perfect fit.

Niro and his siblings were a joy to create, especially with their genetic modifications. I listened to a podcast years ago about a woman with the inability to feel fear (She's real! Look her up!), and that got me wondering how such a condition would manifest in a dragon shifter, a creature with incredible strength and abilities, and an extremely long life. Enter Alu.

This led to pages and pages of scribbles as I built a family of draxilios, each modified to lack a certain emotion to make them more ruthless in battle. I hope you enjoyed a peek into Niro's siblings, because you haven't seen the last of them.

And those poor podlings that attempted to reach Earth but died on their journey, aka "the skins." Such tragic deaths.

OR WERE THEY?

Now, I'm sure you're sitting there wondering what comes next for our clan on Oluura. I've got good news for you! I have many more stories planned for them, so this is not the end. Not even close. In fact, our dear Bruvix, sad and lonely with nothing but his ale to comfort him, is finally getting his own story. And since we've officially run out of human women, there will be some new faces in the village.

Stay tuned!

Love,

Ivy

P.S. - A special thank you to my amazing editors, Tina and Jenny, who spent hours helping me clean up my ramblings. And Mandi, who gave this one a beta read and offered brilliant suggestions to boost the dynamic between Kate and Niro.

And to you, my dear readers, for supporting my work and gobbling up my books the moment they go live. I wouldn't be here without you.

RESOURCES

SAMHSA (Substance Abuse and Mental Health Services
Administration Hotline)
1-800-662-HELP (4357)
TTY: 1-800-487-4889
samhsa.gov

RAINN (Rape, Abuse, & Incest National Network)
1-800-656-4673 (call or chat)
rainn.org

National Suicide Prevention Hotline
1-800-273-8255 (call or chat)
suicideprevention.org

National Domestic Violence Hotline
1-800-799-SAFE (7233) (call or chat)
thehotline.org

ABOUT IVY

Ivy Knox has always been a voracious reader of romance novels, but quickly found her home in sci-fi romance because life on Earth can be a drag. When she's not lost on faraway worlds created by her favorite authors, she's creating her own.

Ivy lives with her husband and two neurotic (but very cute) dogs in the Midwest. When she's not reading or writing, she's probably watching *Superstore, The Good Place, What We Do in the Shadows,* or *Fall of the House of Usher* for the millionth time.